A
Harlequin
Romance

OTHER
Harlequin Romances
by JANICE GRAY

STAR LIGHT, STAR BRIGHT

by

JANICE GRAY

HARLEQUIN BOOKS   TORONTO
WINNIPEG

Original hard cover edition published in 1970
by Mills & Boon Limited.

© Janice Gray 1970

SBN 373-01852-5

Harlequin edition published February 1975

Printed in Canada

CHAPTER ONE

"ISN'T it just too *marvellous*," gushed the opulently dressed, heavily made-up woman in the seat next to Jenny, "how one can leave London in the middle of the morning and arrive in Nice in time for lunch? Really, it's much easier and quicker than taking a tube train across London!"

To ensure that she made herself heard above the noise of the engines she spoke a shade too loudly. Then, although they had been airborne for less than five minutes, she leant across Jenny to peer eagerly out of the window, almost as though she expected to see the coast of France appearing at any moment.

Jenny permitted herself the ghost of a smile. For her part she wasn't in the slightest hurry to reach Nice, in fact, she almost wished that it was possible to tell the pilot to turn the plane around and fly back to London. For her, the journey was likely to prove only too short, inasmuch as something of an ordeal lay in front of her.

"Your first flight?" Her companion's sharp eyes had noticed how awkwardly Jenny had fumbled with her seat belt and the slight tension in her slim figure as the plane had taken off.

"Yes," Jenny answered briefly. She didn't feel in the least like talking and had a suspicion that, given the least encouragement, her fellow passenger would carry on a non-stop conversation until they reached Nice.

"I thought so. One can always tell, you know." There was a faint note of condescension in the woman's voice and she eyed Jenny with an interest that was not altogether untinged by envy. Not more than twenty, she judged, and very pretty, with those large, wide-apart grey eyes that looked mistily out from under straight dark brows and the silky fair hair.

"Going on holiday?" she hazarded.

"I—yes, sort of."

"Alone?"

"No, I'm staying with—friends." Jenny saw the next question already forming itself and said a little desperately, "Please do you mind if I don't talk? I—I've got rather a headache."

"Oh, of course. Suit yourself." Obviously a little offended, the woman settled herself back in her seat and ostentatiously flicked over the pages of a glossy magazine. After a time, however, this pastime palled and she began to rummage through her expensive leather handbag for a pocket mirror.

"Heavens, I look a fright!" she said, frowning critically at her reflection. She shot a half-resentful glance at Jenny as she spoke, envying the younger girl's cool and fresh appearance. It owed nothing to artifice, either: why, she wasn't even wearing powder or lipstick!

Jenny had not even heard her. She had put a hand over her aching temples and had closed her eyes. She was trying hard to relax, but her mind had begun, in spite of herself, to turn over the events which had led up to her presence today in a BEA Trident aircraft destined for the Côte d'Azur.

Jenny, who was two years older than her companion had supposed her, had lived most of her life with her maternal grandmother in a quiet London suburb. An only child, her mother had died when she was only ten and her father, instead of being suitably heartbroken, had immediately abandoned any pretence of living what his mother-in-law described as a "decent God-fearing life" and had begun to travel all over the world in search of experiences and backgrounds for the books he claimed he had always wanted to write.

Success in the shape of one best-selling novel after another had not been his only reward. Three years after his wife's death he had met Gabrielle de Vaisseau, a beautiful French widow with three children and a considerable inheritance, and after their marriage he had promptly removed himself to his new wife's luxurious villa on the outskirts of Nice.

Much to Jenny's secret heartbreak, apart from an occasional and admittedly lavish cheque he had then appeared to forget about his young daughter's existence and the burden of her upbringing had fallen upon her grandmother's shoulders. A singularly humourless woman with narrow, rigid ideas, she had watched anxiously for any signs that might have indicated that Jenny was taking after her father in character or temperament, but her fears soon proved to be groundless. A quiet child with a poised reserve which some people mistook for shyness, Jenny was fortunately quite happy to dwell in her own ivory tower, absorbed in the music which she loved better than anything else and allowing very little to ruffle her characteristic serenity. Her father and his French home and family always seemed completely remote : what was real, what mattered, was her grandmother's undoubted affection for her and the wonderful chance she had been given of studying at the Royal Academy of Music.

After gaining her L.R.A.M. she had taken a teaching post at the local girls' High School. It wasn't what she really wanted to do, but her grandmother was becoming progressively frailer and Jenny tried to spend as much time with her as possible. She had died shortly before her seventy-fifth birthday, and two weeks later letters had arrived from Stephen Challoner and Gabrielle asking Jenny to pay them a long visit as soon as she possibly could.

There had been similar invitations before, but Jenny had always been forced to refuse them. To have accepted would have been to cause untold anxiety to old Mrs. Barrington, who was insular and prejudiced to the *n*th degree and who genuinely believed that her beloved granddaughter would not be safe for one moment amongst a pack of "dirty foreigners". Useless for Jenny to protest, with tender amusement, that the days of the white slave traffic were over : her grandmother had remained unconvinced and so Jenny had stayed in England.

Her first instinct had been to refuse this latest invitation. She remembered so little about her father and she had never seen her stepmother or her two stepbrothers, Piers and Raoul, and her stepsister, Dominique. They were total strangers. She knew that Piers, who was over thirty, had taken over the management of the pottery works which the family had owned for just over a

7

hundred years and that he had recently become engaged to the beautiful daughter of a distinguished French diplomat, but that was about all she did know. What career Raoul, the younger brother, followed she had no idea, and though somebody had once mentioned that Dominique wanted to become an actress it seemed that the idea had never been followed up.

It was odd and even a little frightening, she thought, to have a family which was a completely unknown quantity. On her mother's side there were no surviving relatives at all, and ever since her grandmother's death she had been unable to help feeling that she was very much alone. Not even the warmth of her father's and stepmother's letters had succeeded in dispelling this feeling. What was the point of going to France? It was unlikely that she would ever be accepted as a real member of the family circle, she would probably merely spend an uncomfortable few weeks trying to wear the guise of intimacy among a group of perfect strangers!

She had said as much to old Dr. Roberts, who had been the family doctor for as long as she could remember, and quickly found that he did not share her misgivings.

"A holiday in the South of France? Best thing out for you at the moment, my dear," he said bluffly. "Getting away from all this is just what you need. Complete change ... different environment, new things to think about. Do you all the good in the world."

He glanced at her keenly as he spoke. During the last months of Mrs. Barrington's life Jenny had nursed her devotedly, and he thought that the strain had begun to tell. There were dark shadows under her eyes, and it seemed to him that her mouth was too firm and her expression too reserved. That quiet, mask-like look ... it wasn't natural for a girl of her age!

Jenny had protested, but in point of fact she was between the devil and the deep blue sea. She could either face an unknown family or remain in England to see her home sold—old Mrs. Barrington had leased the property, not owned it—and to continue in a job that she cordially disliked. Better by far, she eventually decided, to give in her notice, spend a few weeks in France while she

8

gradually adjusted herself to her new and bewildering independence, and then return to carve out a new life and career for herself, preferably not in London.

Now, trying hard to suppress her growing apprehension, she turned her head to stare out of the window, but instead of the bank of fleecy clouds she found herself visualising an entirely different scene. Her stepmother had once sent her some colour photographs of the Villa Buichi, so she knew exactly what to expect . . . a cloudless sky, smouldering with an unbelievable blue, and a big white house standing on a sun-dusted hill, surrounded by bleak cypresses and the silver and green iridescence of olive groves and glowing orchards of orange and lemon trees. To Jenny it had seemed the equivalent of a fairy-tale palace and not even her grandmother had been able to tarnish the bright image she had held in her mind ever since.

Well, she would soon find out whether the reality came up to her expectations! She noticed that several of the passengers were beginning to fasten their safety belts, and realising that they were coming in to land she did likewise. Her companion, having mercifully preserved a somewhat chilly silence throughout the journey, suddenly embarked on a running commentary, but this time Jenny did not object to her chatter. It kept her thoughts at bay.

They landed, and Jenny was one of the first to leave the plane. There was the inevitable crush, however, at the Customs barrier and she had to wait for some time, feeling as lost and bewildered as she supposed most people must feel on their first visit to a foreign country. She found her ears assailed by a flood of French chatter and was thankful that she could understand quite a lot of what was being said. (At school she had been told that she had a natural flair for languages, and though she had never bothered to keep her French up after 'A' levels she was surprised how much was now coming back to her.)

"Mille pardons, mademoiselle, excusez-moi!"

A small, thin man in a rather shiny suit, pushing his way through the throng, had bumped against the girl who was standing behind Jenny, sending her handbag flying to the floor and tearing a swift startled exclamation from her lips. He bent to retrieve it, reiterating his apologies, and the girl answered him pleasantly.

"*Ce n'est rien, monsieur.*"

Her accent was good, but her exclamation had given her away. English, even though her clothes announced discreetly that she had been to France before. Jenny gave her a quick glance. Lovely auburn hair, and a face which, though it had no claim to beauty, had character and humour. Her eyes met Jenny's and she smiled, showing perfect white teeth.

The *douanier*, chalk in hand, was pausing over Jenny's two shabby suitcases. "*Vous n'avez rien à déclarer?*"

Jenny started and turned. She said firmly in English, "No, nothing. Nothing to declare at all."

He believed her, and she was through the barrier, scanning the crowd of alien faces for one that she knew, if only from photographs. Surely, oh, surely her father would have come to meet her! But there was no one who even remotely resembled Stephen Challoner, and as all about her uttered little cries of recognition, excitement and pleasure and were claimed by waiting friends and relations, Jenny found herself gripped by a feeling akin to panic.

The crowd was dispersing rapidly. She was just beginning to think that she had been completely forgotten when a voice at her elbow enquired tentatively, "Mademoiselle Barrington?"

Turning swiftly, Jenny found herself confronted by a swarthy-faced little man who explained, in broken English, that he had been instructed to meet Mademoiselle Barrington and to take her to the Villa Buichi. His taxi was waiting outside, if Mademoiselle would please step this way . . . ?

Absurdly, irrationally, Jenny felt tears prick her eyelids. So neither her father nor her stepmother had bothered to come and meet her, to give her the personal welcome which would have meant so much!

She realised that the taxi driver was looking at her curiously and managed to summon a smile. "*Merci,*" she said not quite steadily, and followed him to where his taxi was waiting outside. Subconsciously she noted the dazzling blue of the sky and the warmth of the still and golden air, and remembered wryly that when she had left London, less than two hours ago, it had been raining fast and everyone had looked damp and chilly.

"The Villa Buichi, is it far from here?" she asked. The taxi driver answered her, but this time in such voluble French that she could not understand a word. She felt it wasn't worthwhile to ask him to repeat what he had said more slowly, and she got into the cab without further ado. Her cases were heaved in beside her, the door slammed, the engine roared and then they were off, tearing towards Nice as though pursued by demons.

Jenny, peering eagerly through the window, was disappointed to find that her first glimpse of one of the most famous tourist centres in the world was tantalisingly brief. They roared through the broad straight boulevards at a speed which made it impossible for her to recognise any of the features described in the guide book she had purchased before leaving England, and were soon making for the low, villa-covered hills which shielded the city from the tramontana. Trying desperately to photograph each new panorama on her mind's eye, she clung tightly to the edge of her seat as the driver swerved violently to avoid a stationary vehicle, and wondered a little dazedly whether there were any traffic restrictions in France. Certainly her driver didn't seem to know of any!

Just at that moment the taxi checked momentarily as the car in front made a right-hand turn, and out of the corner of her eye Jenny saw a girl walking slowly along the dusty road. She had noticed very few pedestrians, possibly because it was the siesta hour when most people were still digesting their lunches and only the most fanatical sun-worshippers were roasting themselves in the dazzling heat, and something about this one caught her attention. The sun was beating down on a bright auburn head, burnishing it with gold, and with a little shock of surprise she recognised the girl who had been standing behind her at the Customs barrier.

"Why, I believe she's limping! She must have hurt her foot! I wonder why she's walking? Perhaps we could give her a lift!"

11

Without giving herself time to think she banged on the glass partition which separated her from the driver and spoke imperatively.

"Stop! Please stop!" Then, as he turned his head to look at her in surprise, *"Arrêtez! Arrêtez, s'il vous plaît!"*

The taxi ground to a reluctant halt amid outraged hooting from the vehicles behind. Without bothering to explain—her French would never be up to it, anyway—Jenny wrenched open the door and darted back along the road. Yes, the girl *was* limping, and her face was pale under its golden tan.

"I say! Have you hurt your foot? Can we give you a lift anywhere? I saw you at the airport, I know you're English and so am I." Jenny spoke breathlessly, her usual reserve forgotten in her anxiety to help someone who, like herself, was an English girl in a foreign land.

The girl's face lit up. "Gosh! A Good Samaritan!"

"Well, yes, if you like," Jenny said, laughing. "Where are you going? Have you hurt your foot badly?"

"Only turned my ankle, I think. These shoes weren't meant for walking!" the girl said, directing a rueful glance at the slender heels of her delicate shoes. "My taxi broke down, you see, and I was quite literally abandoned while the driver stumped off to find a mechanic. I knew that that might take him the rest of the day, so I thought the best thing I could do was to ring up for another cab. Unfortunately, when I looked in my bag I found I had no purse and consequently no money for the call."

Jenny's eyes widened. "You've lost it? Your purse, I mean?"

"Stolen," the girl said succinctly. "A horrible little man knocked my bag out of my hands at the airport—oh, did you see him do it?" as Jenny gave a startled exclamation. "I suppose he was a professional pick-pocket and he removed the purse before he handed the bag back! Luckily there wasn't an awful lot in it, but it was a bit of a shock suddenly to find I hadn't a bean! I was just wondering if I should try to thumb a lift, though that can be a bit dicey sometimes!"

"Definitely a last resort," Jenny agreed. "Look, here's

my taxi. Will you have a word with the driver and tell him where you want to go? I do speak French, but I'm afraid I'm rusty, I don't think I'm up to giving directions just yet!"

"Right! I'll talk to him and see what he says. Luckily my French is quite passable: I've had lots of practice!"

She exchanged a few rapid words with the driver, then joined Jenny in the back of the cab.

"It's all right, he's quite accommodating!" she said, smiling. "I've assured him that there won't be any difficulty about paying the fare once I reach my destination!"

She looked at Jenny with frank and friendly eyes. "It really was nice of you to come to my rescue! I think I'd better introduce myself, don't you—I'm Sally Chalmers."

"And I'm Jenny Barrington. Are you on holiday in Nice?"

Sally shook her head. "No, I work here. I'm a nurse." She grinned at Jenny's startled expression. "Is it so surprising? My cousin, David, came out to join the medical staff of a rather swish nursing home a couple of years ago, and he wrote such glowing letters home that last summer I decided to join him. I was fed up to the back teeth with Manchester—that's where I did my training—and the Côte d'Azur just seemed too good to be true!"

"I can understand that," Jenny said, thinking somewhat wryly of the contrast between a great industrial city in the North of England and this tropical paradise, with its quality of intense, scintillating colour and all the chi-chi of the glamorous South.

"Of course I felt a little strange at first, but I soon got over that," Sally went on gaily. "And luckily I've got marvellous parents: they send me the fare every time they want to see me, so there's no problem there! I've just been home for a few days now, as a matter of fact. My sister Pat's become engaged, so we had to have a bit of a celebration. You know what families are about things like that!"

Jenny didn't know. She said nothing, and Sally shot her a quick glance.

"Is it your first visit, or have you been here before?"

"It's my first visit." Jenny hesitated, but though she had been acquainted with Sally for such a short time she knew instinctively that she was a person in whom one could safely confide. Very briefly she outlined the events of the past few weeks and the situation in which she had found herself, though pride made her conceal the disappointment she had felt when she had found that her father had not even bothered to come and meet her at the airport.

"So you see I've been busy wondering what my family will be like and how I shall fit in," she concluded with a slightly rueful laugh. "I've seen photographs of the Villa Buichi and it looks enormous: Grandmother's three-bedroomed 'semi' is an absolute hovel in comparison!"

For a moment her mind went back to the quiet suburban house, with its neat front garden and discreetly curtained windows, which had been 'home' to her for so many years. She returned to the present to find Sally staring at her in something akin to stupefaction.

"The Villa Buichi? You *did* say the Villa Buichi?" Then, as Jenny assented, "But the Englishman—the author—who lives there is called Challoner! You said your name was Barrington!"

"I took Grandmother's name when I first went to live with her. It was what she wanted, and Father didn't seem to mind." Jenny was regarding her with puzzled eyes. "What's the matter? Why are you looking so surprised?"

"Because I know the Villa Buichi! I mean, I know of it! It's a marvellous place!" Sally gave an excited little laugh. "*And* I know the de Vaisseau family! At least, I suppose it might be more accurate to say I know one of them, and that I've heard of the other two!"

She paused, her vivid face full of interest and amusement. "Dominique de Vaisseau—she's your stepsister, I suppose?—was a patient at the Home some six or seven weeks ago, she had her appendix out. David did the operation, and I was her nurse for part of the time, though luckily someone else took over at the end."

"You didn't like her?" Jenny spoke sharply.

"I thought she was a brat," Sally said simply, then stopped, colouring a little. "I'm sorry, I suppose I oughtn't to have said that! But—well, I'm afraid you'll find out for yourself soon enough! Perhaps it isn't really her fault: she's been so terribly spoilt, you see. She's been used to having her own way and I don't think she gives a damn for anyone but herself. She led us all a frightful dance, including poor David! He told me that what she needed more than anything else was a good hiding, but I guess the majority of men feel more like kissing her than spanking her! She's extremely pretty, as you probably know: lovely black hair and eyes the colour of lapis lazuli!"

There was a moment's silence. Then Jenny said, with would-be lightness, "Well, thanks for warning me! What about my stepbrothers—Piers and Raoul?"

"Well, I don't know much about Piers, but I've heard plenty about Raoul de Vaisseau!" Sally had evidently decided on complete frankness. "He's supposed to be quite devastating, if you like the hard-bitten, sophisticated type. He has the reputation of being one heck of a ladykiller: nice girls beware!"

Her expression, as she regarded Jenny, was a mixture of amusement and sympathy, but what more she would have said the latter never knew, for just at that moment the cab turned into a gateway between high white walls and drew up outside a big house, the frontage of which was flaming with bougainvillea and hibiscus.

"Oh, here we are!" Sally exclaimed, and then, as Jenny, momentarily mystified, peered out of the window, "This is the Home: I live in, you see. The nurses' quarters are at the back. Quite decent, though I envy David his flat and his independence!" She turned the handle of the door as she spoke and prepared to get out.

"If you don't mind hanging on for a minute or two I'll go and borrow some money off someone: David if he's on duty. Luckily it's pay day the day after tomorrow, so I shan't be broke for long!"

"Oh, look, please don't bother!" Jenny spoke quickly. "I'll settle your fare with the driver, it can't possibly amount to much. Yes, really!" as Sally protested.

15

"There's no earthly need for you to bother. It may take you ages to find your cousin, anyway, and I'd rather not wait."

Sally hesitated, then laughed. "All right! But I must pay you back some time, you know; it's awfully nice of you to want to settle my debts, but I can't possibly allow it! I know your address: I shall ring you up and insist on a rendezvous!"

"All right, if it will make you feel better." Jenny saw the obstinate tilt to Sally's chin and did not argue further. "I'd like to see you again, anyway."

"That goes for me, too. You must meet David, I think you'd like each other," Sally told her. She held out one slim brown hand. "Thanks again for being a Good Samaritan and—and *bonne chance*, Jenny!"

Good luck! Yes, it sounded as though she might need it, Jenny thought wryly as Sally spoke to the driver and then limped slowly away. The taxi moved off with a jerk, swinging out of the driveway and accelerating down a wide palm-lined avenue. Feeling that she had at one and the same time found and lost a friend, Jenny leant back in her seat and tried almost dazedly to recall the gist of Sally's remarks. Her mind was so busy with new and disturbing conjectures that though she stared out at the scenery it was with unseeing eyes, and it came as a complete surprise when after some time the cab again ground to an abrupt halt. This time, however, the driver got out and opened her door.

"*Voilà!*" he said, grinning, and Jenny realised that they had stopped at the bottom of a flight of wide stone steps which led up to a spreading white house at the top of a small hill. The slope was cut into terraces aflame with oleander and bougainvillea, veronica and hibiscus, and thick with orange and lemon trees, palms and mimosa, so that her first confused, delighted impression was of sunlight and space and colour and scent.

She didn't need to be told that this was the Villa Buichi. This was her fairytale-come-true. For a moment she stood staring, wide-eyed, then the taxi driver picked up her suitcases and began to climb the steps. Her heart beating fast, she followed. At the top she gave him the money he asked for—she had no way of telling whether

16

she was being overcharged or not, but the amount did not seem to be excessive—and rang the bell.

After what seemed an eternity but was in reality only a moment or two the door was opened by a stout, comfortable-looking woman dressed in severe black. Obviously, Jenny thought, the housekeeper. Gabrielle had mentioned her in one of her letters.

She had been desperately rehearsing what she should say, but immediately the housekeeper saw her standing on the step her fat, round face creased into a smile and she broke into a torrent of English and French. Jenny, trying desperately to catch a few intelligible words in either language, eventually learned three things. Firstly, that her identity was known, secondly, that tea was laid for her in *le petit salon*, and thirdly, and far more important, that she would be having it alone. Her father and stepmother, it seemed, were out and were not expected back before dinner and there was no other member of the family at home.

"But—but they knew what time I was arriving?" Of course they did, she thought, chiding herself for the stupidity of the question. Hadn't a taxi been sent to meet her?

"*Mais oui!* Mademoiselle Dominique—" but here the housekeeper suddenly broke off, looking unaccountably embarrassed, and fidgeted with her hands.

After her disappointment at the airport this singularly cheerless reception seemed to Jenny to be the last straw. Why had her father and stepmother invited her here if they cared so little about her that they could not even be bothered to bid her welcome? Even the ordinary laws of hospitality demanded that much from a host and hostess, she thought indignantly.

Tired, lonely and a little dispirited, she silently acquiesced when the housekeeper offered to show her to her room. This proved to be the loveliest she had ever seen : a large, luxuriously appointed apartment with a wonderful view from its tall windows and with its own private bathroom decorated, like the bedroom, in ivory and gold.

After a quick shower Jenny changed into a crisp cotton frock, but decided to leave her unpacking until later. What she wanted more than anything else at the moment was a cup of tea, and remembering what the housekeeper had said about *le petit salon* she made her way slowly downstairs.

The door of *le petit salon* stood open. It was a delightful room, but though the beautiful Aubusson carpet must have cost a king's ransom and at least two of the paintings would have been welcome in the Louvre, there was a quiet subtlety about its luxury which might have deceived the uninitiated. It was predominantly a family room, combining dignity and elegance with an easy grace of daily living.

Each place Jenny's eye fell a new object of beauty met her gaze, yet at the same time she noticed books and magazines on a small table, a piece of embroidery flung carelessly down on a Louis Quinze chair, a tobacco jar and pipes standing alongside a fine bit of sculpture and large, silver-framed photographs on an exquisite little escritoire. Tea was daintily laid on another small table which had been positioned in front of open french windows, and after some wafer-thin bread-and-butter and a cup of very hot, very good tea—who said that the French couldn't make tea? or was this perhaps the result of her father's influence?—she felt very much more refreshed.

She got up and crossed over to the escritoire. Two photographs, both of young men, were standing beside a bowl of fragrant red roses, and she picked one up and studied it with interest. Piers, or Raoul? Not, she thought, the latter, if Sally's description of him was to be believed. It was certainly quite a good-looking face, but there was a hint of austerity about the features, a certain grimness to the jaw-line. This was no gay Lothario!

Frowning a little, she replaced it and picked up the other. Almost immediately she caught her breath. The face that smiled at her from behind the glass was not only strikingly handsome but also disturbingly devil-may-care. The recklessness, gaiety and audacity of his expression was so riveting that she stood for several moments with the photograph in her hands, until a soft, musical voice with only the suspicion of an accent made her spin round like a startled fawn.

"Getting acquainted with my demon brother? Attractive, isn't he?"

An extremely pretty girl about eighteen or nineteen years old stood in the doorway. She had a perfect oval face, glossy black hair and large, brilliant eyes that were the exact colour of lapis lazuli.

CHAPTER TWO

JENNY carefully put the photograph back in its original place.

"Dominique?" she asked hesitantly, though she knew quite well it couldn't be anyone else. Not with eyes like that.

"*Moi-même.*" Dominique advanced into the room, moving with a swift, feline grace. She was wearing a very brief, sleeveless shift dress, its simplicity doing nothing to disguise the fact that it was expensive. Her beautiful, sun-tanned limbs were bare and her only ornament was a heavy gold bracelet which gave emphasis to one slender wrist.

She flung herself into a chair and helped herself to a cigarette from a small inlaid box before subjecting Jenny to an intent, almost critical scrutiny.

"Goodness, you aren't a bit like I thought you'd be!"

There was a note of surprise in the clear, child's voice and Jenny raised her brows.

"Disappointed?" she asked lightly.

Dominique chose to ignore the question. "I see you've had tea. Good. I told Berthe to offer you some directly you arrived." She smiled suddenly and charmingly. "I intended it as an *amende honorable.* Tea is a ritual with Stephen and I thought you might be like him."

"It was very welcome. But I don't see why—" Jenny began.

Dominique extended a sandalled foot and regarded it. "I was supposed to meet you, you see. Maman and

Stephen had to go to St. Tropez to see Tante Louise: she is ill, perhaps dying, and they couldn't put it off until tomorrow. Maman made me promise that I'd meet you at the airport and look after you until they got back, but—" with a shrug of her slim shoulders—"me, I lack the good conscience! I make other plans!"

"It was you who sent the taxi to meet me?" Jenny recalled the housekeeper's embarrassment and now understood why. Well, at least it was nice to know that there hadn't been deliberate neglect on the part of her father and stepmother! She looked hard at Dominique. No wonder Sally Chalmers had called her a brat!

She said, just a little dryly, "Well, I'm glad you didn't allow me to stand in your way."

"I never allow anyone to do that," Dominique said superbly. She smiled again, that extraordinarily disarming smile.

"I did mean to keep my promise at first, you know. But Alex asked me out to lunch and I couldn't bear to disappoint him. He is a Count, you see, and divinely handsome, and he is—oh, how you say—a dish!" She jumped to her feet. "I will tell you all about him, but later. We must be friends, Jenny! I think I shall probably like you after all. I was afraid I wouldn't, you sounded so dull, but Maman is always telling me that I shouldn't jump to conclusions! Why haven't you come before? You have been asked so many times!"

Impossible she might be, yet there was something extraordinarily likeable about her. Amused in spite of herself, Jenny answered calmly.

"Because I couldn't leave my grandmother. She had nobody except me."

The beautiful eyes opened wide. "But you would have liked to have come?" Then, as Jenny assented, "Me, I do not bother about other people! I please myself what I do. Raoul and I, we are the black sheep. It is Piers who is the good one!"

Jenny glanced involuntarily at the photographs on the escritoire, and Dominique chuckled, a hint of mischief in her lovely face.

"Perhaps you have already decided that for yourself? But it was not my virtuous brother Piers' photograph that you were studying when I came in, it was Raoul's. What a pity that sinners are so much more interesting than saints, *n'est-ce pas*, Jenny?"

Jenny was saved from answering by the appearance of Berthe. Dominique spoke to her in rapid French, and the housekeeper answered with the ease of an old servant. It was obvious, Jenny thought, that she adored Dominique and equally obvious that her stepsister serenely accepted this adoration as her right.

She turned to Jenny with raised brows. "Berthe says you haven't yet unpacked. Do you want to do it yourself? Because if not—"

Jenny interrupted her quickly, repelled by the thought of strange hands unpacking her few simple possessions.

"Oh, please! I'd much rather!"

"Then let us go to your room. You can unpack and I will sit on your bed and watch you work and answer all your questions. You have some, have you not? In your place I would have thousands!"

Jenny laughed, and Dominique looked at her approvingly. "That is better! You are beautiful, Jenny, when you do not look so *très sérieuse*!" She gave a sudden mischievous chuckle as she led the way up the polished staircase to Jenny's bedroom. "I must write and tell Raoul that after all he was quite, quite wrong about you!"

"Wrong?" Jenny echoed blankly.

"He was quite sure you would be a pudding-face, you see." Dominique's eyes danced. "At first Maman said that no, you could not be because you were Stephen's daughter, but there has to be two parents, yes? And your grandmother once wrote and told Stephen that she was making sure you had a decent respectable upbringing, and Raoul said that the only respectable English girls he had ever met had pimples and frizzy hair and fat legs and were of a dullness quite extraordinary!"

She paused for a moment, then, heedless of Jenny's indignant protest, swept on.

"Then *you* wrote, and your letters were so very prim and proper and you mentioned that you were a schoolteacher and Raoul said—" She stopped, clapping her hands over her mouth, her eyes still alight with mischief. "But you look so ferocious, Jenny, perhaps I'd better not tell you the rest!"

By this time they had reached the bedroom and Jenny, inwardly seething, was glad to hide her hot cheeks by bending over her case.

"Your brother Raoul seems to have some very peculiar ideas!"

"I do not think they are peculiar!" Dominique sounded genuinely surprised. "Raoul likes pretty girls. What is wrong with that?"

Nothing, except that he sounded completely insufferable, Jenny thought grimly. Arrogant and—and unprincipled!

"What about Piers? Does he share the same liking?" she asked dryly.

Dominique had perched herself on the bed, hugging her bare brown knees. At the mention of Piers her face suddenly wore a closed expression, but all she said was, "Piers thinks—dreams—eats—sleeps ceramics! He has a one-track mind, that one!"

"How nice for his fiancée!"

Dominique shot her a swift, uncertain glance. "Oh, you've heard about Céleste, have you? What did Maman tell you?"

"Only that she was the daughter of a distinguished diplomat and very beautiful. Do you like her?"

"I detest her!" Dominique said, and Jenny was almost shocked by her vehemence. "She is a snake! A traitress! But don't ask me why, for I shan't tell you!"

There was a moment's silence. Jenny, at a loss for words, carefully removed her best dress from its tissue wrappings, and proceeded to smooth out some entirely imaginary creases. Then she said quietly, "Well, I don't expect you see much of her, do you?"

Dominique gave a derisive little laugh. "Oh, don't I? Her father has a villa near here and when they're in residence Piers comes home practically every weekend. The rest of the time we don't see much of him—thank goodness!" She paused. "We see even less of Raoul. He is always on the move: he never stays anywhere very long."

"You mean he hasn't got a settled job?"

Dominique shrugged. "He likes variety. He has been a racing driver and he has climbed mountains and he has been a pilot for a South American charter company which went bust because there was a revolution or something. Raoul was in a tight spot, that time. At present he is tied up with a mining company in Colorado and he tells Maman that he is about to make his fortune, but of course he won't. He is always losing money on unlucky ventures, poor Raoul. It is very sad."

Dominique spoke so cheerfully that it was obvious that she did not find it sad at all. Jenny, horrified by her disclosures, said tartly, "Get-rich-schemes seldom do work, I believe."

"No, but there is always the possibility, *n'est-ce pas?* Stephen says that Raoul is a born gambler and I think that's true. And yet...." She stopped abruptly, almost as though she had been on the brink of some confidence and had then thought better of it. Instead she gave Jenny her swift, enchanting smile.

"But here I am talking about my brothers when naturally it is your father in whom you are most interested." She paused. "You are lucky to have such a father, Jenny. He is—oh, *très gentil*! We do not always agree, you understand, but he and Maman are very happy together and I am glad. She was lonely for a long time after my father died." She gave Jenny a thoughtful glance. "You are very like Stephen, I think, except for your expression. You are still sad, aren't you? It is in your eyes."

Jenny gave an unsteady little laugh. "I suppose I've been living in a kind of vacuum. It's felt so odd ... not having Grandmother to worry about, not to have my duties to perform. Everything's changed and I haven't got used to it yet."

Dominique gave a little shrug. "I think if I were you I should feel as though I had been let out of prison!" She glanced at her watch and jumped to her feet. "I must go and get ready for dinner. Stephen and Maman will be back soon, I think: Maman said that they would not be late.".

Jenny, left alone to finish her unpacking, found that

she had much food for thought. She had just hung the last of her cotton dresses in the magnificent wardrobe—three times the size of the one she had used at home!—when she heard a commotion of footsteps in the hall downstairs, a dog barking happily and Berthe's voice talking to it. Then came a man's deep tones and a woman's answering, clear and lovely. Stephen and Gabrielle, home at last. Ridiculously, her heart missed a beat and she was conscious of a feeling of trepidation. What would they think of her? What would she think of them?—and, particularly, of her father?

Despite the closeness of their relationship she thought that it would be impossible for them to meet as anything but complete strangers, and yet, when eventually she found herself face to face with the man who for years had had little more substance in her mind than a vaguely remembered dream, she was amazed to find how little constraint existed between them.

Perhaps luckily, she was unaware how much this was due to the *savoir-faire* for which Stephen Challoner was noted. A handsome man with black hair winged with silver at the temples and dark-browed grey eyes, like Jenny's, he had for years rarely given more than a passing thought to the young daughter he had left in England. Now as he saw Jenny, slight and fair, her quiet reserve contrasting so strongly with the vivacity of her stepmother and stepsister, his conscience smote him. He ought to have made more effort to persuade his mother-in-law to let Jenny visit him ... ought to have visited her himself. Troubled, as Dominique had been, by the seriousness of her expression when she was not actually smiling, he found himself conjecturing about the kind of life she had led. Pretty dull, he imagined, for after all, her constant companion had been a very old lady with violent prejudices and a fastidious abhorrence of anything that was unconventional and unordinary. Heaven only knew that it was time she had a change! He smiled a little wryly at the thought. There was never anything dull about life at the Villa Buichi, what with his stepchildren and their friends coming and going and his wife involved in her usual whirl of social activities!

Jenny, for her part, was reassured by the kindliness of her father's eyes and smile and fascinated by her stepmother's beauty and charm. Gabrielle was one of those rare women who keep their loveliness unmarred by the passage of years. She had ripened and matured, but she had not grown old and she had, besides a lively sense of fun, a kind heart.

"*Ma chère*, I cannot tell you how glad we are to see you here at last!" she said warmly to Jenny. "Without you Stephen and I have never felt our family to be complete. You must look upon this as your home from now on, and stay with us for just as long as you wish."

Jenny, horrified at the thought of ever living permanently in France, murmured an incoherent answer. She had been relieved to find that in her presence, at least, everyone seemed determined to speak English. That, at any rate, made her surroundings seem a little less strange.

"I am so sorry that we were unable to meet you at the airport," Gabrielle went on. "My aunt is very ill and she wished to see us both. You did not feel that we were neglecting you? Dominique, I hope, has taken good care of you. I did not want you to arrive in Nice without a welcome from at least one member of your family."

Jenny, shooting a quick glance at Dominique, was amused to find that the younger girl was looking slightly uneasy. She had, however, no intention of giving her away.

"Thank you, yes. She has been very kind," she said quietly, and smiled as Dominique, sitting next to her at the beautiful refectory table, gave her hand a surreptitious but grateful squeeze. Evidently, for all her proud boast that she pleased herself what she did, Dominique preferred that the real circumstances surrounding her stepsister's arrival should not be known.

Dinner was such a friendly, comfortable meal that Jenny felt her spirits rising. The food was the most delicious she had ever tasted—a bewildering selection of hors d'oeuvres, golden brown chicken bursting with truffles and served with tiny peas and puffed-out, golden potatoes ... a froth of ice and whipped cream dashed with kirsch ... fruit crystallised whole in sugar—and seemed a far cry from the plain, simple fare upon which her grandmother had insisted. (Even omelettes had been regarded by old Mrs. Barrington with a certain amount of suspicion!) She refused wine almost automatically, but was unable to drink the tepid, queer-tasting water which was brought to her instead. Perhaps another time ... and at the thought her lips curved into a faint smile. Grandmother would probably have said that the rot was already beginning to set in!

It was not only the food which she found enjoyable. The conversation sparkled, and as she was allowed to listen rather than to talk she was able to relax and watch the play of expressions upon the three faces. Dominique was very like her mother, except that Gabrielle's eyes were dark. From whom, then, had Dominique inherited hers? Her dead father, to whom, otherwise, she must surely bear little resemblance?

The telephone rang and a few seconds later a maid came into the room and murmured something into Gabrielle's ear. She immediately excused herself, returning a few minutes later with a glow in her eyes.

"That was Piers. He will be home this weekend." She looked smilingly at Jenny. "I have told you about my elder son, have I not? He has recently taken over the management of the pottery works founded by my late husband: a great responsibility for so young a man, although he appears to revel in the opportunity."

"Piers enjoys hard work," Stephen said, leaning back in his chair and touching his lips with the napkin. "He is an industrious soul."

"Which is more than can be said for his brother!" Gabrielle laughed, but there had been a slightly rueful note in her voice. Again she looked at Jenny. "You will find Piers and Raoul as different as chalk and cheese, Jenny. Piers is a hard-headed and very successful industrialist: Raoul, I fear, is—" she sought for the right word and brought it out triumphantly—"an adventurer!"

"Maman, that is not fair!" Dominique's eyes sparkled with indignation. "An adventurer is someone quite horrid who lives by his wits, and Raoul is not like that at all!"

"I am quite sure your mother didn't use the word in that sense," Stephen said, laughing. "I think she meant that he enjoys an adventurous life. Didn't you, my dear?" and he looked across the table at his wife.

"I did indeed. I haven't many grey hairs, but all those that I have are on account of *mon cher* Raoul!" Gabrielle's eyes twinkled as she put her hand to her glossy dark hair where, sure enough, an occasional silver thread gleamed. "He was a mad scamp when he was a boy and even now that he is a man—" She laughed and shrugged and left the sentence unfinished. "My one consolation is that he seems to have as many lives as a cat!"

Jenny, who had never taken a risk in her life and who secretly thought that for the most part they were foolish and unnecessary, searched in vain for something to say. More and more the conviction was growing that she was going to dislike Raoul de Vaisseau very much indeed.

Dominique was staring down at her glass, her brow creased into a slight frown. It was as though her mother's last words, light-hearted though they had been, had set her off on an unpleasant train of thought.

She said sombrely, "Raoul was luckier than Marcel was. I sometimes wonder whether he has ever forgiven himself for that fact."

"Marcel?" Jenny looked up.

There was a moment's silence. Then Gabrielle said quietly, "Marcel was Raoul's best friend. He joined Raoul in South America and flew for the same charter company until a revolution broke out. Marcel's plane was hi-jacked and, tragically, there was a crash in which everyone, including Marcel, was killed."

Jenny's eyes widened. "And—and Raoul?"

"As Dominique said, he was luckier. After some hair-raising adventures he escaped from the country by the skin of his teeth." Gabrielle sighed. "Normally Raoul would have treated the whole affair as a huge joke, but of course Marcel's death made that impossible. And what made it very much worse was that Marcel left a wife and three young children."

"Then surely—why on earth did he go to South

America in the first place?" Jenny looked and sounded completely mystified and Stephen smiled a little grimly to himself. There spoke a true Barrington!

It was Dominique who answered. "The money was good. It had to be, because of the risks involved." She looked at her mother, her eyes suddenly wistful. "I wish Raoul would come home again soon, Maman. It seems ages since he was last here."

"He'll turn up sooner or later. No one should know better than you that Raoul is completely unpredictable," Stephen said, smiling as he rose to his feet. He laid his hand on Jenny's shoulder.

"If you are not too tired, my dear, would you allow us the pleasure of hearing you play? We have a very fine piano, but it's rarely touched, alas, except by the tuner."

Jenny hesitated, but it was the first request he had ever made of her and she felt unable to refuse.

The beautiful grand piano, open though Stephen had said that nobody used it, was in a large, square room with panelled walls and a marble floor scattered with rich rugs. Jenny, seating herself on the stool, ran her fingers up and down the keys, rejoicing to find that it was as fine an instrument as her father had promised. Stephen asked for Mozart and Gabrielle for Chopin, and she played both, losing herself as always in the sheer joy of the music, unconscious of time or her surroundings. Even when her fingers fell from the keys after the last rippling chords and she looked up to receive her father's and stepmother's appreciative thanks the spell was not broken. Warmed by kindness, soothed by the music, she felt at that moment more at home than she had ever dreamed possible.

Almost inevitably, it was not a feeling which was destined to last. Despite Stephen's and Gabrielle's unfailing kindness, she found the next two days the most bewildering she had ever spent. Every facet of her new life contrasted so strongly with the life she had led with her grandmother that it almost seemed as though it bore no resemblance to it at all.

Thanks to an excellent staff, domestically the household ran on well-oiled wheels, but peace as Jenny understood it simply did not exist at the Villa Buichi, except perhaps in Stephen's study, which was a sanctum respected by everyone. Gabrielle entertained lavishly and the house always seemed to be full of people, even when she herself was out. Both she and Dominique seemed to spend most of their time in the pursuit of pleasure, and Jenny, brought up to believe that life held a serious purpose, found their frivolity hard to understand. In addition, she felt almost guilty about the opulence with which she was surrounded. Old Mrs. Barrington's only source of income, apart from Stephen's cheques, had been a modest annuity and there had never been any money to spare for even small luxuries. Jenny had little jewellery and even fewer cosmetics and she had always been accustomed to looking after her own hair and making most of her own clothes. Consequently she had something of a shock when she first saw Dominique's wardrobe, which was literally crammed with beautiful, elegant clothes which must have cost a small fortune.

"But I like clothes—I find them *fort amusant*!" Dominique protested. "What would you? I cannot go naked!" She looked thoughtfully at Jenny, then, searching along the rows of dresses, took one out and held it towards Jenny. It was a slim sheath of gentian blue lace and it had obviously never been worn.

"Let me give you this, Jenny. I have never felt that it was quite right for me, but it would look perfect on you."

Jenny shook her head. "Thank you, Dominique. It's kind of you, but I have plenty of dresses," she said quietly.

"Those!" Dominique said scornfully, then, seeing Jenny flush, she added, "I suppose it is pride that makes you say no! Me, I think you are silly. You do not make the best of yourself : it is a waste!"

Her lips set in a sulky line. Jenny had learnt that although she was all charm when she was getting her own way, the least hint of opposition annoyed her.

"You forget I'm a working girl, not a film star!" Jenny strove to speak lightly.

"Bah! Who wants to work?" Dominique demanded.

"You, presumably. Didn't someone tell me you wanted to be an actress?" Jenny retorted.

"Oh, that was ages ago!" Dominique's shrug was expressive. "I found out that it was not as nice as I thought. I fear I am the butterfly, *n'est-ce pas*? Maman and Stephen will have to support me until I find a suitable husband!"

"Suitable?"

"Rich and clever and handsome. What more could a girl want?" Dominique mocked.

"You might perhaps want to be a little in love with him as well," Jenny suggested.

Dominique's brilliant eyes danced. "My dear Jenny! I do not expect miracles!" She waited for Jenny's reluctant grin, then flung herself on her bed with a laugh. "Have you ever fallen in love, *ma soeur*?"

"Never. Have you?" Jenny asked the question equally bluntly.

Was it her imagination, or did a shadow pass over Dominique's expressive face? At any rate she seemed to hesitate before answering.

"Oh, many times! But not seriously, you understand. I think perhaps I am like Raoul. He makes love to all women, that one, but he is careful not to become too involved." She looked teasingly at Jenny. "It is a pity he is not here now, for I am sure that you would find him very attractive. Women do: there are few who can resist him!"

"Dominique!" In spite of herself Jenny blushed scarlet.

"Well, what is wrong? He is only your stepbrother! He would expect you to fall in love with him, you know, and it would not do you any harm, so long as you remembered that you must not take him too seriously!"

That was a bit too much. Jenny got to her feet and said decidedly, "I don't think the contingency is in the least likely. Stop being so silly, Dominique, and finish dressing. I thought you said you had an appointment at your hairdresser's? You'll be fearfully late."

"You sound just like a schoolteacher!" Dominique grumbled, but much to Jenny's relief the subject of Raoul de Vaisseau was dropped, at any rate for the time being. Later, however, she found herself remembering Dominique's words with something approaching indignation. Did her stepsister really imagine that she, Jenny, would be silly enough to let herself be attracted by a good-looking philanderer who seemed, from all accounts, to stand for everything she most despised? It was so absurd that it was almost laughable—except, of course, that Dominique had been perfectly serious!

She wandered along the esplanade, torn between the desire for a cool drink in one of the pavement cafés and the feeling that now she'd got the chance to do a bit of exploring on her own it would be as well to make the most of it. She had agreed to accompany Dominique into Nice, but had firmly resisted the suggestion that she, too, would benefit from a visit to the beauty salon.

"What's the point of paying someone an astronomical number of francs to do what I can quite well do for myself?" she had asked practically, and had laughed at Dominique's disgusted expression. In actual fact there was no real need for her to worry about money since Stephen had already told her that whatever she wanted she could charge to his account, but Jenny's pride would not allow her to do this. To accept her father's and stepmother's hospitality was one thing: to become a dependant was another.

Nevertheless Nice was obviously not an ideal spot for anyone with modest resources. It seemed to Jenny that practically everyone she saw looked almost terrifyingly rich and elegant and as though they regarded money as the most important thing in life. The modern city, with its opulent hotels, expensive shops, broad straight boulevards and never-ending stream of cars and buses, was doubtless what they wanted, but Jenny found the old town, still very Italian in character, far more to her liking. Even so she quickly realised the truth of Stephen's remark that Nice was essentially a town for living in and not for sight-seeing and was not sorry when it was time to return to the beauty salon, where, surprisingly, Dominique was already waiting for her.

"You wish to go down to the beach?" Dominique asked.

Jenny thought of the hundreds of bikini-clad bodies lying, sardine-wise, on the pebbly beach below the Promenade des Anglais and shook her head. "I'd rather go home, thank you."

"*Bon.*" Dominique, who had emerged from the salon with a new and ravishingly pretty hairstyle, appeared to be in an excellent mood. She chatted away gaily as she drove back to the villa in a series of jerky dashes and stops which made Jenny bounce, and eventually parked the car with an insouciance which proclaimed a fine disregard for the possibility of scratched paintwork. She was in the middle of a lively and somewhat malicious account of a conversation she had overheard at the hairdresser's when Berthe came running to meet them.

"Mademoiselle Jenny! You are wanted on the telephone."

"Me?" Jenny stared at her in surprise. "Who wants me, Berthe?"

"It is a Miss Chalmers. I was about to take a message when I heard the car," Berthe explained.

Sally! Jenny's face lit up and she hurried past Dominique to the telephone.

"Hello! Jenny Barrington here."

"Hello, Jenny! It's me—Sally Chalmers." The warm, gay, very English voice was music in Jenny's ears: she had not realised until then that she had been feeling slightly homesick. "How are you enjoying the Côte d'Azur?"

"Very much, thank you." Jenny was acutely conscious of Dominique, standing only a few feet away. "How are you? Foot better?"

"Oh, quite, thanks. When can we meet, Jenny? I want to pay you the money I owe you. Are you free next Monday? It's my day off and I thought we might have lunch together, if you'd like that. There's rather a nice little café in the Rue Masséna, a place called Maxime's."

Jenny thought rapidly. As far as she knew no plans involving herself had been made for next Monday.

"That would be lovely. What time?"

"Oh—half-past twelvish. I'll book a table. The food is so good and relatively inexpensive, for Nice, that the place is apt to get a bit crowded. It will be nice to see you again, Jenny: I'm looking forward to it."

"Me too." Jenny put the receiver down and turned to find Dominique staring at her.

"I did not know," the younger girl said in an odd voice, "that you had any friends in Nice, Jenny?"

Jenny laughed. "This one I owe to you, Dominique. We shared the taxi that you booked for me on the day I arrived," and she explained what had happened.

There was a faint crease between Dominique's brows. "Her name is Chalmers? I seem to know that name."

"I'm not surprised. By an odd coincidence she's one of the nurses who looked after you when you had your appendix removed. Lovely red hair and lots of freckles and a nice smile—remember her?"

"Oh! Oh, yes, I think I do." Dominique's eyes sparked. "But I'm not at all sure that I agree with you about the smile! She was very officious and full of her own self-importance. I didn't like her much." She paused, then added casually, "I suppose she thought she could do more or less what she liked because she was related to one of the doctors. There was a Dr. Chalmers, and somebody said they were cousins."

"Yes, she talked quite a lot about him," Jenny agreed. She hesitated, then added, "I think you probably got the wrong impression of Sally, Dominique. She struck me as being an awfully nice girl."

Dominique gave a disagreeable little laugh. "You haven't been her patient! She was quite horrid to me, and so was her odious cousin! He's the most bumptious young man I've ever met, and I believe I told him so!"

The good humour of a few minutes ago had disappeared completely and there was a distinct edge to her voice. Before Jenny could answer she added tartly, "You are not planning to meet this Sally person to-morrow, I hope? Piers will be home and Maman will expect you to be here."

Puzzled by her attitude, Jenny looked at her, her brow pleated by a frown. Why should Dominique care what friends she made? All she said, however, was, "I'll be here. I'm not meeting Sally until next Monday, so that's all right."

Secretly she was devoutly thankful that it was Piers who was coming home and not his younger brother. So far she liked all that she had heard about Piers, but she had a shrewd suspicion that the qualities she was most disposed to admire were not really appreciated by his mother and sister. Gabrielle obviously loved both her sons, but Jenny thought it likely that the graceless Raoul was her favourite and Dominique, of course, was unashamedly partisan.

She was forced to admit, after actually meeting Piers, that he had neither the striking good looks nor the easy charm which characterised the rest of his family. He looked older than his photograph and the suggestion of hardness about his mouth and square chin was accentuated. He greeted Jenny pleasantly enough but without a great deal of interest, and she was a little chilled by his attitude until she realised, from something that Gabrielle said, that his mind was still completely preoccupied with business problems.

What about Céleste? Jenny wondered. Was she also relegated to the background of her fiancé's life? At the moment it appeared that she was in Paris with her father, for whom she acted as honorary secretary.

"Poor Piers! You don't see much of each other, do you?" his mother said sympathetically.

Piers shrugged. "Circumstances are against us, Maman. Madame de Courville has not been at all well lately and Céleste has not felt able to leave her."

"Except, of course, for really important reasons!" Dominique's eyes were wide and innocent. "She always seems to be getting photographed, going to this social function or that."

There was a moment's uncomfortable silence. Then Piers, his face impassive, said smoothly, "Naturally Monsieur de Courville entertains, and is entertained, a great deal. Luckily Céleste has been able to help him by taking her mother's place on a number of occasions." He turned to his mother. "Naturally we both hoped that she would be able to accompany me this weekend, but it simply couldn't be managed."

This time Jenny thought that she detected an oddly defensive note in his voice and she noticed, too, a mock-

34

ing gleam in Dominique's eyes. She had a feeling that the younger girl was not prepared to leave it at that, but since her mother adroitly changed the conversation she had to content herself with murmuring something under her breath. Jenny did not catch the words, but evidently Piers did, for although he pretended not to hear a slow red flush crept up under his skin.

It seemed to Jenny that although outwards all seemed pleasant enough there were definite undercurrents, and she found herself wondering about the cause. Dominique, of course, disliked her brother's fiancée, she had made that perfectly plain already. In itself her antipathy was not particularly remarkable, "in-laws" often didn't get on together, but why had Dominique called Céleste a "traitress"? It was an odd word to choose, however much she detested her! She had meant it, too, just as a few moments ago she had meant to needle her brother.

"When are Piers and Céleste getting married?" She found Gabrielle sitting alone in the *petit salon* before dinner that same evening and asked the question out of sheer curiosity. No wedding plans had been mentioned by anyone, yet surely it would be a huge affair involving much preparation?

"Some time in the late autumn, I believe. They haven't actually fixed the date yet." Gabrielle frowned down at the glass of sherry she was holding in her hand. "They haven't been engaged very long, you see, and Madame de Courville's illness has been an unforeseen complication." She paused for a moment, then sighed and added, half to herself, "I only wish that they would settle something soon."

"Settle what?" Dominique, wearing a lovely amber dress that accentuated her vivid colouring, appeared in the doorway.

"Jenny was just asking me when Piers and Céleste intend to get married," Gabrielle said quietly, and it seemed to Jenny that she gave her daughter a warning glance.

If so Dominique either didn't see it or she chose to disregard it. "I don't suppose Céleste will want to fix a date until she's quite, quite sure that she can't have her cake and eat it, too," she said with a hard little laugh.

"Dominique!"

Jenny had not the slightest idea what Dominique meant, but evidently Gabrielle did, for she spoke with unwonted sharpness. Her daughter shrugged, shooting an oblique defiant look at Jenny as she did so.

"Well, I wish her joy of dear brother Piers, anyway. Do you know, Maman, he's just taken it upon himself to read me another lecture? He doesn't approve of me or anything I do, it seems. He even told me I ought to get myself a job!"

"Well, it would probably be good for you," Gabrielle said, laughing. "And you know Stephen has told you the same thing many times before."

"Maybe. But it isn't Piers' place to tell me what to do!" Dominique retorted, and Jenny saw that her brows had drawn together in an angry frown. Not a happy united family, this, she reflected wryly. Its members were strong and varying personalities and it was only too obvious that Piers and Dominique, at least, were at loggerheads most of the time.

And what about Raoul, the other "bad" de Vaisseau? How did Piers get on with him? She had a slight clue to the answer to this question when at dinner Stephen made a casual reference to his younger stepson which seemed to give Piers an opening he had been looking for.

"I suppose there's no point in asking whether you've heard from Raoul?" There was a sardonic inflection in his voice which spoke volumes.

Gabrielle bit her lip. "No, not recently. But the last time he wrote he was wildly enthusiastic about this new mining venture. He's sure it's going to pay off: the chance of a lifetime, I believed he called it."

Piers gave a short laugh. "I don't suppose it will be any more successful than his other ventures! It's a thousand pities that he can't seem to settle down to something useful!"

"I think perhaps he needs a touch of excitement." Gabrielle spoke lightly, but her words seemed to act as an irritant on Piers, for his face darkened.

"What he needs is a sense of responsibility! He's been in and out of some kind of trouble all his life, and it seems to me that it's high time he began to grow up!"

Dominique's face flamed and she glared at her brother. "How *dare* you say that? I suppose you would like Raoul to be as dull and solemn as you are yourself? At least he knows how to enjoy life, and that is something that you have never learned to do!"

What Piers would have answered no one ever knew, for just at that moment a laughing voice said from the doorway, "What a dramatic pronouncement, little sister! Has Piers again been taking my name in vain, that you need to take up the cudgels on my behalf?"

There was a stunned silence. Then "Raoul!" Dominique squeaked, and flew out of her chair with outstretched arms to meet the tall, dark-haired man who came striding towards her. Then she stopped stock still and said in an entirely different voice, *"Céleste!"*

A willowy, golden-haired girl had followed Raoul into the room and now stood, graceful and smiling, by his side.

Beside her Jenny heard Piers catch his breath. Then there was the unmistakable sound of splintering glass and when she looked she saw that the slender stem of his wine-glass had snapped. He was holding the fragment in his hand, while a pool of red Chateau Gruard Larose Sarget was already spreading slowly across the white damask tablecloth.

CHAPTER THREE

"DARLING, couldn't you manage to look a little more welcoming? I shall begin to think you aren't pleased to see me!" Céleste's voice was low and lilting. She bent over Piers to kiss his brown cheek and Jenny caught the delicate, elusive fragrance of the scent she was wearing.

Piers rose to his feet. He was master of himself again, his feelings, whatever they were, hidden behind the mask-like expression that made his face so often inscrutable.

"Of course I'm delighted to see you—but also very surprised. You told me you couldn't possibly manage to get away this weekend."

Céleste laughed. "I know. That's what I thought. But Maman suddenly took it into her head that she wanted to come down here for a week or two: Paris is a bit too stuffy for her at the moment, I'm afraid. I've come on ahead to open up the house and to make sure that everything is as it should be. You know what servants are, they're so unreliable." She directed a smiling glance at Raoul, who was being embraced by his mother and sister. "Raoul arrived in Paris yesterday and dropped in to see us. I told him my plans and he was an absolute angel, insisted on driving me down. We didn't bother to let you know: we thought it would be such fun to give you a surprise." She paused, then added lightly, with a flicker of her long, gold-tipped lashes, "It appears that we've succeeded."

It did, indeed, seem as though everyone was stunned. After the first rapturous welcomes an odd feeling of constraint had pervaded the atmosphere and there was an awkward silence after Céleste had finished speaking. For once even Gabrielle's usual composure had deserted her and it was with a visible effort that she pulled herself together.

"My dear, it's lovely to see you both, however unexpectedly." She turned to Jenny. "As you've probably gathered by now, Jenny, this is Céleste, Piers' fiancée, and this is Raoul, my younger son."

Céleste extended a slender, languid hand in Jenny's direction. She was, Jenny thought, quite the most beautiful girl she had ever seen, with masses of red-gold hair, a long, slender neck and a very white skin.

"So this is Jenny!" Raoul said.

Because of what Dominque had told her, Jenny knew quite well why there was a note of surprised amusement in Raoul's deep voice. Flushing a little, she forced herself to meet his gaze and raged inwardly at the gleam of impudent approval in the intensely blue eyes which were so like his sister's. He was, she realised

38

half-resentfully, even more good-looking than his photo-graph, and so charged with vitality that it almost seemed to brim over.

"What a delightful addition to our family Allow me to congratulate you, Stephen!" Raoul said, and instead of shaking Jenny's hand, as Piers had done and as she had expected, he bowed over it and kissed the fingertips.

Taken aback by what she considered the flamboyance of the gesture, she snatched her hand away. Too late she realised that for a Frenchman it was merely a com-monplace: sudden laughter was already dancing in the blue eyes and she saw the corners of his firm mouth lift. Luckily, no one except Raoul seemed to notice her confusion. Dominique was trying to attract her brother's attention, Céleste had arranged herself decoratively on the arm of Piers' chair and Stephen and Gabrielle were both of them talking at once. There was a ring of nervousness in Gabrielle's voice and her words almost tumbled out of her mouth, as though she felt that only by keeping the conversation going would it be possible to avoid the further straining of what was already a badly overstrained situation.

Jenny, so sensitive to atmosphere that after a time she felt acutely uncomfortable, decided that it might be tactful for her, the outsider, to leave them to them-selves as soon as possible. For the life of her she could not imagine why what should surely have been a happy family reunion had turned so sour, but it was nothing to do with her, and explaining that she had letters to write she excused herself as soon as an opportunity arose and went up alone to her room.

She did not, however, do much writing. Her mind was too crowded with new impressions for concentration to be possible, nor was it easy for her to dismiss the dramatic arrival of Raoul and Céleste from her thoughts. The impact upon the rest of the family had definitely been shattering—but why? And though Raoul, at least, had acted as though everything was perfectly normal, surely he must have seen—couldn't have avoided seeing! —the expression on Piers' face as he had walked in!

She sucked the end of her pen meditatively. There

39

was no love lost between the two brothers, that much was certain. Inevitably her sympathies were with Piers, who, she thought wryly, was the only member of the whole family of whom her grandmother might grudgingly have approved. It couldn't be easy for him, obviously a respectable, hardworking type, to contend with a brother and sister like Raoul and Dominique. Both of them seemed to have an extraordinary sense of values : both of them were potential dynamite.

In spite of herself her face grew hot as she remembered her gauche reaction when Raoul had kissed her hand. After that she had several times found his eyes upon her, wickedly teasing under down-dropped lids, and each time, to her helpless annoyance, she had had to make a conscious effort to retain her composure. She believed that she had succeeded, but nevertheless her dislike of Raoul de Vaisseau had increased. Dominique might believe in her brother's fatal fascination, she thought grimly, but that was simply because she was too young, as yet, to realise the worthlessness of superficial charm. Thank goodness for her own sensible, rigid upbringing, which, however the de Vaisseaus might sneer, did at least enable her to tell the gold from the glister !

Gradually she became aware that the house was very quiet, and glanced at her watch. Nearly eleven o'clock. She supposed she had better go down to say good night. That much would be expected of her and she did not want to provoke comment.

Gabrielle was alone, working on her embroidery. On a low table by her side was a lamp and silks of every colour, from delicate tints to deep shades, all piled carelessly together.

She looked up and smiled as Jenny entered. "Hello, my dear. Finished your letters?"

"Not all, I'm afraid." Jenny sank down into a chair and watched her stepmother's busy needle. "That's simply beautiful ! I love those delicate colours !"

"Céleste chose them. This is for her trousseau." Gabrielle spoke calmly, setting a stitch with delicate care. The light shone softly on her slender white hands and her face was in shadow, so that Jenny could not see her expression.

"Oh!" For a moment Jenny could think of nothing to say, then she said awkwardly, "She is very beautiful, isn't she? I don't think I've ever seen such wonderful hair."

"Yes, indeed. And she has brains as well as beauty. She will make a perfect wife for Piers." Gabrielle spoke with perhaps just a shade too much enthusiasm. She paused, then added, "I am so glad that they will be able to be together this weekend after all."

"Is Céleste staying here?"

"No. Her family has a charming villa not far from here and Piers has taken her home now."

"Is everyone else out? The house seems very quiet."

Gabrielle raised her delicate brows. "I suppose it is. I hadn't noticed. Stephen, of course, is working and Dominique has gone out. Raoul, I think, has gone to his room. I gather that he's had very little sleep since he left Colorado two days ago and I expect he wants an early night." She hesitated a little. "I believe he and Dominique have made arrangements to go riding tomorrow morning. Perhaps you'd like to join them, Jenny?"

Jenny's colour rose. "I'm sorry. I don't ride."

"It doesn't appeal to you? You prefer swimming or dancing, perhaps?"

Jenny shook her head. "I've never had time for anything but music."

"You are like Piers—an industrious soul!" Gabrielle's voice was a little rueful. "I wish that my bad Dominique was more like you, *ma petite*. She worries me sometimes : she is so restless and unpredictable."

"Growing pains. It's a pity she isn't interested in a career : that would absorb some of her energy," Jenny said, smiling.

"As I think I told you in one of my letters, she wanted to be an actress once, but that was some time ago. Before she went into the nursing home to have her appendix removed, in fact." She sighed, then laughed. "I don't think that having operations agrees with her! She has been far more difficult since."

"I expect she'll settle down sooner or later." Jenny tried to speak encouragingly.

"I hope so. Piers insists that she needs a job, but he refuses to be more specific. He forgets that she has not been trained for work and she has, also, an innate dislike for discipline." Carefully Gabrielle selected a new thread. "Of course, she'll probably marry quite soon. She is an attractive girl and she has a host of admirers."

"So I've noticed. I haven't met her Count yet, but I'm told he's a dish," Jenny said, laughing.

Gabrielle frowned. She looked as though she was about to say something, then changed her mind. Instead, she let her embroidery fall from her hands into her lap.

"I must remind Berthe to take Stephen some coffee. Would you like some too, *ma chère?*"

"No, thank you. I'm just going to get a breath of fresh air, then I'm going to bed."

It was a warm, still night and the wine-dark sky was spangled with stars. Jenny, glad to escape from the confines of the house, went slowly down the terrace steps, taking deep breaths of the sweet-scented air. Instinctively she made for what had become her favourite spot, a secluded corner shaded by an old magnolia tree, where roses and oleanders grew in profusion. Here she dropped down on to a rustic bench and sat perfectly still, her hands clasped in her lap, looking up at the blue-blackness of the sky. Even at home she had loved to star-gaze, and here the stars were more brilliant and more numerous than she had ever imagined.

Several minutes had passed before she gradually became aware that she was not alone. There was a tall shadow under the bougainvillea which was not cast by any tree, and a small glowing light which could only be the tip of a cigarette. Hastily she rose to her feet, intending to flee precipitately back to the house, but before she could do so the shadow moved. The moonlight fell strongly on Raoul de Vaisseau as he came forward, its pale glow blanching and dramatising his handsome features.

"Don't go." There was a suspicion of laughter in the

deep voice. "Most things are better shared, and moonlight is one of them."

"I only came out for a breath of fresh air. I'm just going to bed: it's late." Jenny knew that she sounded stiff and unfriendly, but she couldn't help it.

"You aren't frightened of me, are you?" This time the amusement in his voice was unmistakable. "I won't eat you, you know."

Jenny drew a short breath. "I never imagined you would. You find English girls unpalatable, I believe!"

Raoul did not seem in the least put out. "My young sister has been talking!" he said, laughing. "Is it only that that you hold against me?" His gaze was quizzical and it disturbed her oddly: nobody had any right to such bright, challenging eyes!

She said coldly, "Your opinions really don't interest me," and made as if to brush past him. She was not quick enough, however, for his hand caught at her arm and almost before she could divine his intention he had pulled her round to face him.

"But yours interest me." His voice was amused and there was mockery in every line of his body. "You've looked at me like a disapproving dowager from the moment we met! Why? Just because I didn't dare to hope that you'd be as beautiful as you are? One doesn't usually expect Aphrodite for a sister, you know!"

"Stepsister!" Jenny retorted sharply, and then wished she hadn't, for Raoul grinned.

"Ah yes! That subtle distinction is definitely worth remembering!"

His arrogance was insupportable, Jenny thought indignantly. She turned quickly away and this time, instead of stopping her, Raoul fell in beside her. They ascended the steps side by side without speaking until they reached the top, then Raoul said teasingly, "Are you really determined to go to bed? Such a night is not made for sleeping. What about going for a bathe? Not in the pool, I know a perfect cove where the beach will still be warm from the day's sun and where the water is like silk."

He wasn't joking. After one stunned moment Jenny

43

said incredulously, "Go for a bathe? At *this* time of night?"

Raoul gave a low laugh. "Haven't you ever bathed after dark? It is an exhilarating experience. One has such a sense of freedom, of being at one with the sea and the sky." His voice again held that hateful note of amusement. "Your education has been sadly neglected, *ma belle.*"

Jenny stiffened. "I imagine that we hold very different views on the meaning of education!" she said crisply.

"I imagine we do," Raoul agreed, unruffled. "Some day we must pool our ideas. We might learn from each other." This was said with a smile and a quick whimsical glance, daringly irrepressible, which left Jenny feeling oddly shaken. "He would expect you to fall in love with him. . . ." Dominique's careless words came back into her mind and she lifted her chin.

"I'm sorry, I'm very tired and you certainly ought to be if you haven't slept for two days. Good night."

If he was disconcerted he did not show it. "Good night. Sweet dreams," he said pleasantly, and quelling an impulse to tell him that she never had anything else (which would have been untrue) Jenny slipped through the open french windows and went swiftly upstairs to her room.

The following morning, when she went down to breakfast, she found only Piers and her father at the table.

"Gabrielle is tired: she is having breakfast in bed this morning," Stephen explained, handing Jenny a basket of freshly baked *brioches.* "Dominique and Raoul had theirs early: they've gone for a ride, I believe." He smiled across the table at his elder stepson. "You should have gone with them, Piers. You used to enjoy a canter."

Piers was certainly not dressed for riding. He was wearing an immaculately-cut suit of lightweight grey cloth, a white silk shirt and a sober tie, just as if today was a normal working day and he had to be at the office by ten. He looked tired, Jenny thought, and his

face was thin in profile. He obviously drove himself
hard, but then he had to. He had said himself that his
brother wasn't much help to him.

"Céleste will probably be here soon. I've promised
to take her out for the day: she has friends at Avignon
she's anxious to see." Piers pushed back his chair and
stood up. "Will you excuse me? I've got some telephoning to do before she comes, and there are one or two
letters I want to write."

There was a moment's silence after he had left the
room. Then Stephen looked at his daughter and smiled
a little ruefully.

"That's the kind of bondage I ran away from, Jenny.
Do you blame me very much?"

Jenny coloured, crumbling her roll nervously between her fingers. It was the first time that Stephen
had made any reference to the past.

"There isn't any question of blame. You did what
you had to."

He sighed. "Yes, but I can't pretend, even to you,
that my motives were anything but selfish." His eyes
rested with something approaching tenderness on his
daughter's downbent head. A real-life Sleeping Princess, Gabrielle had called her last night, and though
she had only been joking there was enough truth in
her words for the anxiety he already felt on Jenny's
behalf to be increased. It was this odd prickling of guilt
which made him add, now, "It wasn't fair to you, I'm
afraid. You might have had a happier life if I'd stayed."

Jenny's head jerked up. "But I *was* happy! I loved
Grandmother and she was always so good to me!"

Stephen smiled faintly. "That's how I've salved my
conscience for the past twelve years. The fact remains
that you haven't had any playtime, child. You must
make up for it now ... learn to take life a little less
seriously." His eyes twinkled, suddenly, under the bushy
brows. "Dominique and Raoul will show you how, if
you're in any doubt!"

Jenny's lips tightened. She said nothing, but her
father, reading her expression aright, wisely decided
not to pursue the matter further.

"I must go. Gabrielle has inveigled me into taking

her into town this morning. You wouldn't like to come with us, I suppose, Jenny?"

Jenny shook her head. "No, thank you. I didn't finish my letters last night, I'd better do them now."

She was, in fact, occupied for the next hour. She addressed the last envelope with a sigh of relief and then, pushing the writing materials away from her, got up and went out into the sunshine. At first she found the light so brilliant, after being indoors, that she was dazzled, and stood with her hand in front of her eyes. Then her vision cleared, and the first person she saw, coming slowly up the terrace steps, was Céléste.

The previous evening the only fact that had really registered with Jenny was that Piers' fiancée was extremely beautiful. Now, however, she looked at her with increased interest, wondering why it was that Dominique had spoken of her with such bitter dislike and what had attracted Piers, so quiet and self-contained, to a girl who seemed the complete antithesis of himself. Was he really in love with her? He seemed so wrapped up in his work that it was difficult to believe that he was capable of loving any woman, but perhaps love did not come into it. Perhaps he wanted to marry her because she was beautiful and well-born and intelligent—"a perfect wife", as Gabrielle had said.

The sun was bright on Céléste's red-gold hair and she was wearing a slim dress and jacket of white shantung which even Jenny, inexperienced in such matters, recognised as having indubitably come from an extremely expensive and exclusive shop. Her figure was faultless and she moved with a kind of fluid grace.

"Hello." Céléste's look was appraising, almost critical. Suddenly Jenny became painfully conscious that her green cotton dress, though freshly laundered, had been designed and made by herself, and that the material had only cost a few shillings per yard.

"Where is everybody?" The cool gaze flicked over the empty garden.

"Piers is working, in the library—" Jenny began, and Céléste laughed.

"But of course Piers is working! He never does anything else, if he can possibly help it! I really meant the rest of the family. Where's Raoul?"

"Out riding, with Dominique." Jenny glanced at her watch. "They'll be back soon, I expect."

Céleste seemed in no hurry to drag Piers from his work. She had jerked a spray from a vivid crimson rose and was twisting it round and round in her slim white fingers. Looking at her, Jenny thought that for some reason she seemed strangely on edge.

After a few moment Céleste dropped the bruised rose on to the ground and said abruptly, "Why didn't you go riding with Raoul and Dominique? Didn't they ask you?"

Jenny flushed. "I don't ride." Something made her add, "Do you?"

"Oh, yes." A tiny smile curved Céleste's red lips. "Raoul taught me. I believe he gave me a lesson the first time he ever brought me here."

Jenny stared at her. "*Raoul* brought you?" She could not keep the astonishment out of her voice.

"Why, yes." Céleste spoke calmly. "I knew Raoul long before I knew Piers. It was Raoul who introduced us, in point of fact." She paused, then smiling, added lightly, "I had a hard job to choose between them. They're both so attractive, aren't they—each in his own way."

What was she trying to say? That Raoul had been in love with her as well as Piers? Was *that* the reason for the strained atmosphere when she and Raoul had walked in, together, last night?

Before she could think of an answer Céleste turned quickly towards the steps.

"I heard Dominique laugh. They must be back. Let's go and meet them, Jenny—I may as well give Piers a few more minutes to finish his work. He'll only fret if I turn up too soon."

She began leading the way down the steps, the slender heels of her fashionable shoes clicking on the grey stone. Jenny, a faint frown etching her brow, followed, albeit reluctantly.

They saw Dominique first, slim and supple in her riding kit, her face flushed and laughing. Behind her was Raoul, wearing breeches and high brown boots and

47

a white shirt, short-sleeved and open at the neck. He looked bronzed and fit and handsome.

"Had a good ride?" Céleste asked pleasantly.

The laughter had died out of Dominique's face: she made her dislike of Céleste very plain, Jenny thought ruefully. It was Raoul who answered, his eyes vivid under the black lashes, laughing yet watchful.

"Not bad." He smiled at Céleste and then over her head at Jenny, who was hanging back. "Good morning, *ma soeur*." (Oh, that hateful teasing voice!) "I tried to prevail upon Dominique to drag you from your slumbers this morning, but she insisted that we left you in peace. You don't ride, I understand?"

Jenny shook her head, colouring as Dominique said quickly, "Raoul will teach you if you want to learn. Won't you, Raoul?"

"I'd be delighted."

"It will be a little difficult, won't it, since you're planning to return to Colorado quite soon?" Céleste laughed, but there was a slight edge to her laugh.

Raoul shot her a bright, teasing look. "Oh, I don't know. It's sometimes surprising what one can achieve in a comparatively short time," he said, smiling, and lightly though he spoke Jenny saw the sudden glimmer in Céleste's grey-green eyes.

So, perhaps, did Dominique, for she thrust her arm through her brother's.

"Oh, come on, do, Raoul! I'm dying for some coffee!" She looked at Céleste. "Aren't you supposed to be going out with Piers this morning?" she asked pointedly.

"She is." A voice from the top of the steps spoke crisply. "I've been waiting for you, Céleste."

Piers' face, as always, was expressionless, but it seemed to Jenny that there was tension in the way he held his shoulders and some sort of strain about his eyes.

Céleste shrugged, looking almost sulky. "Jenny said you were still working, so I thought I wouldn't disturb you. Nothing I ever do is right, is it?"

Piers ignored that. He turned and walked towards the house and after a moment Céleste, with another shrug of her slender shoulders, followed him.

Raoul's brows had drawn together and for once the laughter in his eyes was stilled. Dominique, with a quick glance at his face, began chattering gaily, but Jenny had the feeling that he was not really listening. His expression was abstracted and looking at him, she wondered what he was thinking. It surely couldn't be that he grudged Céleste to his brother, and that his careless manner was merely a cloak for the inward bitterness he felt because she had preferred Piers to him? Not, apart from the huge emerald ring that she wore upon her left hand, that Céleste made her preference very clear....

She became conscious that Raoul was watching her and smiling a little sardonically. She coloured and looked away, for not for anything would she have him guess that she took the slightest interest in anything he said or did.

The trouble, as she had already begun to discover, was that Raoul was a difficult person to ignore. This was probably because of his tremendous inner vitality ... which was like a fire, a flame ... coupled with his infectious gaiety. He was so eminently likeable that Jenny, fighting to preserve her instinctive prejudices against a man of his type, had constantly to remind herself that charm was his stock-in-trade. "Nice girls beware...." Sally's words came back into her mind. And of course it wasn't just Sally. Dominique, too, had made it abundantly clear that Raoul, for all his charm, was completely unprincipled. Laughing eyes and lazy grace, what did they count when there was a complete lack of more solid virtues?

Her guilty feeling that unfortunately they *did* count, just a little, resulted in her manner being rather more reserved and aloof than usual when Raoul was around. After lunch a crowd of Dominique's friends descended upon the Villa and they all congregated in the huge green-tiled swimming pool, with its chute and two diving boards. At first Jenny joined them, but when she saw Raoul, tall and lithe in brief black bathing trunks, being practically mobbed by several attractive young women she hastily retreated to the side. Trying not to feel too much of an anachronism in her sedate,

49

one-piece costume—everyone else wore a bikini—she looked on with a half-scornful expression in her clear eyes at the romping, laughing, splashing crowd.

Raoul, looking round, suddenly caught the expression on her face and swam over to her side. Hoisting himself out, dripping wet, he stood looking down at her, the water glistening on his bronzed skin and a lock of black hair falling in a wing over his forehead.

"Come and join us," he said, smiling, and holding out his hand. "You look *très ennuyée* sitting there, all by yourself."

"I certainly shouldn't feel any happier behaving like a mad thing!" Jenny spoke rather more crisply than she had intended and Raoul's brows arched derisively.

"Thank you!" he said drily. "Meaning me, of course! Well, I certainly can't imagine you behaving like a mad thing, as you call it, but it would do you good."

Jenny bit her lip and for a few moments Raoul studied her intently, a half-smile in his eyes.

"You know, I can't think how on earth Stephen managed to produce a daughter like you! You're a delight to look at, but"—shaking his head sadly—"I was right about you in the first place, *ma mie*. You're too prim and self-righteous for anything. If I didn't know better I'd say you were by Baden-Powell out of Mrs. Grundy, and even then I don't know that I'd be doing them justice!"

He dived back into the water before she could think of an answer. Furious, she marched into the house and changed out of her wet bathing costume and into a cotton dress with all possible speed. How *dare* he talk to her like that, she thought, doing up buttons with fingers that trembled. "Too prim and self-righteous for anything..." the words stung even though she would not admit their justice.

It was unfortunate that the gibe was still rankling when later on Gabrielle, obviously searching round in her mind for suitable entertainment for her stepdaughter, suggested that Raoul might take Jenny out to dinner and then perhaps on to the casino.

"With pleasure, *ma mère*," Raoul answered promptly. "But"—and he turned to Jenny, his eyes glinting—"I

50

have a sad presentiment that such a programme would not be to your taste?"

He was baiting her. Jenny's chin lifted and she said coolly, "You're right. It wouldn't. I don't like gambling."

"I was sure you wouldn't," Raoul said, grinning.

"Oh, nonsense, Jenny!" Dominique, who had been listening wide-eyed, broke in indignantly. "Everyone goes to the casino at least once—it is *comme il faut!*" She looked at her brother, her blue eyes, so like his, sparkling. "Take me, Raoul, even if Jenny doesn't want to go!"

"What—no one else willing to be your escort to-night?" Raoul teased.

"No one who is as much fun as you," Dominique said simply. "Please, Raoul."

It would have taken a hard heart to resist her plea. Raoul laughed and assented, then shot a mocking glance at Jenny.

"Think how my reputation will suffer, *chère* Jenny, if I spend the whole evening in the company of my sister! Won't you change your mind? We need not go to the casino, you know—Nice has many other *divertissements.*"

Humour the victim...Jenny felt the colour rush into her cheeks and she shook her head.

"Thank you, but I'd rather stay at home. There's a concert on the wireless that I'd like to hear."

Raoul shrugged and turned aside. He did not seem at all put out by her refusal, but Jenny was horrified to find herself experiencing a definite pang of regret that she had not answered differently. It was absurd, of course: the concert would be first-class and they were playing Brahms' Fourth and the Schumann piano concerto that she loved. Nevertheless, when eventually she sat listening to the music, alone in her own room, she was conscious that it was not providing her with the pleasure and spiritual refreshment that usually she could expect. Instead it was more of a background to a host of disquieting thoughts, and after it was over she found it impossible to go quietly to sleep. She was still reading when the sound of subdued voices and footsteps told her that Dominique and Raoul had arrived home, and a few moments later there was a discreet tap at her door.

"May I come in?" Dominique, looking, despite the lateness of the hour, as gay and sparkling as the rhinestones at her ears and wrists, effervesced into the room. "I saw that your light was still on, so I knew that you were still awake. What is the matter? Can't you sleep?"

"I shall now, I expect." Jenny put down her book, one of her father's which she had taken from the big, oak-panelled library with its well-stocked shelves. "Heavens, it's two o'clock! I hadn't realised that it was so late."

Dominique regarded her thoughtfully, a puzzled frown in her blue eyes. "We've had a simply marvellous evening, Jenny, it was such fun! You ought to have come with us, I'm sure you'd have enjoyed yourself far more than staying here and listening to that stuffy old concert!"

She flung herself down on the foot of the bed, careless both of her lovely amber-coloured dress and the exquisite rose-embroidered quilt. "We had dinner at a marvellous little place Raoul found, not particularly smart, but the food was out of this world! And then we met some people we knew and we all went somewhere to dance, and then I said I thought I'd got a lucky number and we all ended up at the casino." She laughed. "The only thing was, it wasn't a lucky number after all. I lost and so did Raoul."

"Too bad, but I believe it's quite usual, isn't it?" Jenny asked dryly. "How much did you lose?"

"Me—not much. Raoul lost quite a bit, I think," Dominique said carelessly. She looked at her stepsister with puzzled eyes.

"You do not like Raoul much, do you, Jenny? Me, I find that *incroyable!* If it were Piers, now....!" She gave an expressive little shrug.

"Tastes differ. I like Piers very much better than I like Raoul," Jenny said stiffly.

"*Incroyable!*" Dominique said again, shaking her hand.

"Why?" Jenny retorted, nettled. "Céleste preferred him to Raoul, too, didn't she?"

She saw Dominique's lovely face go blank, all expression wiped away as if with a sponge.

"Who told you that?"

"Céleste herself—more or less. She said that she knew Raoul a long time before she knew Piers and that she had a hard job choosing between them," Jenny said coolly.

"She had a hard job all right—but not to choose between Piers and Raoul!" Dominique was now sitting bolt upright, two little spots of angry colour burning in her creamy cheeks. "Her choice was between Raoul and Piers' money! It was Raoul she loved—until she discovered that under my father's will it is Piers who has a controlling interest in the family business and that Raoul and I have nothing except a few shares! We can't even sell those without Piers' consent!" She paused, then added vehemently, "And even though it is Piers to whom she is engaged, it is still Raoul who comes first in her heart! Even you ought to be able to see that!"

There was a moment's silence, stretching out like a gossamer thread. Then Jenny said slowly, "She loved Raoul but she chose Piers? Is that why you called her a snake? A traitress?"

"Of course!" Dominique said, flashing her an impatient glace. "I hate her because she betrayed Raoul!"

"I thought you said he was careful not to become too involved?" Jenny forced herself to speak lightly. "Did he love her very much?" To her annoyance she found herself waiting almost breathlessly for Dominique's answer.

'I don't *know* that he did," the younger girl admitted. "But I think so. She is very beautiful. Even I have to grant that." She studied the toe of her dainty sandal. "Of course, we all know quite well that Céleste is only marrying Piers for his money. I expect he knows it, too, but naturally his pride will not let him admit it. He thinks he has taken Céleste away from Raoul and it is to him—how you say?—a feather in his cap. But sometimes, I think, he has suspicions and then there is an awkward situation, like last night." She gave a rueful laugh. "Of course, it was very silly, what Raoul did.

It made Piers very angry and he will make Raoul pay, sooner or later."

"He had a right to be angry," Jenny protested.

Dominique shrugged. "It is up to him to take care of his own," she said coolly, and this time Jenny was silent. So much, now, seemed to be clear to her. She said goodnight to Dominique, but tired though she now was, it was a long time before she got to sleep.

CHAPTER FOUR

BREAKFAST at the Villa Buichi consisted of freshly baked *brioches*, fruit and coffee, and it was always such an informal meal that it was rare to find more than two members of the family partaking of it at one and the same time. When Jenny went down to breakfast on Sunday morning, however, she was very much a late arrival. Everyone else was gathered round the huge table and had, it seemed, nearly finished eating.

Her surprise must have showed in her face, for Gabrielle laughed and held out her hand.

"We have all been to early Mass. Come and sit next to me, *petite*, and tell me about the concert. Raoul, coffee for Jenny, please."

Stephen smiled at his daughter. "Perhaps you would like to go to church this morning, Jenny? There's a rather nice little Protestant church not too far from here : I could drive you there in time for Matins."

"Thank you. That would be very kind of you," Jenny said gratefully.

Dominique was frowning out of the window. Her late night had left no discernible mark on her amazing vitality but she did not seem to be in a particularly good mood.

"I wanted to play tennis, but I've a hunch it's going to rain," she said gloomily.

"You and your hunches !" Raoul scoffed. "They cost me a pretty penny last night, *ma mie!*" He looked wickedly under his lashes at Jenny's disapproving face.

54

"I wish very much that you had come with us, Jenny. I feel sure that you would have been a most steadying influence!"

"Did you lose much?" his mother asked anxiously.

"More than I could afford," Raoul said wryly, and Piers looked up, his mouth twisting.

"I suppose it's something that you acknowledge that. Since you consistently appear to live well above your income, one is apt to gain the impression that you enjoy a perpetual state of insolvency." He spoke smoothly, but with a definite edge on the carefully pedantic words.

Raoul smiled at him and said, very pleasantly, "Insolvency is never enjoyable, *mon frère*. However, unlike you I have never believed that the best things in life have to be bought!"

In the sharp little silence that followed Jenny saw the flash of anger in Piers' eyes. He said nothing, but his mouth thinned to a straight line.

Gabrielle, with one quick glance at the two faces, Raoul's faintly amused and Piers' cold and bleak, said hurriedly, "I've invited the Montels to lunch. Such amusing people. Céleste is coming too, isn't she, Piers? We haven't seen nearly enough of her lately."

"Speak for yourself, Maman." Jenny, sitting next to Dominique, hoped that only she had caught the younger girl's provocative murmur. The atmosphere was loaded enough already. Had there always been conflict like this between the two brothers or was the root cause— Céleste?

"You'll probably see a little more of her in future, Maman." Piers was answering his mother, his voice carefully controlled. "Madame de Courville arrives on Thursday and will stay until the end of the month. Céleste then plans to accompany her to Geneva, where they will both spend a week or two with some old family friends."

"Then we shall have the pleasure of your company next weekend, Piers?"

"But of course." It was Raoul who answered, his expression bland. "How can true love flourish apart?"

Jenny held her breath, for Raoul's lively, mocking

air said much that was offensive. She thought that it said a great deal for Piers' self-control that he did not lose his temper, but she was later to discover that apparently there were limits even to his patience.

She had made herself ready for church, adding a white floppy-brimmed hat and plain white gloves to the blue courtelle dress she was already wearing, and was fairly satisfied with the result. Blue, she knew, suited her, and the dress was one of which even Dominique approved. She was looking for her father to remind him of his promise when she heard the sound of loud and angry voices issuing from the library. They were speaking in French, but it was evident that a bitter quarrel was raging. She caught the name "Céleste" and then, a moment later, Raoul almost hurled himself out of the room. He looked as black as thunder and his eyes were blazing.

Jenny, startled and embarrassed, shrank back as Raoul brushed past her. She caught a glimpse of Piers, his face hard and set, and then fled in the direction of the study. She felt almost as sick and shaken as if she herself had been embroiled in the dispute, and just at that moment she longed desperately for the correct, well-ordered life she had led with her grandmother. Dull it might have been, but at least there had been none of the wrangling and feuding which seemed a commonplace among the de Vaisseau family!

She did not doubt for one moment that the nigger in the woodpile was Raoul. He had an inflammatory personality and seemed, moreover, to take a delight in needling his elder brother. Jealousy, of course, was probably at the bottom of it. What he and Piers had been arguing about just how she did not know, but since she had definitely heard Céleste's name mentioned she thought that it was more than likely that indirectly, at least, Piers' fiancée had somehow been involved.

At any rate it was no concern of hers. It was odd, Jenny thought, that she should have to remind herself of that fact. She had always had a gift for removing herself from any possible trouble zone and it was a gift that she valued. She had not the slightest desire to become embroiled in a family conflict, and though her sympathies were definitely with Piers she had every intention of remaining neutral.

After the violent impact of the de Vaisseau personalities, the tiny Protestant church to which Stephen subsequently drove her was refreshingly restful. Glowing with lovely stained glass which shed pools of colour on to the grey stone floor, and steeped in an atmosphere of ages of prayer, the interior was also richly adorned with sculptures of the life of Christ. Stephen had told her to look out for these, and at the end of the simple service she lingered behind for a closer inspection. Consequently, when she finally emerged into the sunshine the rest of the congregation had dispersed.

There was one car waiting. Not Stephen's grey Chevrolet but a red Mercedes-Benz. Jenny hesitating in the porch, just had time to think, *Raoul has a car like that ... and then the door opened and Raoul himself got out. He waited by the off front door, for once unsmiling, as she came up to him and when he spoke it was with unaccustomed brusqueness.

"Stephen is tied up with friends who called unexpectedly. He asked me if I would fetch you instead."

"Oh! Well ... thank you," Jenny said feebly. She got into the car and Raoul slammed the door after her, walked round the front and slid into his seat beside her.

The car glided forward and Jenny leant back, trying to give the impression that she was completely at ease. In point of fact she felt completely the reverse, but it soon became obvious that no subterfuge was necessary. As far as Raoul was concerned she might not have been in the car at all.

It was after he had been driving for some time in frowning abstraction that Jenny, stealing a surreptitious glance at his silent profile, realised with almost a sense of shock that in his present mood he was a stranger. There was something in his face, something dark and difficult, which contrasted so forcibly with his former carefree expression that she began to think that his quarrel with Piers must have been serious. He was undoubtedly driving as though he was in a bad temper, not recklessly but certainly skirting danger, and fast... very fast.

At last Jenny could bear the silence no longer. In a polite, frozen little voice she said, "I hope you didn't mind waiting for me? Stephen said he wanted me to look at the sculptures."

(She had fallen, almost unconsciously, into the habit of calling her father by his Christian name, as did all his stepchildren.)

"That's all right." Raoul answered her absently and kept his eyes, narrowed against the glaring sun, fixed on the road ahead. Just as well, Jenny thought wryly, gripping the edges of her seat as the car roared into a bend with a protesting scream from the tyres. If anything had been coming then....

Desperately she tried to concentrate on the splendid view. It was like a highly-coloured picture postcard, all brightness and light and sea and flowers. The sunshine was beating down on the roof of the car and it streamed through the windows. Dominique had been as wrong about the threat of rain as she had been about her lucky number, Jenny thought, but in spite of the heat she was conscious that gooseflesh was creeping out all over her. There wouldn't be much of a chance for anyone who went off the Middle Corniche, not with those cruel rocks so far below!

Watching the speedometer, she saw the needle flick up ... sixty ... seventy ... seventy-five.... Everything rushed past them in a kind of Technicolor blur and the tyres tore at the tarmac. If this was Raoul de Vaisseau's usual mode of travelling, she reflected grimly, he certainly had need of his nine lives. The only question was, how many had he got left?

Just as she was nerving herself to ask if there was any need to go quite so fast, Raoul abruptly slackened the car's headlong pace. As if he had only just become aware of her presence he shot her a swift, oddly inimical glance. His first words showed that his thoughts were still on, or had harked back to, the quarrel with his brother.

"What were you doing outside the library? I suppose

you realised that Piers and I were having a first-class row?"

The question sounded almost like an accusation. Anyone would think he suspected her of deliberate eavesdropping, Jenny thought indignantly.

Aloud she said crisply, "I was looking for Stephen. And I could scarcely avoid realising what was going on, considering that you were both shouting at the tops of your voices!"

The corner of his mouth turned down cynically. "I suppose you consider it undignified to shout?"

Jenny flushed at his tone. "Yes, and very unwise, unless you prefer to do your brawling publicly," she retorted.

"You were the only one within earshot." Momentarily he sounded faintly amused. "Be thankful that your knowledge of French is limited. You might have heard some words which are not usually included in the vocabulary of a *jeune fille bien élevée*." He gave the ghost of a laugh. "But at least we didn't resort to physical violence. Wasn't that civilised of us?"

Strangely, she preferred the familiar mockery to his earlier remoteness. That withdrawn, brooding look had made her feel ridiculously uneasy. She clasped her hands tightly in her lap and said coldly, "I think your brother Piers would always try to act in a civilised manner."

She saw the glint in his eyes as he turned his head towards her. "Oho! You like Piers, do you?"

I prefer him to you. She longed to say it, but she didn't quite dare. Instead she said briefly, "I respect him."

Raoul threw back his head and laughed. "What a lukewarm sentiment!" he said derisively. "What's the matter, *ma chère?* Is it too untidy to show any stronger emotion? Respect . . . duty . . . admiration . . . that's about your lot, isn't it? Love . . . hate . . . fear, I don't believe you know what it is to feel any of those things!"

Before Jenny could answer he had put his foot down hard on the accelerator. The needle swung to the right and held there. They rounded a bend on the wrong side and the back of the car skidded round in the dust.

Jenny felt her stomach turn over and she was sure that her hair must be standing on end. Then the car straightened out and roared along the crown of the road and Raoul was laughing, but without amusement.

"You see what I mean? Nine hundred and ninety-nine women out of a thousand would be screaming their heads off, after a piece of driving like that. You sit there and look as ice-cool as if you'd just stepped out of a refrigerator!"

Jenny stared at him. "You mean ... you were deliberately trying to frighten me?"

He grinned. "Just trying to shatter that terrifying composure of yours. You needn't look so indignant—after all, I didn't succeed, did I?"

Jenny almost choked. She sat in frigid silence, thankful that they were nearly home. Raoul was humming something under his breath : apparently he had recovered his usual cheerful flippancy. He swung the car into the drive and it jerked to a stop as he slammed on the brakes. There was a curious glint in his dark blue eyes as he said, "I wonder if I'd have better luck if I tried to make you angry?"

"I doubt it. I haven't a Gallic temperament." Jenny put her hand on the handle of the door and spoke with as much cold hauteur as she could muster. She was completely unprepared for what happened next. Raoul reached across her, not to open the door for her as she had imagined, but to pull her roughly into his arms. His mouth came down hard on hers and for the first time in her life she found herself being kissed.

It was not a tender kiss. Raoul's lips were hard and demanding and when he raised his head his blue eyes glinted with challenge.

"W-e-ell," he said, drawing a long breath. "Well. After that I must say that I'm very glad you are *not* my sister, *chérie!*"

Oh, he was impossible! Jenny, thoroughly shaken, rigid with fury, reacted instinctively. She raised her hand, but even as her arm lifted steely fingers gripped her wrist.

"How unladylike!" he drawled teasingly. "I may deserve the slap you are obviously itching to give me, but I really cannot allow you to do something which later you would so bitterly regret, *ma mie*."

She tried to wrench free. "Let me go!"

"In a moment." The blue eyes danced wickedly. "You really are quite safe, you know. I am not a maniac, nor am I a ravisher of the young and innocent. I kissed you merely to satisfy my curiosity. You look so very lovely, Jenny, when you are really angry. For the first time I am convinced that it is blood and not ice which flows through your veins." He paused, then added very softly, "Especially as you did not exactly ... resist ... when I held you in my arms just now."

Jenny's cheeks burned. It was true. She had been so completely taken by surprise that she had been powerless to move. Worse, she had an uneasy feeling that for one brief treacherous moment she had even responded to the fierce pressure of Raoul's lips. Her fury gave way to a wave of humiliation. She had allowed him to make a complete fool of her. He had kissed her on purpose to make her angry ... had deliberately tricked her into losing her temper!

"Oh, I hate you!" she said passionately.

"Good!" Infuriatingly, Raoul grinned. "At least that's a start in the right direction! Keep it up, and you may be surprised at the dizzy heights you can achieve!"

To her horror Jenny felt a strong inclination to burst into tears. Swallowing rapidly, she blinked, and when Raoul felt in his pocket and pulled out a clean white handkerchief she felt miserably certain that he had seen the shine of tears in her eyes.

It transpired he hadn't. All he said, very gently, was, "Your lip is cut: I'm afraid it's bleeding. You'd better dab it with this."

How *dared* he sound so solicitous, when all the time there were dancing devils in his eyes and it was all his fault that her lip was bleeding, anyway? Now that he had mentioned it she could taste the blood on her tongue, bitter-sweet. Unable to trust herself to speak, she ignored the proffered handkerchief, almost flung herself out of the car, slammed the door furiously behind her and stalked up the wide sweep of steps which led to the front door. She hoped to convey an impression of outraged dignity, but halfway up the heel of her shoe stuck in a small crack and she was left to hop on one foot in a far from dignified fashion.

"Allow me." Raoul, close behind her, retrieved the shoe and handed it to her with excessive politeness.

Controlling an impulse to fling it at his head, she rammed her foot into it and stormed up the rest of the steps. Not that her troubles were over. Raoul opened the door for her and she walked past him as though he didn't exist, almost straight into the arms of Céleste de Courville.

Céleste, a slender, fragile figure in a dress which was the perfect complement to her exquisite red-gold colouring, looked from Jenny to Raoul and her brows lifted incredulously. Jenny, burning with humiliation, anger and embarrassment, felt sure that the story of the last few minutes must be plainly written on her face. In any case Céleste herself was probably quite used to Raoul's insufferable behaviour—except, of course, that he would never have kissed *her* just as a mere experiment!

"What on earth—?" Céleste began, but Jenny did not wait to hear the end of the sentence. Her head held high, she turned abruptly and ran upstairs.

To her great relief, Raoul was not present at lunch. Céleste was, and Jenny writhed inwardly under the elder girl's look of amused speculation. She wondered bitterly what Raoul had said to her. Probably they had both had a good laugh at her expense!

Piers was as quiet and as self-contained as he usually was on these occasions, but for once his silence went almost unnoticed. Besides the Montels there was one other guest, the "Alex" of whom Dominique had often spoken. Jenny, sitting opposite, had a good opportunity to study him closely and took an instinctive dislike to him. He was certainly very handsome, with his bold black eyes, very white teeth and olive skin, but he struck her as being extremely egotistical and the touch of arrogance in his manner repelled her. Did Dominique really find him attractive or was she, perhaps, over-impressed by his title—and his bank balance? She smiled a little ruefully to herself. Dominique suspected Céleste of a mercenary streak and was unable to forgive her for it, yet it was perfectly obvious that she herself had every intention of finding a rich husband. Love in a garret would not appeal to Dominique—she had been used to a life of luxury for too long.

Nobody commented publicly on Raoul's absence, but Jenny overheard a significant exchange between Piers and his mother as they all filed into the dining room.

"You do not know where Raoul has gone, Piers?" Gabrielle spoke in a puzzled undertone.

Piers shrugged with seeming indifference. "I am not his *confidant*, Maman." Then, with a rather bitter laugh, "Probably just as well. I should find it difficult to condone the kind of irresponsible behaviour he goes in for, even if he is my brother."

"You are not being fair, Piers. Raoul is not wholly irresponsible. He has changed a lot since Marcel died."

"I haven't noticed it," Piers said shortly, and then Céleste was beside him, tucking her arm into his, and the subject of Raoul was dropped.

After lunch the party split up. Dominique and her handsome Count went off somewhere in the latter's large and impressive car—everything about Count Alex was calculated to impress, Jenny thought wryly—and Piers and Céleste disappeared into the garden. Céleste's beautiful face wore a somewhat bored expression, though she had been animated enough during lunch.

Gabrielle and Stephen were, of course, occupied with their guests. Jacques Montel was an artist, a thin dark man with a clever, ugly face, and his wife was an exotic creature with heavy, copper-coloured hair and a vivacious manner. Jenny quite liked them both, but though every effort was made to draw her into the conversations—both the Montels spoke impeccable English—she still felt as though they were all talking a different language. Eventually, feeling herself to be hopelessly in the way, she excused herself and slipped quietly away to her room. For some reason she felt lonelier than at any time since her grandmother's death. She had been right in the first place, she thought desolately. She simply did not fit into life here. She ought never to have come.

Raoul did not return to the Villa Buichi until late that night and he left for Paris very early the next morning, before Jenny was up. Alarmed to find that her relief at his departure was tempered by an odd feeling of dissatisfaction, she eventually decided that this was merely because an apology was due to her and it hadn't been forthcoming. And it was certainly natural to miss someone who, however detestable he 'was, made such a violent and irrevocable impact upon everyone around him! Without Raoul and without Piers—who also left, for Toulouse, on Monday—the house seemed strangely quiet and empty.

Gabrielle, Jenny thought with a rush of sympathy, looked very pale and tired, and there were unaccustomed shadows under her brilliant eyes. Stephen, when questioned, confirmed that she was not feeling too well.

"This weekend has been a bit of a strain for her, I'm afraid." Stephen pulled his pipe and pouch from his jacket pocket and began to pack the pipe carefully, without looking at his daughter.

"Yes. There has been rather an atmosphere," Jenny said quietly.

This time Stephen did shoot her a quick glance, as if surprised by her perception. "You noticed it too?"

"The friction between Piers and Raoul? It's not exactly a secret, is it?"

Stephen sighed. "I suppose not. There has been trouble between those two since they were babies. They are so completely unalike, and neither makes the slightest attempt to understand the other. Piers is solid and painstaking and conscientious, and Raoul is gay and easy-going and mercurial. Piers is completely wrapped up in his work: it is his life. Raoul . . . well, for Raoul there has to be a spice of excitement, even of danger, in whatever he is doing. Piers resents his lack of interest in the family business, and Raoul resents Piers' resentment. It's a vicious circle."

Jenny bent her head so that her face was hidden by the shining bell of her hair. "And then there's—Céleste."

Stephen did not pretend to misunderstand her. "Yes, there's Céleste. Even now I don't think Piers can believe his luck—that she actually preferred him to Raoul. Women don't as a rule."

Not by word or look did Stephen betray the fact that there might be an underlying motive for Céleste's preference. Jenny said quickly—perhaps a shade too quickly—"I think she made the right choice."

"You do?" Stephen looked at her and smiled, a little sadly. She was all Barrington, this child of his, he thought. And yet what Barrington had ever had eyes like hers, wide and misty with dreams?

"Jenny! Where's Jenny?" At that moment Dominique came into the room, pulling on white gloves which ruckled over her slim brown wrists. She was wearing a slim-fitting cotton dress, the colour of lemon-ice, and over one arm she carried a little jacket of the same crisp material as the dress. Her dark hair, brushed into an elaborate and very attractive style, had the gloss of a raven's wing and her eyes were very bright and sparkling. There was nothing remotely dreamy about his young stepdaughter, Stephen thought amusedly. In point of fact, she and Jenny made a perfect foil for each other.

"Aren't you supposed to be meeting that Chalmers girl for lunch today?" Dominique's eyes swept over her stepsister. "I'm lunching with a friend, too. I'll run you in to Nice if you like."

"Thanks." Jenny accepted the offer gratefully. It was nice of Dominique to have remembered, she thought, and tried not to feel too surprised. Consideration for others wasn't exactly the younger girl's strong point!

As they passed through the hall she gave herself a quick look in a splendid antique mirror which, in years gone by, must have reflected the smiling face of many a Court beauty. In her simple white blouse and blue skirt, belted tightly to her slim waist with a wide leather belt, she certainly lacked Dominique's crisp elegance but, she reminded herself with a flicker of wry amusement, they would doubtless be lunching in two very different places. Almost certainly nothing but the very best hotel would be good enough for Dominique: she wouldn't even have heard of the "nice little café" in the Rue Masséna!

65

Dominique's driving was even more atrocious than usual, perhaps because she seemed to have something on her mind. She was an odd mixture, Jenny thought. Wilful and obstinate, but also honest and passionately loyal to those whom she loved. Raoul, of course, could do no wrong in her eyes. She obviously adored him, and was as blind to his faults as she was to Piers' virtues.

"I suppose you're looking forward to seeing Sally Chalmers again?" Dominique's voice broke in on her thoughts.

"I am, rather. I liked her a lot," Jenny admitted.

"I wouldn't have said she was exactly your type." There was a slight edge to Dominique's voice. "I believe she goes in for quite a gay life—off-duty, that is. Not like her cousin! Now *he* really *is* your type, Jenny! Dour and solemn and exuding conscientiousness at every pore!"

"Professional façade. What about off-duty?" Jenny asked, laughing.

"I wouldn't know. I asked him to a party, after I got home, but he didn't come. Too busy, he said." Dominique gave a short laugh. "Not that I lost any sleep over that! I only asked him out of—oh, perversity, I suppose! He told me to take things quietly for a bit and I wanted to show him that I had no intention of doing any such thing!"

That was typical of Dominique, Jenny thought ruefully, and sat in silence as they wove their way in and out of the teeming traffic. In spite of several hold-ups they arrived in Nice shortly before twelve. Dominique parked the car without much difficulty and after arranging to meet again at three o'clock, she and Jenny went their different ways. Jenny, with half an hour to kill, strolled down the famous Promenade des Anglais, admiring the palms, flowers and tropical shrubs and enjoying the effect of the dazzling sunlight on the sparkling, dancing sea. When finally she turned her footsteps in the direction of the Rue Masséna, however, it was with a certain amount of eagerness, for what she had told Dominique was perfectly true. She was looking forward to seeing Sally again. Perhaps it was partly because they shared the same nationality but also Sally's own personality was very attractive. It was odd that Dominique seemed to dislike her so!

It was exactly half-past twelve when she arrived at the little café where she and Sally had arranged to meet. It was a gay little place with red and white check curtains and a small patio which was a positive riot of colour. There was, however, no sign of Sally's slim figure and splendid red hair, and after a moment's hesitation Jenny found herself an empty table and settled down to wait. She hoped it wouldn't be for long, for the place was beginning to fill up rapidly and there was constant coming-and-going at the café door.

"Miss Barrington?"

A voice spoke rather diffidently beside her and she looked up with a start to find a tall, fair-haired young man regarding her cautiously. He looked, she thought, as though he might be in his late twenties, though he had an air of dignity and quiet assurance which usually belonged to a far older man. He had a strong face, firm-chinned and firm-browed, and an expression of thoughtful solemnity.

Jenny was taken aback and showed it. "Why, yes, but. . . ."

"But you don't know *me*." The young man smiled, a rather shy but singularly attractive smile which transformed his whole face. "You're waiting for Sally, aren't you? I'm her cousin, David Chalmers, and I'm frightfully sorry, but I'm afraid she isn't coming. It's supposed to be her day off, right enough, but at the last moment she was asked to 'special' a very sick child and she felt she couldn't refuse, even though it meant disappointing you."

"Of course not!" Jenny exclaimed. "But why didn't she phone me? There was no need to trouble you! I would have quite understood—"

"Just what Sally thought you'd say!" David Chalmers said, laughing. "There were several reasons, actually. One, she was anxious to repay her debt! She has a very independent streak, has Sally, and she hates owing anyone a penny! Two, she knew I was off duty and would probably be going into Nice, anyway. Indeed"—and by now his solemnity had almost completely vanished—" 'trouble' doesn't come into it at all. She thought I'd probably welcome the opportunity of meeting a charming compatriot and of course she was perfectly right." He gave her his disarmingly shy grin. "In point of fact I'm very much hoping that you'll accept me as a substitute, however poor, for Sally, and allow me to buy you lunch. Apart from everything else it really is wonderful to talk English to someone!"

"What about Sally?" Rather to her surprise Jenny found herself laughing back at him. "Don't tell me you speak in French to her!"

"Sally doesn't count," David said firmly. "We've known each other for so long that we generally know what each other is thinking, so conversation seems a bit of a waste of time!" He picked up the menu. "What will you have? Are you hungry? I'm ravenous!"

There seemed to be a bewildering choice, but in the end Jenny plumped for *ratatouille Niçoise* (a mixture of egg-plant, pimentoes, tomatoes and small marrows all cooked in rich olive oil), fruit and a carafe of wine, served by a plump, rosy-cheeked girl with sloe-black eyes. It was a delightful meal, for Jenny and David found that they had a lot in common and were soon chatting away like old friends. Jenny found herself drawn to him in the same way that she had been drawn to Sally : perhaps, she thought, because they seemed to be very much alike. David was nice ... kind ... friendly, though underneath his good-humoured exterior she was also aware that he had a very strong character.

Suddenly she found herself remembering Dominique and the caustic comments she had made about David Chalmers. Her brow creased into a little frown. Why was she so bitter about him? Undoubtedly, if she'd behaved badly while she was under his care, he would have made it plain he wasn't going to stand any non-sense—he was that sort of man. Even so, it was odd that she hadn't realised his essential niceness.

David was twirling the stem of his wineglass between his lean, supple fingers. Without looking up he said casually, "How is Dominique? I suppose you know that she was a patient of mine quite recently?"

68

Dominique? Not Mademoiselle de Vaisseau? A little surprised, Jenny said awkwardly, "Yes, she has mentioned you."

He gave the ghost of a smile. "Not very charitably, I imagine. I'm afraid we didn't hit it off too well."

"I don't suppose you found her an easy patient." Jenny found it impossible to be less than frank with David's blue-grey eyes, as honest as water, looking straight at her. "She seems to hate restrictions of any kind."

"Don't I know it!" David's expression was rueful. "I made the mistake, when she left the Home, of advising her to take things quietly for a bit. The first thing I found, when I opened my mail next morning, was an invitation to what I have no doubt at all proved to be a very hectic party!"

Jenny laughed. "She told me about that! You refused, didn't you? To show your disapproval?"

David was tracing a little pattern in spilt wine on the table top. He said: "Partly. And partly because I had the sense to realise I'd stick out like a sore thumb among her sort of crowd."

Jenny thought of all the friends of Dominique's that she had met so far: glossy, sophisticated and well-dressed, and knew exactly what he meant. Wasn't that how she herself felt, a misfit?

David did not give her a chance to reply. He glanced at his watch, then beckoned to the waitress and asked for the bill.

"What about a visit to the wholesale flower market? Have you been yet?" he asked. "It's famous the world over, and is well worth a visit if you've got half an hour to spare."

"I'm not meeting Dominique until three o'clock. I'd love to see it," Jenny said warmly, and together they went out into the sunlit street. She found that she had not the slightest desire to rid herself of David's company and that was odd, because up to now she had always fought shy of men friends. There had never been a time for anything or anyone except music and her grandmother, and she was pleasantly surprised to find that David was so likeable. With him she felt none of the disquietude, tinged with apprehension, that she experienced when she was with Raoul de Vaisseau! Of course, they were completely and utterly different. Raoul was—But here she took a firm hold of her thoughts. She would *not* spoil a pleasant excursion by thinking about Raoul!

The wholesale flower market was situated just behind the Quai des Etats-Unis in the Cours Saleya, once the centre of the old town. Its two long covered halls held a fabulous combination of colour and fragrance and Jenny wandered round, wide-eyed and enchanted, until David was reluctantly forced to remind her of the time.

He accompanied her back to the car. Dominique was already there and Jenny wondered a little uneasily what her reaction would be when she saw David. She had, however, watched them cross the square so that there was no element of surprise in their meeting and her greeting was, in fact, a model of cool indifference.

Her eyes flickered over David's tall, loose-limbed figure and Jenny felt reasonably sure that she was registering inward disapproval of his well-worn tweeds with the leather-reinforced elbows and cuffs. All she said, however, in a light, brittle voice, was, "How funny not to see you in a white coat! You look quite different!"

"You look quite different, too," David said pleasantly. "Up to now I've only ever seen you in a nightie or negligée!"

A woman strolling past obviously overheard the remark, for she turned round and stared curiously. Rather to Jenny's amused surprise Dominique flushed scarlet and for a moment her poise was in flinders. She recovered herself quickly, however, and gave a little laugh.

"I suppose I ought to be surprised that you remember me at all—Dr. Chalmers!"

"Oh, I always remember my patients—especially the difficult ones." David was affability itself. "And don't you think that you could now drop the 'Dr. Chalmers'? We aren't doctor and patient any more, remember."

"Thank goodness!" Dominique snapped, so rudely

that Jenny almost blushed for her. David, however, did not seem in the least put out.

"Yes, indeed. It was a trying period—for both of us," he said calmly. He turned to Jenny. "Well, thanks for a very pleasant meeting, Jenny. I hope I'll see you again before long: I'm sure Sally will be getting in touch." He gave her his swift, warm smile, nodded to Dominique and then was gone, his tall figure striding purposefully across the square.

"Well!" Dominique stared after him, her face stormy, then swung round and shot an angry, almost suspicious glance at Jenny.

"I thought you told me you were meeting Sally Chalmers? How did you come to get mixed up with *him*?"

Jenny explained, with Dominique listening in tight-lipped silence. Obviously, Jenny thought in amused despair, her friendship with Sally and David Chalmers, if it developed, was the last thing her stepsister was likely to approve of and she'd better take great care, in future, to keep the three of them apart!

CHAPTER FIVE

PERHAPS, Jenny thought, she was being ultra-sensitive, but it did seem to her in the days that followed that Dominique was rather less friendly than she had been at first. For some reason she appeared to be in a reckless, defiant mood and Gabrielle was obviously worried both by her long absences from home and the many late nights which eventually began to result in heavy shadows under her amazing blue eyes.

Jenny, during this period, was left very much to her own devices. Gabrielle was always kind and considerate, but she had many social engagements and Stephen was busy with his latest book. Raoul was still away and Jenny gathered that he had business in Paris which was taking him longer than he had anticipated.

"It's something to do with money and that mine of

his, Maman said," Dominique told her, giving that little shrug of her slim shoulders which meant that she did not find that aspect of Raoul's absence particularly interesting. "As soon as it's all settled I suppose he'll go straight back to Colorado. It's too bad of him, when we haven't seen him for such ages." She shook back her thick black hair. "At least I'm not the only one to feel disappointed! I bet Céleste is furious, she probably thought they'd be able to spend some time together without dear Piers being any the wiser!"

She grinned a little unkindly at Jenny's expression. "That shocks you? But surely, *ma chère*, you have heard that old saying about forbidden fruit?"

She was, of course, being deliberately provocative, Jenny thought, and then reminded herself that in any case she was not the slightest bit interested in anything that Raoul did or did not do. He and Dominique were not her kind of people and she infinitely preferred solitude to wasting time in their company! Yet the fact remained that here on the Côte d'Azur, the playground of Europe, the natural thing seemed to be to enjoy its wonderful sunshine and amenities in the company of someone else … someone young and gay. Unconsciously she began at times almost to envy her stepsister, who had a host of friends her own age and who never lacked invitations for this, that and the other. It was a butterfly existence, of course, she reminded herself sternly, and locked herself in the music room and plugged into a spate of five-finger exercises, scales and arpeggios as if to atone for her guilty thoughts.

It was after one particularly lonely day that Sally again rang up, this time to invite her to spend an evening at David's flat.

"He's lending it to me because of course I can't very well invite people to the Home," she said cheerfully. "Some friends are coming round and we'll probably end up by having a bit of a party, nothing elaborate, but it's bound to be fun. We'd love it if you could come, Jenny. David says he'll fetch you." Then, laughing, "You made a terrific impression on him the day you met him in Nice!"

Later, when telling Gabrielle of the invitation, Jenny

saw her own pleasure reflected in Gabrielle's beautiful face.

"But how nice! You must tell me what time you want the car, *chérie*."

"Thank you, but my friend's cousin—Dr. Chalmers, I expect you know him?—will fetch me. I shan't need to bother anyone," Jenny said quickly.

Gabrielle raised her brows. "Dr. Chalmers? The young man who removed Dominique's appendix? But of course I remember him! A very pleasant young man. You wouldn't like to invite him to dinner before you go on to the party?"

Jenny shook her head, albeit a little regretfully. Dominique and David obviously struck sparks off each other and another confrontation was to be avoided at all costs, she decided. She'd make quite sure that she was ready when David called so that there would be no fear of an awkward contretemps.

Unfortunately, thanks to a broken zip, things did not work out quite as she had planned and when she arrived downstairs, flushed and a little breathless, it was to learn that David had already arrived and was waiting for her in what was known as the Blue Salon.

"By himself? Or is Madame with him?" Jenny asked Berthe anxiously.

"*Oui*, Madame is with him—and so also is Mademoiselle Dominique and Monsieur le Comte," Berthe replied, and Jenny stifled a groan. Bother! Just what she'd tried to avoid, but it couldn't be helped. She only hoped that Dominique had managed to curb her unruly tongue!

When she walked into the Blue Salon David was standing by the window, a glass in his hand, talking to Gabrielle. He was wearing a grey suit which, though it might once have been "good", had obviously seen better days and his hair was a little tousled. Alex, who was standing beside him, not only topped him by at least two inches but completely overwhelmed him as far as physical splendour went. In fact, the contrast between the two men was so marked that Jenny, shooting a swift glance at Dominique, was not surprised to see an odd expression in her eyes as she watched them.

Handsome is as handsome does . . . no, Dominique had probably never even heard of that particular proverb! It struck her that her stepsister, although looking beautiful in a dress of flame-coloured silk, was somewhat paler than usual and her usual vivacity was missing. Evidently she was not the only to receive this impression, for when they were in David's car—a battered relic of dubious age—he said abruptly, "Useless, I suppose, to ask whether Dominique ever gets to bed early?"

"I'm afraid she doesn't. I can't think where she gets her energy from," Jenny said ruefully.

"It's nervous energy." David was frowning at the road ahead. "She isn't nearly as tough as she thinks she is, and she's obviously overdoing things. I saw that from her face tonight." He paused, and Jenny noticed a sudden hardness in the set of his mouth. "Who is the handsome boy-friend? She forgot to introduce me, but I don't seem to remember him among the hordes who danced attendance on her when she was ill."

Jenny told him. "I don't know much about him, except that he has a very impressive car and an equally impressive yacht," she said flatly, and saw David's lip curl, though he did not make the caustic comment she had half expected. After a moment he began to talk lightly of other things and Jenny, relieved, followed his lead.

It was growing dusk when David stopped the car outside his flat, which was at the top of a tall, grey building. Judging from the noise the party was already in full swing, and when they went in they found that the place was crowded. The other guests proved to be gay young people who were so charming and friendly that for once Jenny's usual shyness and reserve melted. David was kind and attentive—so attentive that at first she found herself wondering rather anxiously if Sally minded. Then she saw her dancing cheek-to-cheek with a tall, dark-haired young man who had been introduced to her as "Louis" and guessed from the rapt, blissful expression on Sally's face that he was the man of the moment and that temporarily, at least, she had no time for Cousin David!

74

She did, in fact, make this perfectly clear. She whirled up to Jenny while David was engaged in changing the records on his radiogram, rattled off a few breathless remarks and finished with, "You are enjoying yourself, aren't you? David's nice, isn't he?" Then, without waiting for an answer, "He likes *you*, and I'm so glad. He's such a poppet and he deserves somebody nice, he really does!"

Jenny went pink. Surely Sally wasn't trying to matchmake? The thought was oddly disconcerting. She liked David immensely, but the thought of falling in love with him was simply absurd. In fact, for her the thought of falling in love with anyone was absurd!

"Respect ... duty ... admiration ... that's about your lot, isn't it? Love ... hate ... fear, I don't believe you know what it is to feel any of those things!" Infuriatingly, Raoul's mocking voice rang again in her ears and she coloured and bit her lip. The sooner she forgot all about Raoul de Vaisseau and that disastrous last meeting the better!

It was well after midnight when the party finally broke up and David took her home. The lights were still burning brightly in the Villa Buichi, but when Jenny went in the only person she saw was Dominique. Evidently she, too, had only just come in, for her wrap was still around her slender shoulders.

"Hello, Jenny! Had a good time?" Dominique kicked off her high-heeled sandals as she spoke and unpinned the flowers on her dress, throwing them carelessly on to a chair. Orchids ... lovely, flamboyant blooms as exotic as the wearer. From Alex, of course, Jenny thought. He sent flowers to Dominique every day, huge boxfuls which must be costing him a small fortune!

"Yes, thank you." Jenny answered guardedly, but she need not have worried. Dominique's smile was brilliant.

"Maman is so glad that you have made friends here in Nice. She said she wanted you to invite Dr. Chalmers to dinner but that you wouldn't. That wasn't because of me, was it, Jenny?"

"Well, I thought . . . you seemed to dislike him so much. . . ."

"Oh, I expect I could bear to see him around, just occasionally," Dominique said carelessly. She stifled a yawn. "I said he was your type, didn't I?"

"You did, but he isn't a bit as you described him." Jenny spoke crisply and Dominique raised her brows.

"Goodness, don't bite my head off! Or look so disapproving . . . I have enough of disapproving looks from brother Piers!" She bent and picked up her sandals. "Which reminds me, he'll be home again this weekend, I suppose."

Perhaps it was her fancy, but it seemed to Jenny that she had deliberately changed the subject. Without thinking she voiced the question which sprang immediately into her mind.

"And Raoul? Will he be home, too?"

Dominique shrugged. "I don't suppose so. Maman says he is trying to raise some money and he is not finding it easy: people are suspicious of gold mines in Colorado! But he won't come back until he has accomplished what he set out to do: that is not Raoul's way."

She spoke with confidence, but she was wrong. On Friday night it was Piers who telephoned to say that owing to pressure of work he could not get home for the weekend and Raoul who rang, barely half an hour later, to tell Gabrielle to expect him some time on Saturday.

The message did not seem to give his family as much pleasure as might have been expected. Gabrielle's smooth brow was furrowed and even Dominique's reaction was mixed.

"I suppose he's coming because Piers isn't! I just wish to goodness that that wretched Céleste wasn't living on our doorstep!"

She spoke with some vehemence, leaving Jenny in no doubt at all that she believed that the magnet which was drawing Raoul home was his brother's beautiful fiancée. And if so, what would Piers' reaction be to that? "It is up to him to take care of his own. . . ." She remembered Dominique's careless words and frowned to herself. Surely it wasn't absolutely necessary for Piers to work a seven-day week? Must he always put the firm before every other consideration?

At this point she pulled herself up sharply. Obviously duty and not personal inclination was Piers' guiding rule and who was she to question that? If Raoul devoted more of his time to a sensible well-paid job instead of indulging in dreams of El Dorado he would be far better off!

When Raoul arrived the next day, however, she had something of a shock, for he looked very tired and she thought that his face showed unmistakable signs of strain.

"It's like battering my head against a brick wall," he said wearily, in answer to his mother's anxious questioning. "The one man I felt sure would back me—old Monsieur Dupré, you remember him, Maman?—is seriously ill in hospital and cannot see anyone. I've tried several other sources, but in each instance the answer has been the same. No one wants to invest in something which—despite my own faith in it—has a measure of risk involved."

Gabrielle looked troubled. "But that's natural, isn't it?"

Raoul's eyes were very dark and intense. "Nothing is a dead sure thing in this vain and transitory world, but sometimes it pays to take a chance. And this is one of the times, Maman. I know I've backed some wrong horses in the past, but this is different. I *know* it will pay off!" He clenched his hands until the knuckles whitened. "The only thing is, we're up against the time factor. We—my partner and I—have raised one loan, but it wasn't enough and we desperately need more for new drilling equipment and wages. If it's not forthcoming ... well, we've lost our chances of hitting the main vein before the bank forecloses."

Gabrielle bit her lip. "*Mon cher*, how I wish I could help you! But you know how my money is tied up: as of this moment I simply couldn't lay my hands on more than a few thousand francs."

Raoul gave her a crooked smile. "Not to worry, Maman. I shall find someone, eventually, who needs a touch of excitement to keep him cheerful. I've a few weeks left: things aren't desperate yet."

Jenny, who had been listening to the conversation in silence, glanced at Gabrielle's unhappy face and felt a surge of indignation. Didn't Raoul realise how much his get-rich-quick efforts worried his mother?

Piers is right, it's time he grew up, she thought grimly, and then coloured as she felt Raoul's eyes upon her. He seemed now to be pondering some quaint thought, for she saw the corners of his mouth lift and a teasing light in his eyes. Confused, she turned her head away. Although he had greeted her when he had first arrived he had not, since then, addressed any remark exclusively to her and she had been congratulating herself on escaping his attention. Evidently, though, even if overlooked she had not been forgotten. The glint in his eyes told her that. It was a glint which seemed to her to say, as plainly as words, "Don't think I'm fooled by that icy composure... remember I've seen what happens when you're sufficiently provoked...."

After dinner that night Jenny went along to the library, intending to borrow some books so that if she made an excuse and retired to bed early she would have plenty to read. Some new novels that had been sent to her father from London—he still kept an account with one of the big stores—were piled on a big, flat-topped desk by the window and she examined them eagerly. She had never had much time for reading, apart from biographies of the great musicians and histories of music, and now she was catching up on lost time.

She was leafing through one of the volumes, smiling at a phrase here and there, when she realised with a shock of surprise that she could hear Raoul's cultured, deep-toned voice, very faintly but also very distinctly. Wildly she looked round. Where on earth...?

It was another voice speaking now, a husky, caressing voice as unmistakable as Raoul's had been. Céleste... and limited though her French was, Jenny had no difficulty in understanding at least a few of her words.

"It has been so long, Raoul...." and then, "If only I were free tonight!"

But by now Jenny had succeeded in locating the voice. Very carefully she righted the receiver of the desk phone—an extension—which had somehow been knocked awry, perhaps when she had picked up the books. Raoul had not lost much time before contacting Céleste, she thought grimly. Well, presumably that was what he had come home for. Didn't he and Céleste have any decent feelings? And just how long did they think they could play with fire before they got burned—badly?

She selected two books at random and marched out, her lips tightly compressed. She was crossing the hall when Raoul came out of the small *salon* which was used exclusively for telephoning.

"Jenny!" His smile was wholly disarming. "Just who I want to see! I've managed to book seats for the opera tonight: will you do me the honour of accompanying me?" The blue eyes laughed into hers as he added teasingly, "You can't say this time that I haven't studied your tastes!"

Oh, how *dared* he say that, when it was obviously Céleste he had had in mind when he had booked those seats! Then, when he'd telephoned her, she had upset all his carefully laid plans by telling him that after all she wasn't free tonight! But no matter, since he couldn't have his first choice she, Jenny, was to be the grateful recipient of his largesse!

Keeping her voice steady only with an effort, she said coldly, "Thank you, but I'm afraid I'm not interested. Perhaps Dominique will go with you, if she's free."

She saw the laughter die out of his eyes and an odd expression, so fleeting that afterwards she wondered if she had only imagined it, crossed his face.

"Are you still angry with me because of last Sunday? I'm sorry for what I said and did, Jenny, really I am. I—well, I was in a vile mood, though I know that's no excuse for the way I behaved." He paused, then added very softly, "Please forgive me for everything—except the kiss, that is. I'd be lying if I said I was sorry about that!"

The colour rushed into her face. She said stormily, "You must think I'm very gullible! Do you think I'm going to fall on your neck just because you've said you're sorry? I fully realise that last Sunday you probably felt you had to live up to your reputation! I—I was warned that you'd expect me to fall in love with you, but—" and she choked—"I must say that I didn't think you'd turn out to be as arrogant and conceited as you really are!"

She stopped. Incredibly, infuriatingly, Raoul was laughing. "Jenny! You do not really believe such nonsense?" Then, hastily, as he met her furious eyes, "But I see that you do! *Ma chère,* if you will only accept my invitation I will demonstrate to you that—"

She did not let him finish. "I don't want to go out with you—now or ever!"

Heavens, she thought, how melodramatic she sounded! There was mockery in his eyes now, like little pinpoints of light, but before he could answer Dominique, who had emerged from the library and who had obviously heard Jenny's passionate declaration, came up behind them.

"Jenny does not seem to be impressed by your blandishments, Raoul! Perhaps it is because for once, *mon frère,* you have been slow off the mark—somebody else has got in first!"

"Dominique—" Jenny protested, but Dominique, her smile teasing, ignored her.

"She has a doctor boy-friend, by an odd coincidence the very same one who removed my appendix and was such a frightful bore about it! Very worthy, very English—and oh, so very, very proper!"

With a little trill of laughter she disappeared in the direction of the staircase. Jenny, flushed and angry, would have followed her, but Raoul put out a detaining hand.

"So the ice has begun to melt, has it?" he asked softly. "Well, in that case I shall console myself with the thought that perhaps it was I who precipitated the process! But what a pity it is that it doesn't sound as though your worthy English doctor knows how to turn the first snow-slide into an avalanche. . . !"

The dancing devils were back in his eyes. Not trusting herself to speak, Jenny thrust her way past him and made for the stairs. Halfway up them she could still hear Raoul laughing, and realised with a feeling of sick impotent rage that he knew quite well that once again he'd succeeded in breaching the defences that once she had thought so solid and secure.

Raoul, the next day, behaved as though nothing untoward had happened, but nonetheless Jenny took enormous pains to avoid being alone with him, and she was helped in this by the fact that the house was even more full of people than usual.

Gabrielle had planned a sherry party before lunch and almost inevitably the guests included Céleste. Exquisitely dressed and elegantly groomed, she strolled in just after Jenny had returned from church, and after greeting Gabrielle and lamenting Piers's absence gravitated almost at once to Raoul's side. From then on her golden head and Raoul's dark one were rarely far apart and Jenny, watching them, thought with an odd pang what a handsome-looking couple they made. Céleste, apparently from mercenary motives, had chosen the elder brother—but what if she were now beginning to realise her mistake?

Even as she watched Céleste put her slim white hand on Raoul's sleeve and looked up into his face in an intimate, provocative manner which spoke volumes. Suddenly feeling that because of her sympathy for Piers she could not bear to see Raoul's answering smile, Jenny turned abruptly aside and bumped straight into Dominique, causing her to spill her drink.

"Céleste is not exactly pining for Piers, is she?" Dominique spoke ironically as Jenny, apologising profusely, dabbed at her dress. Luckily it was patterned material and the splashes did not show. "I'd feel almost sorry for him, if it weren't entirely his own fault. He should be here."

"Lots of men have to make their business their whole life." Jenny, answering quickly, thought of something that her grandmother had once told her, that her

81

grandfather had never taken a holiday from his small business in his entire life.

Dominique shrugged. "It might not matter if she were in love with him. She might accept it. But as things are. . . ." She left the sentence unfinished.

Jenny was silent, and after a moment Dominique, sipping the rest of her drink, and watching her stepsister over the rim of her glass, spoke again. This time there was a faintly quizzical note in her voice.

"Incidentally, Jenny, what is it that you have done to *la belle* Céleste?"

"I?" Jenny stared. "Nothing that I know of. What do you mean? I've hardly seen her."

Céleste had, in point of fact, visited the villa once or twice during the week, but only briefly. The second time she had brought her mother, a silver-haired woman whose air of fragility, Jenny strongly suspected, was very largely assumed. Madame de Courville, from all accounts, positively enjoyed ill-health, but just at the moment this peculiarity seemed to suit her daughter. Not that she appeared to spend any large part of her time cosseting the invalid: even Gabrielle had remarked on that fact!

"Well, you must have done something," Dominique told her. "She was saying something frightfully catty about you a little while ago. Oh, not to Raoul"—as Jenny glanced involuntarily in that direction—"but to someone else."

Jenny flushed. She had realised last weekend that Céleste did not like her but could not think of a possible reason.

"It must be a case of 'I do not like thee, Dr. Fell. The reason why I cannot tell'," she said, striving to speak lightly.

To her relief Dominique adopted the same tone. "I could understand it if you were making a play for Piers—or Raoul. But you couldn't have shown more clearly that you don't give a rap for either," she said, laughing. "Only David Chalmers seems to have met with your approval so far—and that's possibly only because he's English! Which reminds me, Jenny, I've been invited to a sort of dance-cum-barbecue next

Wednesday. I suppose you wouldn't care to bring David and Sally along?"

Jenny's eyes widened, for up to now Dominique had not seen fit to include her in the many invitations which came her way. "They may not be able to get the time off. But I could ask," she said doubtfully.

"Yes, do that," Dominique said airily, and Jenny, recovering from her surprise, made a mental note to phone David either that evening or the next day.

The rest of the day passed without event. Raoul disappeared soon after lunch and Céleste made her excuses, too. Jenny thought it likely that they had gone off somewhere together, though nothing was said. It was most improbable that Stephen and Gabrielle were at all happy about the situation, but they obviously felt that their wisest plan was to remain silent and let things take their course.

Raoul returned to Paris on Monday morning and later in the day Jenny telephoned David at his flat to tell him of Dominique's invitation. Rather to her surprise he accepted after only a slight hesitation.

"I'd like to come, Jenny. Sally won't be able to, I'm afraid : she told me yesterday that she hasn't got a day off until Saturday and in any case she's spending all her free time with Louis at the moment."

"Well, it's nice to know that I shall see you," Jenny told him, and meant it. She wouldn't feel half such an outsider among Dominique's friends if David was there as well.

"Why the sudden affability—on Dominique's part, I mean?" David asked the question casually. "Or is the idea to lull me into a sense of false security? I shan't need to bring along my scalpel in order to defend myself, I hope?"

Jenny laughed. "I don't think so. Perhaps now you're no longer doctor and patient you'll find it easier to get along with each other." She hesitated, then added, "I know you think she's spoiled, David, and of course she *is* maddening sometimes, but she has her good points as well. She's loyal and affectionate and those are both qualities to be respected."

"I'm sure you're right." David sounded dour and

Jenny sighed as she replaced the receiver. Oh, for the pleasant uncomplicated days when there had been no disruptive elements to worry about! She'd always got on well with everyone, and though of course it had been obvious that other people were not always quite so lucky in their relationships, at least it had never affected *her*. How was it that now she had managed to become so involved?

Obeying a sudden impulse, she glanced at herself in the nearest mirror. She looked just the same.... wide, smoke-grey eyes, broad brow and fine cheekbones and small pointed chin ... and yet somehow she didn't *feel* the same person. The Jenny of three weeks ago had never been torn by conflicting emotions ... never been known to lose her temper ... never acted impulsively ... never been kissed by warm, strong lips! At the last thought she shivered involuntarily, although it was so warm. She had an uneasy feeling that it was all wrong that she should remember that kiss so vividly, and it was certainly all wrong that Raoul de Vaisseau should have such a disquieting effect upon her!

The barbecue was held at the opulent home of one of Dominique's girl-friends, Marie-Louise, who was the only daughter of a wealthy banker. It was an uncomplicated, lively affair and Jenny, with the reassurance of David's presence, found that she was enjoying herself far more than she had expected. As friends of Dominique she and David were automatically accepted, and even David, who had at first been slightly on the defensive, relaxed sufficiently to laugh and joke in a way which was obviously a revelation to at least one member of the party.

Jenny, catching sight of Dominique's amazed expression as David exchanged a piece of light-hearted badinage with Marie-Louise, smiled to herself. It would do her stepsister no harm to see how ill-founded her prejudices were! Not, however, that she was ever likely to admit that they were ill-founded. She was nothing if not stubborn, Dominique de Vaisseau!

Alex, of course, was Dominique's escort for the evening. Jenny found, on closer acquaintance, that she liked him even less than she had at first, and wondered with astonishment how Dominique could have so little judgment. The only thing she could find in his favour was that he was a superb dancer and he and Dominique certainly combined well. They danced on the wide verandah far more than anybody else, seemingly untiring, though nearly everyone else was complaining that it was much too hot for sustained energy.

"What about a bathe?" Marie-Louise broke away from her partner to sparkle at her guests. "I think we could do with something to cool us all down!"

"Good idea!" Dominique was the first to applaud the suggestion, though it seemed to meet with everyone's approval. Or nearly everyone's. Jenny, glancing at David, was surprised to see his brows draw together in a quick frown. He seemed about to say something, then thought better of it.

Most of the guests, it seemed, had brought swimsuits. Moonlight bathing appeared to be popular with the Riviera set, Jenny thought wryly, remembering how Raoul had tried, one starry night, to lure her to "a perfect cove where the beach will still be warm from the day's sun and where the water is like silk".

She and David were possibly the only two who had come unprepared for a swim, but several other guests preferred to watch rather than to participate, including Alex. His excuse was that he wanted to watch Dominique, who was not only a strong swimmer but also excelled at diving. Tonight her friends were insistent that she show them a spectacular new dive she had just perfected, and since she was never averse to being in the limelight she was easily persuaded to comply with their demands.

She did not, however, find it easy to satisfy them. "*Mon Dieu*! No more!" she protested laughingly as, clambering out of the pool after her fourth dive, she was greeted by a chorus of, "Oh, do it again! Please do it again!"

David was looking at her intently, but there was no admiration in his eyes for the slender perfection of her figure as revealed by the scanty costume. Instead he said quietly, but with an underlying note of authority,

"You've done enough, Dominique. Have a rest for a few minutes."

Jenny, glancing first at him and then at her stepsister, realised that Dominique was indeed looking very tired and she was pale under her golden tan. At David's words, however, she flushed vividly.

"Thank you, Dr. Chalmers! When I need your advice I'll ask for it!" she said pertly, and there was a ripple of laughter.

"Your professional services are not needed tonight, *mon ami*." Alex, who was lounging against the side of the pool, smiled, showing his very white teeth. Then he turned to Dominique. "Just one more dive for me, *chérie*."

The idiot! Jenny thought indignantly. Couldn't even he see that after all she had done this evening Dominique was almost exhausted? She was about to add her voice to David's when Dominique took the matter into her own hands.

With a gay, brittle little laugh she ran towards the high diving board and a few seconds later her slender body flashed like a sword through the air. She hit the water with barely a splash and there was a sound of enthusiastic applause.

Jenny, waiting for her to surface, saw that David was looking grim. He ought to have known better, she thought ruefully. He might have known that Dominique would not be prepared to accept advice from him, however well-meant.

Time seemed to stretch out forever. Why doesn't she surface? Jenny thought uneasily, and even as she felt the first prickings of apprehension there was a hoarse cry from Alex.

"*Mon Dieu*! She isn't coming up!"

In the moonlight the surface of the pool was perfectly still, unbroken by a single ripple. For a moment there was a stunned silence, then Marie-Louise began to scream.

"For God's sake do something!" somebody shouted, but it seemed as though David was the only one who was not completely paralysed by shock. Kicking off his shoes and shrugging off his jacket, he dived into the water and struck out with a fast crawl towards the spot where Dominique had disappeared. He reached it in less time than Jenny would have believed possible, dived, came up spluttering and empty-handed, and then dived again. After what seemed an eternity but was in reality only a few seconds he surfaced once more, and this time he held Dominique's limp body in his arms.

Afterwards Jenny could never clearly recall the next few minutes. The white scared faces of the guests as David, dripping wet, carried Dominique into the house ... the horrifying stillness of her slender form and the deathly pallor of her face ... David's speed and efficiency as he carried out the work of resuscitation ... the moment when at last Dominique opened her long-lashed eyes and looked up into their anxious faces ... all formed a mass of jumbled kaleidoscopic impressions which whirled madly around in her head.

Predictably Dominique, on recovering full conscious-ness, reacted in a typically feminine fashion. The moment the full significance of what had happened hit her she burst into tears, her shoulders shaking with sobs, and David held her, saying nothing, until the worst of the reaction passed. Only Jenny, hovering in the background, could and did appreciate the signific-ance of a fleeting look that crossed his face as he held her and the surprise, on top of everything else, was so great that she almost gasped aloud.

Luckily at that moment Dominique claimed her attention by asking for a handkerchief. She blew her nose and rubbed her eyes and then, as if belatedly realising whose arm was supporting her, she pulled herself away.

"What happened?" she asked weakly. Then, faint surprise colouring her voice, "You're wet!"

This remark David ignored. Instead, he answered her question. "I imagine you 'blacked out' when you hit the water. I shouldn't worry too much about it: it was probably the result of extreme fatigue and over-exertion."

Dominique bit her lip. "I suppose you're going to

say I told you so!" she said with a flash of her old spirit, and David's lips twitched.

"Hardly necessary, is it?" he asked dryly.

Before she could answer Alex, who up to now, Jenny thought grimly, had played a far from creditable rôle came bustling into the room and assumed full charge. David, catching Jenny's eye, rose to his feet and walked over to her side.

"There's nothing else I can do for Dominique. If you're ready, I may as well take you home," he said curtly. Then "No, it doesn't matter about my suit," in answer to an anxious question from Marie-Louise's mother. "I'll change when I get home."

It was a silent journey back to the Villa Buichi. David seemed immersed in thought and Jenny was struggling to dismiss from her mind the strong suspicion that Dominique's *bête noir* was actually head over heels in love with her. She felt no jealousy or resentment, merely an overwhelming sympathy. It was obvious enough how it had happened. Dominique, for all her faults, was lovely enough to turn any man's head—even a man as sensible and well-balanced as David. The really awful thing was that his love was so hopeless, for not only did Dominique appear to dislike him intensely but his material assets, from her point of view, were negligible.

At any rate, she decided, even if he were in love with Dominique it certainly did not preclude a friendship with her, Jenny. Both of them knew that there was no vital spark between them, but that did not mean that they could not enjoy each other's company. David was the kind of brother she would have loved to have and he, for his part, might be glad of her as a tenuous link with Dominique. In time, of course, he'd get over his infatuation—or so she hoped—and find someone far more suitable to be his wife!

She frowned a little at the thought. Grandmother had always emphasised the importance of "suitability" when it came to choosing a marriage partner. That, she had clearly indicated, was where her own daughter—Jenny's mother—had made such a disastrous mistake, for Stephen Challoner had definitely *not* been a suitable match for a quiet, home-loving, respectably brought-up Barrington! Like to like, Grandmother had always said. Was that why Stephen and Gabrielle were obviously so happy together? And why the gay, sophisticated Céleste so often gravitated towards Raoul although she was wearing his brother's ring upon her finger?

She sighed. No doubt Grandmother had been right and yet—and yet, if so, why hadn't she, Jenny, fallen in love with David, who would almost certainly have met with Grandmother's wholehearted approval? It was all very odd!

Odder still was Dominique's behaviour the next day. Jenny was sunbathing in the garden when her stepsister, looking very little the worse for her misadventure, joined her. She was looking rather more subdued and more vulnerable than usual, for she was wearing a very simple white cotton dress and very little make-up.

"Hello," Jenny smiled at her and feeling that it would be tactful not to refer to the events of the previous night, made a bright remark about nothing in particular.

This Dominique ignored. She began twisting a flower stalk around her little finger as she said, almost awkwardly, "I suppose I ought to apologise to you for last night, Jenny. I rather spoilt things for you and David, didn't I?"

"Spoilt things?" Jenny raised her brows.

"Well . . . I don't suppose David exactly enjoyed doing what he had to do for me." Dominique sounded almost sullen. She paused, and then added, "They said you were marvellous, too, rushing around organising blankets and hot water bottles and brandy and telling everyone to shut up and keep out of the way. You never lose your head, do you? Must be nice to keep calm and collected, whatever!"

Jenny flushed. Somebody, last night, had had to do all those things and David's job had been to rub life and warmth back into Dominique's flaccid limbs. The rest of the party had been useless : some of them semi-hysterical.

She said crisply, "You'd better keep your thanks for David. It was he who saved your life, not I!"

"You needn't rub it in!" There was a sulky curve to Dominique's wayward mouth and Jenny, after one incredulous stare, felt an urge to shake her. Of all the ungrateful brats . . . !

She opened her mouth to utter a blistering retort, but the words never came out, for just at that moment she heard the sound of footsteps behind them. She turned to see Gabrielle coming across the patio and something in the way she moved . . . almost like a sleepwalker . . . alerted Jenny to disaster even before she saw her stepmother's ashen face and dazed look.

"Maman! What's wrong?" Dominique raced to her mother's side, her eyes widening in apprehension as she, like Jenny, realised that the tautness of Gabrielle's expression portended bad news.

"It's Raoul." Gabrielle spoke unsteadily and she clung on to the stone balustrade as if glad of its support. "There—there's been an accident. It wasn't Raoul's fault, but—but he's been injured, I don't know how badly. He's in hospital now."

CHAPTER SIX

"HE'S not—dead?"

It seemed to Jenny that Dominique's hoarse little voice had come from a very long way away.

Gabrielle's lips pinched, but she made an effort to pull herself together. "No! He's not dead, thank God! But—but they don't yet know the extent of his injuries. There seem to be no broken bones, but he's suffering from shock and concussion and—and there may be some internal damage. The doctors are examining him now."

"Do you know how the accident happened?" Jenny wondered why she had felt such a queer turning over of her heart and why her mouth had suddenly gone so dry. Raoul meant nothing to her. It must be the shock, she thought vaguely.

"There was a passenger in Raoul's car: he was unhurt and I spoke to him. He says that a lorry came out of a side turning and ran right into them. Raoul swerved, but he hadn't a chance."

Dominique choked back a sob, and turned blindly towards Jenny. Instinctively Jenny put her arm around her, trying hard to maintain her own composure.

Somewhere in the house a telephone rang. In the last few minutes Gabrielle had regained a little of her normal colour, but now it ebbed again and she was white and shaking as she rushed to answer it. Dominique went with her, but Jenny remained where she was. Her hands clenched at her sides, she stared with unseeing eyes at the kaleidoscopic masses of flowers. Impossible, somehow, to think of Raoul lying white and still ... perhaps badly injured ... in a narrow hospital bed, shorn of that amazing vitality which seemed so much a part of him!

A big, sleek black and white cat stalked up to her and began rubbing against her bare brown legs, purring loudly. Automatically Jenny bent to stroke it. She loved animals, and possibly the only time she had ever been at odds with her grandmother had been when old Mrs. Barrington had firmly resisted her impassioned plea for a cat or dog of her own. Nasty dirty animals, breeding germs and spoiling carpets and furniture, the old lady had said firmly, and though Jenny had wept her opposition had never weakened.

This cat, Jenny, knew, belonged to Berthe, though usually it disdained the servants' quarters and had a marked preference for the more luxurious apartments. It was an affectionate animal and now, as Jenny tickled its throat, its purr became almost thunderous. It had purred like that for Raoul last Sunday morning, she remembered, and Raoul had laughed and buried his strong brown fingers deep in the long silky fur while Céleste had shuddered and moved away. Céleste was another one who couldn't bear cats!

"Nice puss." Jenny murmured the words automatically but saw, almost with disbelief, that the hand stroking the cat was trembling. She straightened abruptly, and as she did so Dominique came out of the house and walked quickly towards her.

"It's all right, Jenny!" The younger girl's face

was radiant in her relief. "The doctors have seen Raoul and though he's still unconscious they say there's absolutely nothing to worry about except the shock and concussion, and even that ought to wear off fairly soon. He'll have to stay in hospital for observation, of course, but when we think what might have happened . . . !" She stopped and gave a shaky little laugh. "I think I must have aged about ten years in the last twenty minutes!"

"Well, luckily the grey hairs don't show!" Jenny said, laughing. Unable to find words to express the relief she felt, she picked up the cat and hugged it hard. Outraged, it stiffened, struggled and shot out of her arms with a protesting "Miaow!"

"You'll be in hospital next!" Dominique said. "It's got sharp claws, *cette mauvaise bête*!" She linked her arm in Jenny's, the sullenness of a short time before completely forgotten.

"Come and help Maman to pack. She insists on going to Paris immediately, so Stephen, bless him, is going to drive her. I'd like to go, too, but I suppose it would be silly. Raoul will have to be kept very quiet for a few days and he won't be allowed many visitors, if any."

Gabrielle and Stephen did not, in fact, stay in Paris for longer than one night. They returned to Nice late on Friday evening, arriving almost at the same time as Piers, who had driven from Toulouse.

"We've left Raoul in good hands!" Gabrielle made the announcement with something akin to her old gaiety. "He's recovered consciousness and the doctors are quite satisfied with his condition. His only trouble at the moment is a perpetual headache and he is suffering a little from blurred vision, but apparently that is only a temporary disability."

"I don't expect it prevents him from singling out the prettiest nurses," Stephen said jokingly, and Gabrielle laughed.

"Well, he certainly won't die for lack of attention! It seemed to me while I was there that every nurse in the hospital was making it her business to attend to his needs!"

Jenny smiled politely, but oddly enough the picture Gabrielle's words conjured up did not really amuse her. It did not seem to amuse Piers either. He was standing silently in the background, even more withdrawn than usual, and Jenny wondered what he was thinking. Was he concerned about his brother or was he, on the other hand, completely lacking in sympathy and was that why he was saying so little?

She discovered later on that whatever was troubling Piers it was certainly not anxiety on Raoul's behalf. There was an oppressive atmosphere all day on Saturday, and the chief factor was undoubtedly the tension which existed between Piers and his fiancée, who arrived for lunch. She had, it seemed, only just learned of Raoul's accident and the news had unmistakably been a severe shock.

The impression she gave was that she was spoiling for an argument with Piers and one or two of her snappy remarks did, in fact, result in an ominous tightening of his rather thin lips. Jenny, looking from one to the other, realised with a slight sense of shock that Céleste was finding it increasingly difficult to play the part of a loving fiancée. She had elected to marry Piers because from a worldly point of view he was a better match than his younger brother: what she could not have bargained for was that her heart would try so hard to betray her head!

The relationship between her and Piers became so strained that Jenny was not surprised when Dominique burst into her bedroom late that night to tell her that the couple had had a bitter quarrel.

"I haven't been eavesdropping, Piers told Maman all about it and Maman told me," she said airily, in answer to Jenny's sharp question. "Piers has evidently seen the red light at last and he's trying to make Céleste fix a definite date for their wedding. She's been putting him off with one excuse or another, but now I think he's more or less presented her with an ultimatum: an autumn wedding or no wedding at all. She's got to tell him what she's decided when she comes back from Geneva. She leaves for there next week, you know, with her mother."

Jenny stared down at the rose-patterned coverlet on her bed. What would it be like, to marry one man when you were in love with another? No wonder Céleste, for all her greed and selfishness, was inwardly dreading the day when the bars of matrimony should close irrevocably behind her!

"What do you think she'll do?"

"Marry Piers, of course." Dominique spoke with certainty. "She won't like it, but she'll do it—in the end. She's always been brought up to believe that what money can buy ought to be hers, and Piers is certainly rich enough to be able to provide her with all the things she wants." She gave a hard little laugh. "Of course, it's Raoul's gold mine which is giving her nightmares! If Raoul really *is* right about it . . . !"

Jenny was silent. It didn't seem to occur to Dominique that there might be a doubt as to whether Raoul, under such circumstances, would still want Céleste. She seemed to take that for granted, and perhaps she had good reason to do so.

She said slowly, "I can't understand Piers . . . wanting to marry Céleste even though he must know that she isn't really in love with him."

Dominique shrugged. "Who can tell how Piers' mind works? I think perhaps she is something of an obsession with him. He collects things, you know, and Céleste would look well in any collection. He won't let her go without a struggle. And perhaps he is also hoping that she will change towards him after they are married." Her mouth curved into an oddly bitter little smile. "As if you can love someone to order . . . or stop loving them, come to that!"

For a moment her lovely, vivid face was wistful. Jenny, watching her expression, spoke abruptly.

"Dominique, are you happy?"

Immediately the mask was back in place. "Happy? Of course I am! Heavens, Jenny, what a question to ask—and at this time of night, too!"

She uncurled her slim legs and jumped up. She was laughing as she went out, but nevertheless Jenny was left with the uneasy conviction that she had not received an entirely truthful answer to her question.

The bulletins from the hospital in Paris continued to be satisfactory. The doctors still insisted on absolute quiet for their patient and though Gabrielle and Dominique were allowed to see him on a couple of occasions, all other visitors were frowned upon.

Jenny half-wondered whether she ought to write him a polite little letter saying that she was sorry about the crash and that she hoped he would soon be better, but after half a dozen attempts at producing something between formality and friendliness she gave it up as a bad job. Her good wishes would mean nothing to Raoul, anyway. According to Gabrielle and Dominique he had been deluged with messages and flowers and fruit —"Most of them from ex-girl-friends, of course!" Dominique said, laughing, and Jenny was left wondering what flowers, if any, Céleste had sent.

It was after her second visit to the hospital that Dominique surprised Jenny by saying casually, "Raoul sent his love to you. Oh, and he seemed to want to know how your romance was progressing."

Jenny's cheeks flamed. "My romance?"

Dominique was buffing her long, pointed fingernails and did not look up. "He meant you and David, I presume." She spoke carelessly, as though her mind was on something else.

"But—" Jenny began, and then stopped, biting her lip. As if Dominique—or Raoul either, for that matter! —could be in the least interested in the true state of affairs that existed between her and David!

In any case, she did not hear from either him or from Sally until nearly a week after Marie-Louise's near disastrous party. Then David rang up one evening to ask her if she would like to see a film with him. He explained that he had unexpectedly found himself at a loose end and would enjoy her company.

It would be silly, Jenny thought, not to accept. Dominique was out with Alex, Gabrielle was busy catching up with some important correspondence and Stephen was writing. The evening stretched out in front of her, long and empty, and she hesitated no longer.

"Thank you. It would be lovely."

"Good. I'll call for you in twenty minutes' time,"

David said briskly, and was as good as his word. Punctuality, to him, was important. It was something else they had in common.

"I don't know whether there's any film you're particularly interested in? What kind of thing do you usually like?" David asked, meticulously buckling first her safety strap and then his own before switching on the engine. He was the complete antithesis of Raoul, who never thought about such things, Jenny reflected, and then bit her lip. Why, when she was with David, did she have to try to spoil everything by thinking of Raoul?

She realised that David was waiting for her to answer. She said, "I'm sorry, I've very rarely been to the cinema, but I expect I'd like practically anything.".

David looked amused. 'What's your tipple, then? The live theatre?"

Jenny shook her head. "Concerts—before my grandmother became too frail to be left alone at night. Even then I had the radio."

"Oh!" David looked thoughtful. "Well, I don't know much about classical music myself, I'm afraid, but I'm always willing to learn—in the right company!" He turned his head and smiled at her. "I believe there's rather a good concert on next week: one of my patients happened to mention it." He paused, obviously searching his memory. "Someone called Weber—I think that's the right name?—is the pianist."

"Max Weber!" Jenny sat up straight, her eyes suddenly sparkling. "He's giving a concert here next week? Oh, I'd love to hear him!"

"You and half Nice, judging by what Monsieur Chambord told me! Tickets are scarcer than gold-dust, apparently, but would you like me to try to get hold of a couple?"

"Oh, please don't bother—" Jenny began, but David merely grinned and shook his head.

"No bother. I'll see what I can do."

The film they eventually saw was not particularly good and Jenny left the cinema with a slight headache. When he discovered this David insisted on driving her out of the town and towards the hills, where the air was fresher and cooler. He parked the car and they sat for a time in companionable silence.

David was the first to break it. "I've had a letter from Dominique."

"You have?" Jenny could not keep the surprise out of her voice and David gave a grim little laugh.

"Remind me to show it to you some time! It's exquisitely worded. She thanks me charmingly for having acted with such promptitude and efficiency and very much hopes that if my suit was ruined she will be allowed to replace it. The only thing that surprises me is that she didn't see fit to enclose a five-thousand-franc note there and then!"

David's voice was raw with hurt anger. After one dismayed moment Jenny said, "Oh, David, I'm sure she didn't mean . . . she couldn't have thought . . . she's been terribly worried about her brother, you know."

David laughed derisively. "She meant it all right! As far as she's concerned I'm just another lackey! But anyway, what the hell? Who cares about Dominique?"

Before Jenny could answer he reached for her and kissed her, hard upon her lips. Recognising, with a strange wisdom that she had not known she possessed, the hurt desperation which lay behind his action, Jenny did not struggle to free herself from his embrace, but waited until at last he raised his head and drew away. Then she said gravely, "Why did you do that, David?"

For a moment he was silent, then he gave a slightly embarrassed laugh. "Was it so unexpected? You're very lovely, Jenny. Few men could sit beside you on a starlit night and not want to do what I've just done—but I'm sorry if you didn't like it."

"I didn't dislike it." That, Jenny thought wryly, was perfectly true. She hadn't felt any reaction at all. Raoul's kiss had been a shattering experience, but she had emerged from David's embrace without so much as a quickened heartbeat. Even now she could feel nothing but a deep sympathy for his unhappiness.

Looking at him, she saw his sandy brows draw together in a puzzled frown and she spoke quickly. "What I mean is, I neither liked nor disliked being kissed by you. I—I'm very fond of you, David, but I'm terribly sorry, I'm not the least bit in love with you." She drew a deep breath. "Actually, though, I'm not sorry, I'm glad. Because I'm quite, quite sure that whatever happened just now you aren't at all in love with me!"

For a few seconds he stared at her. "What do you mean?"

Jenny spoke steadily. "You only kissed me because you're hurt and angry with Dominique. That's true, isnt' it? You're in love with her. You always have been."

She heard him take a quick breath. Then he opened the car door, got out, and walked a little way away from her. Jenny, looking at his wide shoulders, wondered for one panic-stricken moment whether she had been too outspoken.

Then he turned and came back to the car. In the moonlight his face looked pale and a little grim. "How did you guess?"

"I saw your expression the night that Dominique was nearly drowned—I don't think anyone else has the slightest inkling," she added hastily.

He gave the ghost of a laugh. "For which heaven be praised! Being all sorts of a fool is one thing, having everyone recognise the fact is another!" He paused, looking straight ahead of him, unseeingly. "I—I'm not such a fool that I don't know the score. God only knows I've tried to stop loving her, but I can't. No one realises better than I do that she's spoilt and wilful and stubborn, and yet it doesn't make any difference to the way I feel about her. Crazy, isn't it?"

"That's the best kind of love," Jenny said quietly.

He got back into his seat. "Is it? You're the kind of girl I ought to be in love with, Jenny. Any man would be lucky to get you. Even Sally tumbled to that fact: that's why she was so keen for us to meet." He sighed. "I really have tried to make myself love you, you know, Jenny." He saw her lips curve into a little smile and added, ruefully, "Do you hate me for saying that? It doesn't sound very complimentary, I'm afraid."

She shook her head. "Of course I don't hate you, and I think that you've actually paid me a very sweet compliment." She hesitated. "I—I only wish that I thought you had a chance. With Dominique, I mean."

He shrugged. "Don't let it worry you. As I've told you, I've no illusions. No doubt I'll get over my foolishness—in time." He covered her hand, briefly, with his own. "Thanks, anyway, Jenny, for being so sweet about it. You're a girl in a million, you know. Some day someone with a bit more sense than I've got is going to find that out!"

Jenny laughed, hoping that he could not see the sudden flush which mantled her cheeks. Luckily he did not wait for her to reply.

"In the meantime, Jenny, would it be a fearful cheek if I asked you if we could go on seeing each other? We get on well together and we seem to be the same sort of people—except, of course, that you probably don't know the first thing about the pancreas and I certainly don't know one composer from another!"

"Of course we can go on seeing each other!" Jenny spoke warmly. "I really do like you tremendously, David, and I enjoy your company."

He laughed. "Even if your heart doesn't do a crazy somersault every time you see me! Right, Jenny! Friends it is!" He glanced at his watch. "And now I suppose I'd better take you home. It's getting late."

When they reached the Villa Buichi Jenny said tentatively, "Gabrielle made me promise that I'd ask you in for coffee, David. I—I don't think Dominique will be home yet, if you'd care to come in for a few minutes?"

David smiled at her. They understood each other better now than they had ever done. "Thanks. I will."

Gabrielle, it seemed, had already gone to bed, but Stephen was still up. He emerged from his study just as Jenny, who still hated asking a servant to perform any duty that she felt she could well do herself, was departing kitchenwards to rustle up some coffee and sandwiches. When she returned, bearing three cups of steaming, fragrant coffee on a tray, the two men were chatting amicably and it was obvious that they liked each other. They had, in fact, met before, at the nursing home, and when David had gone Stephen looked smilingly at his daughter.

"Pleasant young chap, that. Good doctor, too, I'm told."

"I'm glad you like him. I think he's nice, too." Jenny began carefully to stack the empty coffee cups on to the tray and Stephen's mouth twitched into a slightly rueful smile. She didn't sound wildly enthusiastic, he thought, but then that was probably because he was so used to Dominique's hyperboles whenever she fell in love—which, up until recently, had been with monotonous frequency! She'd been much less volatile of late, though, and he hoped that that did not mean that she had decided that Count Alex Venescu was her "Mr. Right". Neither he nor Gabrielle liked him, though they had had the wisdom to say nothing. He sighed. His little Jenny seemed likely to make a far better choice. David Chalmers was just the kind of man she ought to marry: they would probably be very happy together.

Stephen was not the only one who realised that somehow there was a sense of fitness about Jenny and David being together. Sally, sounding very gay and also a little mysterious, rang up the following morning to ask if Jenny would meet her for coffee.

"I've something important to tell you and I don't want to do it over the phone!" she explained, and laughing, refused to say more. The first thing that Jenny noticed, however, when they met, was a sparkling sapphire and diamond ring on Sally's left hand, and her face lit up.

"Sally! You're engaged!"

Sally's eyes were very bright. "It happened last night. It's Louis, of course: you met him at the party, didn't you? I never ever thought I'd end up by marrying a Frenchman, but he really is an absolute poppet, my family will adore him!" she said, laughing, then added with a twinkle, "Your turn next, Jenny!"

This and her subsequent remarks made it so plain that she was hoping that at some future date Jenny and David would follow the example set by her and Louis that Jenny, despite her discomfort, felt that she ought to make the position plain.

She did so, of course, without mentioning David's

love for Dominique, and was slightly amused at his cousin's intense and outspoken disappointment.

"Oh, Jenny, are you sure? I earmarked you for David that first day I met you!" she wailed.

Jenny laughed in spite of herself. "Sorry, Sally! You ought to know by now that things like that really can't be arranged in advance!"

"I suppose not, but it would have been *so* suitable!" Sally said grudgingly. "There isn't anyone else, is there? For you, I mean? I know there isn't for David."

So, close though they were, Sally hadn't guessed her cousin's secret! Jenny was saved the necessity of replying because just at that moment Sally, glancing round the café stiffened with surprise.

"I say, Jenny! Isn't that your stepbrother's fiancée over there? Céleste Somebody or other? She came to the nursing home once, with her mother, and one of the patients told me who she was. I'm sure it's her! But look who she's with!"

Startled by the note in Sally's voice, Jenny turned her head and followed Sally's gaze. It *was* Céleste!—though she had to look twice to make sure. Her hair was done in a completely different style and she was wearing enormous dark glasses.

She and her companion, a tall, dark-haired man with a swarthy skin and a little black moustache, were sitting at an unobtrusive corner table. Céleste seemed to be doing all the talking and the man was listening intently, a slight frown on his handsome but dissipated-looking face. Jenny, watching them, was conscious of a faint stir of astonishment. They looked so completely out of place in this small pavement café, the prosperous-looking man in his faultlessly cut suit and immaculate silk shirt and the elegant girl in her creamy dress and the pearl necklace that looked real!

Just at that moment Céleste glanced round. Her eyes met Jenny's and, astoundingly, a tide of vivid colour suffused her face and throat. Jenny, who had started to give her a small, wavering smile of recognition, nearly dropped her cup of *café noir* in her surprise. Why, Céleste looked positively guilty, though why she should, under such unexceptional circumstances, was beyond her comprehension!

"I don't think she's very pleased to see you, do you?" Sally sounded puzzled. "That's Pierre Lamotte, the financier, she's with: have you heard of him? He's as rich as Croesus and—oh, look, she's getting up to leave!"

Sure enough, Céleste had risen hurriedly to her feet. She said something to her companion, snatched up her handbag and left the table without another glance in Jenny's and Sally's direction.

"I say, how rude!" Sally spoke indignantly. "She might at least have spoken to you! What's the matter with her? Anyone would think she had a guilty conscience!" She paused, then added casually, "It's Piers de Vaisseau she's going to marry, isn't it? Funny, when according to the woman I was telling you about everyone was so sure it would be the younger brother—Raoul! How is he, by the way? I heard about his accident from David."

"Improving rapidly, I believe." Jenny gulped down the last of her coffee, burning her mouth in the process, and glanced at her watch. "Didn't you say you had to be back on duty at noon, Sally?"

"Heavens, yes! I'd better fly!" It was Sally's turn to jump to her feet, Céleste de Courville's strange behaviour forgotten. Jenny was conscious of a definite feeling of relief. Much as she liked and trusted Sally, she simply wasn't the right person with whom to discuss family affairs.

Nevertheless, she reflected on the way home, Sally's remark about a guilty conscience seemed peculiarly apt. Céleste *had* looked guilty—frightened almost. But why? Why shouldn't she have coffee with whomsoever she liked? She couldn't possibly think that Piers might mind if he knew? According to Dominique, she was out nearly every night with a different escort! And yet... she'd certainly picked an out-of-the-way spot for a rendezvous, almost as though she'd deliberately tried to avoid being seen by anyone she knew!

She made up her mind that she would mention the matter the next time she saw Céleste. Then she remembered that this was not likely to be for a week or so,

for the next day she and Madame de Courville were
due to leave for Geneva. Away from Piers, away from
Raoul, it seemed that Céleste would finally have to make
up her mind which brother she really wanted ... the
grim-faced businessman whose devotion to his work,
however irritating, meant that he could afford to shower
her with the luxuries she craved, or the blue-eyed adventurer who had staked every penny he owned in a goldmine which everyone but himself believed to be a
phony!

Angrily she tried to dismiss her troubled thoughts. It
was absolutely nothing to her whichever brother
Céleste chose! She simply didn't care, one way or the
other!

Gabrielle's early morning call to the hospital next
day took a little longer than usual. She was smiling
when she reported the gist of the conversation she had
had with the Sister in charge of Raoul's case, but there
was, at the same time, a gleam of anxiety in her dark
eyes.

"Apparently, *mon cher* Raoul is being very difficult!
He is like a caged lion, Sister says: he does not at all
want to stay in hospital now that he is feeling so
much better, but the doctors insist that he still requires
absolute quiet. He still has an occasional blinding headache and it will be some time, they say, before he is fit
to return to Colorado. That has not pleased poor Raoul!
He would get out of his bed and fly there this very
moment if only they would let him!"

"I wish he would never return!" Dominique spoke
with passion. How she adored Raoul, Jenny thought.
Impossible to think of her ever putting anyone else
before him!

Gabrielle sighed. "If he is bored and unhappy and
worried about his mine he will only end up by doing
something incredibly stupid, and that I do not want to
happen! I shall go to Paris tomorrow to see him: perhaps I can coax him into a better frame of mind!"

She pushed away her half-drunk coffee as she spoke
and began to glance through the small pile of letters

which Berthe had just brought in. One she handed to Dominique.

"This is the only one that looks interesting, but unfortunately it is for you, *chérie*. None for you, Stephen, and I, alas! seem to have nothing but bills this morning!"

"That is surely not so unusual!" Stephen teased. He had been very considerate of Gabrielle these last few days, neglecting his own work in order to be constantly with her. Undoubtedly he had done much to alleviate her anxiety, Jenny thought, and wondered, a little wistfully, whether there had ever been such a perfect relationship between Stephen and her own mother. He and Gabrielle were extraordinarily close: even when other people were present it was impossible not to notice some gleam, or flash of understanding, that passed, sparkling, between them.

Dominique looked up from her letter. "This is from Angélique, to remind us that we are dining with her on Friday, Maman."

"But of course! I had not forgotten." Gabrielle smiled at her daughter and then looked somewhat apologetically at Jenny. "Angélique is my godchild, Jenny, and the first of Dominique's childhood friends to have married. She and her husband have just returned from their honeymoon and they have invited us to dinner on Friday so that we can hear all their news and admire their house, which has been specially designed for them by a very well-known architect. You will not mind if we leave you alone for an evening? I would suggest that you accompany us, but as you do not know Angélique or her husband, and they will naturally be very full of their own affairs, I think perhaps you might feel a little bored."

"I won't mind being alone in the least," Jenny assured her stepmother. Solitude, thank goodness, had never worried her: in fact, at one time she had positively welcomed it.

Yet when Friday came and Gabrielle, Stephen and Dominique set out for their dinner engagement, she was conscious of a restlessness which was so foreign to her nature that it almost alarmed her. Instinctively she turned to her beloved Beethoven, Chopin and Liszt to soothe and relax her, and in the dark-panelled music room, heavy with the sweetness of roses growing outside, the magic, as always, worked. Watching the trained rhythmic action of her hands, listening to the strong, true notes that came from the wonderful piano, she was completely absorbed and happy.

She did not hear the door behind her open and then close again, very softly. She did not know that a tall figure moved swiftly, silently, across the darkening room and sank into a deep armchair, and it was not until her hands finally released the keys after the last chords of a Mozart sonata that she realised for the first time that she was not alone, as she had thought.

"You play beautifully, *ma chère*. Allow me to congratulate you—and to thank you for an unexpected treat."

At the sound of the deep, familiar voice Jenny's heart seemed to turn over. She turned swiftly, her eyes wide and incredulous. She had not bothered to switch on the light when it grew dark and the pale moonshine blanched her cheeks to crystal and her hair was silvered.

"*Raoul!*" she whispered, and he got up from his chair and came towards her, moving with all his old, easy grace.

"You sound frightened! See, I am not a ghost!" he said, smiling, and caught hold of her hands. At his touch her heart, absurdly, began to race and she had to tense every muscle in her body in order to still the violent trembling that threatened to possess her. It was, of course, the total unexpectedness of his appearance which had caused such an idiotic reaction, she told herself, but it was disconcerting nonetheless.

She said breathlessly, "I—it's just that you startled me so! You're the last person I expected to see! Gabrielle seemed to think you would be in hospital for several more days at least. Why didn't you let her know you were coming home?"

He seemed amused. "Because I didn't know myself until an hour or so ago."

Perhaps he sensed her perplexity, for he added nonchalantly, "I discharged myself, you see."

"You did *what*?" Jenny stared at him, horrified. "Raoul, you didn't? Not really?" Then, helplessly, "Why?"

His face was pale and carved in the moonlight, but she thought it likely, from the way he spoke, that a smile lurked in his eyes.

"Oh, several reasons. Perhaps I was tired of all the petty restrictions!" Then, laughing, "Have you ever been in hospital, *chérie*? No? You are fortunate. One is treated like a child—and a singularly dim-witted child at that!"

Belatedly, Jenny became aware that he was still holding her hands. Worse, that the clasp of his warm, strong fingers was distinctly pleasant. Blushing scarlet, she pulled quickly away from him and said, as crisply as she could, "Well, in your case I'm not surprised! I've no doubt that while you were there you contrived to break every rule in the book!"

"And a few others they hadn't thought of!" Raoul said, grinning. Then, impudently, "Don't lecture me, *chérie*! Remember I'm still officially an invalid and need to be treated with care and tenderness!"

Jenny moved over to the light and snapped it on. "Then you ought to have stayed in hospital! You might—anything might happen to you!" she said, and in spite of herself her voice faltered. Now that she could see him properly she realised how pale he was under his tan and how tired he looked. His jaunty air, she realised suddenly, was mostly assumed : underneath it all he was probably feeling like death.

With a vague feeling that she ought to suggest that he go to bed, she turned to close down the lid of the piano, but he checked her movement.

"Please don't stop playing!—unless, of course, you're tired? I meant it when I said how much I enjoyed listening to you, you know : you have a great gift. You are wasted as a teacher."

He spoke quietly and with such evident sincerity that Jenny coloured. "I'm not going back to teaching."

"No? Then what are you going to do?"

"I'm not sure—yet." To her intense embarrassment Jenny saw his eyebrows shoot up and realised, with annoyance, that he was probably drawing his own (erroneous) conclusions. Hastily, in order to avoid further questions, she said the first thing that came into her head.

"What about your mine? I suppose you're still trying to raise a loan?"

Unexpectedly he grinned. "Not any more. I can convalesce with a quiet mind : help has been forthcoming from a surprising but nonetheless most welcome quarter. When I return to Colorado it will not be to confess failure, as I had begun to fear. No, we can forge ahead with our venture, thanks to *le bon Dieu* and one Pierre Lamotte, who has given me the loan I wanted."

Jenny wrinkled her brow. Pierre Lamotte! The name sounded oddly familiar. She tried to think where she had heard it before, and suddenly she remembered. The small pavement café—and the man who had been with Céleste de Courville! Sally had said his name was Pierre Lamotte—and also that he was a financier and as rich as Croesus!

Raoul was looking at her, his dark brows tilted enquiringly. "What is the matter?"

"Nothing." Nothing was the matter, she told herself fiercely. The thing was probably a pure coincidence!

She moved quickly over to the piano. "Are you sure you want me to play to you? What do you like?"

He came and stood by her shoulder and she was disturbingly aware of his nearness. "Some Chopin Preludes to begin with, please. After that I leave the programme entirely to you," he said, smiling, and pulled up a chair so that he could watch her face as she played.

His intent gaze made her nervous, but she tried not to show it. She was a little surprised to discover that he had a keen appreciation of music and knew a lot about it. Somehow it seemed an unexpected facet of his personality, but then perhaps it was Céleste, accustomed to moving in the well-bred, cultured society of cosmopolitan Europe, who had influenced certain of his tastes!

The thought was so oddly distasteful that even while the liquid dreaming notes of the "Berceuse" rippled from under her fingers she shivered. Immediately Raoul jumped to his feet.

"You're cold... I'll close the window." He moved swiftly across the room as he spoke, then she saw him stop as though he had been shot, sway slightly and put his hand to his head, where a livid scar marked his left temple.

"Raoul!" Terror sharpened her voice: he suddenly looked ghastly. He seemed to stagger a little and instinctively she put out her hand to steady him.

"Sorry!" he said between clenched teeth. "This pain..." and he sank back into the chair to which she guided him. She rushed for brandy and forced a little between his lips, relieved to see, after a few minutes, his colour slowly return to normal.

She was still bending anxiously over him when he opened his eyes and looked at her.

"Don't worry, I'll be all right now," he said wearily. He put his hand up to his head. "That's what they wanted to keep me in hospital for... these sudden blinding attacks of pain." He gave a rueful laugh. "This is the first one for nearly three days: I thought I was over them. There seemed no earthly reason why I shouldn't come home...."

And every reason why he should? Almost certainly, Jenny thought bitterly, he didn't know that Céleste had left for Geneva or perhaps he might have been content to stay. Well, she wasn't going to tell him tonight that he had flouted his doctors' advice for nothing and that for all he was going to see of his brother's fiancée during the next fortnight he might just as well have stayed in hospital! He could find that out for himself tomorrow!

She said quietly, "I think I heard footsteps. It will probably be your mother and Stephen and Dominique."

"Too bad of them to leave you in solitary splendour!" Raoul looked at her, and suddenly something of the old mockery was back in his eyes. "But what a heaven-sent opportunity for your worthy doctor! Don't tell me he didn't want to take advantage of it!"

The colour rushed into Jenny's face. "David's on duty tonight." (She didn't actually know whether he was or not, but for once she had less than her usual regard for the truth.)

"Oh well! His loss was my gain." This time there was no mockery in Raoul's voice and when, surprised, she looked at him it was to find him smiling at her in a way which she found oddly disturbing.

He added teasingly, "You know, Jenny, I have to admit that you represent something of a challenge as far as I am concerned. Never before has a young and beautiful woman treated me with such shattering disdain: never before have I invoked so many disapproving looks! You have obviously believed all the stories you have been told about my wicked Past, but really I am not as black as I am sometimes painted! Could you not learn to like me just a little, if only to save me from complete demoralisation?"

"I'm not such an idiot as to believe that you care two hoots what I think about you!" Jenny retorted coldly.

"Then that is where you are wrong, *chérie*! I have a nature that simply cries out for love and understanding!—Ah, no!" Before she realised what he meant to do he raised his hand and gently traced the outline of her lips with the tip of his finger. "You have an enchanting mouth: it is a sin to prim it so!"

Jenny jerked away. She opened her mouth to utter a blistering retort, then to her enormous surprise burst out laughing.

"I—oh, you're impossible!"

Raoul was regarding her with astonishment and amused approval. "That is far, far better! Did you know that you have little golden candles shining in your eyes when you laugh? Never before have I seen such a beautiful phenomenon!"

She had no chance to answer. There was the sound of footsteps and voices in the hall, the door was flung open and Gabrielle and Dominique exploded upon them.

Explanations followed exclamations. And Jenny, turning quickly away, took advantage of the hubbub to admonish her sensible Barrington heart, which had begun to behave in a fashion absurd enough to make any true, self-respecting Barrington ask for an immediate heart transfer!

CHAPTER SEVEN

WHEN the sensation caused by Raoul's unexpected homecoming had died down life at the Villa Buichi resumed a more or less normal pattern. Raoul firmly refused to be treated as an invalid, and indeed he was not one, in the strict sense of the word. To his relieved family it seemed as though his gaiety and vitality were unimpaired, and only the blinding headaches from which he still suffered at irregular intervals served to remind them that he was not, in fact, one hundred per cent fit.

At Gabrielle's insistence he reluctantly agreed to return to the hospital in Paris for periodic check-ups, but though the doctors there were forced to admit that his general health was good, they were still worried about the cause of the headaches and strongly vetoed an immediate return to Colorado.

Rather to everyone's surprise, Raoul seemed far more resigned to the prospect of an enforced holiday than might have been expected. Of course, Jenny thought, now that his mind was at rest about the loan he was probably glad of the chance to rid himself of the tension of the past few weeks. Whatever it was, his gay good humour was irresistible and had a profound effect on the whole household.

"Isn't it *marvellous*, having Raoul home? I can't help feeling almost glad that he had that crash!" Dominique, who seemed to prefer her brother's company to that of anyone else, even Alex, so obviously expected Jenny to agree with her that she did not wait for an answer.

Perhaps it was just as well, for even though Jenny would have had, in all honesty, to say "Yes," it would have gone very much against the grain. She had had every intention, after that first night, of keeping Raoul (in a perfectly polite and friendly way) at arm's length, but that was easier said than done. Under the present circumstances it was impossible to avoid his company; even more impossible not to recognise that his home-coming had made all the difference to her life at the Villa Buichi. The loneliness she had experienced during her first weeks in France had melted like an icicle in the sun and each day was filled with a new interest for which she had to admit Raoul was mainly responsible.

She told herself that she had always admitted that Raoul had charm, and the secret—which surely she had learnt!—was to be amused by his easy-going, laughing way of accepting life, laugh with him and never, ever, make the mistake of believing that he was serious about anything he said or did.

Raoul was so different from anyone she had ever met. He could keep up a line of chatter by the hour, half teasing, half amorous : he thought of things to do that were crazy but fun. Jenny, at first bewildered, reluctant to join in, found it impossible in the end to resist. She and Raoul sparred continually, but their arguments always ended in laughter : Raoul saw to that.

And sometimes, when the humour took him, he could be chivalrous . . . the *"Parfit gentil knight"* she had dreamed of in her schooldays. On those occasions he treated her with an odd gentleness which she found disconcerting—disconcerting because it was so unexpected. Like his love of music, it seemed out of character. He often came and listened to her while she was playing : an appreciative, sometimes critical, figure in the background. At these times she was very conscious of him beside her, her absorption in the music less complete than usual, and then Dominique, loudly grumbling about wasted time, would bounce into the room and insist on dragging them both off to the swimming pool, the tennis courts or the stables.

For Jenny, at last, was learning to ride. Raoul insisted on it and brushing away the intrusive memory of Céleste—it was too silly, to refuse to allow him to teach her because, once, he had taught Céleste!—Jenny found herself enjoying the lessons far more than she would have believed possible. As a teacher Raoul was patience exemplified, but he was also very firm and not easily satisfied.

"Don't be so exacting, Raoul!" Dominique said once, laughing as she dismounted from her thoroughbred chestnut mare. "Poor Jenny must be saddlesore after all she's been through this morning! Don't forget you'll have David Chalmers to answer to if she turns up for their next date covered with bumps and bruises!"

There was a moment's silence. Jenny felt her cheeks grow hot, then Raoul said smoothly, "Well, since he's a doctor he could doubtless prescribe some excellent remedies!"

He turned away to lead his mount into the stables. Dominique, stroking the soft muzzle of her mare, spoke over her shoulder, her voice careless.

"Incidentally, you haven't been seeing much of David just lately, have you? You haven't quarrelled, I hope?"

"Of course not. He does work for a living, you know, Dominique. He doesn't get a lot of time off." In spite of herself Jenny spoke a little tartly. Dominique often seemed to forget that the majority of the population had to earn money in order to live. There weren't many people as fortunate as Alex, who from all accounts had been born into millions.

"I suppose not." Dominique said no more, but Jenny, following her into the house, felt a pang of guilt. In the last few days, since Raoul had been home, she had hardly given David a thought. He must have been extra busy or he would have got in touch with her as he had promised, but the fact remained that she hadn't missed him at all.

By sheer coincidence, Gabrielle's first words at lunch related to David.

"Dr. Chalmers telephoned this morning, Jenny, and asked me to give you a message. He says he is so sorry, but although he's tried hard he's been unable to obtain tickets for the Weber concert."

Stephen looked up. "The Weber concert? That's this week, isn't it? I wish I'd thought of it before, Jenny, I might have been able to get tickets for you. Too late now, I'm afraid. I believe every seat has been booked for weeks."

"It doesn't matter." Jenny spoke hastily, but in point of fact it *did* matter, she was intensely disappointed. Max Weber was a brilliant pianist, one of the most famous in Europe, and she would have loved to have heard him play. However, it was no good crying for the moon, and since tickets were unobtainable that, unfortunately, was the end of the matter.

Or so she thought. The following morning, opening a small white envelope which lay upon her plate, she gave a gasp of astonishment as two tickets for the Weber concert fluttered on to the table. Almost incredulously she unfolded the note which was enclosed with them. It was very brief.

"Jenny—Please accept these tickets with my compliments. Don't worry, there are no strings attached!—Raoul."

Raoul! Raoul had succeeded where David had failed! Scarlet-checked, embarrassed beyond measure, Jenny stared down at the small buff tickets. She couldn't possibly accept them! "There are no strings attached..." He meant, of course, that she could ask David to accompany her. It was kind...considerate...of him. But David had only tried to obtain tickets for her sake, he would probably much rather see a Disney film than hear a classical concert! Yet to any music-lover, such as Raoul, the Weber concert would be a rare treat. By what means, fair or foul, he had obtained the tickets she had no idea, but one thing was certain. She couldn't possibly accept the one ticket unless he was prepared to use the other.

She bit her lip. The last time he had wanted to take her out...admittedly as a substitute for Céleste!... she had refused in no uncertain terms. "I just don't want to go out with you—now or ever!" The angry words she had used on that occasion re-echoed in her mind and she almost groaned aloud. What an awful predicament! This time, of course, there was no question of Céleste's being involved, but how could she possibly go back on what she'd said? Almost she wished she'd never mentioned the Weber concert to anyone, except of course that—if she went—it would be an evening in a lifetime!

Raoul was in the study, writing a letter, when she eventually found him. He looked up with a smile as she entered: the smile that, absurdly, always made her heart feel as though it was going to skip a beat.

"*Bonjour, ma chère!* As you can see I am being industrious today!"

"I wanted to thank you for these." Jenny held out the tickets. "I—I don't know how you got them, but it was most awfully kind of you."

Raoul grinned. "I bribed the girl at the box office to let me know if she had any returns. Distinctly dishonest, but definitely worth it, I feel. I'm lucky enough to have heard Weber before: you and Chalmers should have a memorable evening."

Jenny looked at him, her face pink. This was even harder than she'd thought it was going to be.

"Raoul, wouldn't you like to use the other ticket? David doesn't care for classical music at all, really, and it—it seems such a waste. I—I'd be terribly pleased if you'd come with me."

There! It was out! For a moment Raoul stared down at his pen. Then he said, slowly, "You know, I wondered if perhaps you might say something like that. I was going to tell you that I had another engagement for that particular night, to put your mind at rest."

"But you haven't, have you?" Jenny looked at him anxiously. "I—Raoul, I really do want you to come with me, 'if—if you'd like to, I mean. You can always enjoy things better if someone else is enjoying them with you!" Why had she said that? she thought wonderingly. It was true, and yet all her life, up to now, she had preferred to do things on her own.

There was an odd expression on Raoul's face. "You really mean that, Jenny?"

"Yes."

"Then I should love to come." He took her hand and for a moment she felt the warmth of his lips against her knuckles. As always, whenever he touched her unexpectedly on hand or arm, she was left confused and shaken, though if Raoul was aware of this he gave no sign.

It was a wonderful...unforgettable evening, the night of the Weber concert. Jenny felt as though every detail, however tiny, was being indelibly printed on her memory, even the oddly brilliant glance which Raoul gave her when she came downstairs towards him, wearing the white, crystal-embroidered dress that in a fit of reckless extravagance she'd bought especially for the occasion...the drive through the clear, starlit night...the white and crimson and gold of the magnificent concert hall...the tense, excited atmosphere in the auditorium. She would never forget anything, and least of all the exhilaration of Max Weber's superb artistry. A slightly built man with greying hair and deep-set, almost sunken eyes, he played the Grieg Piano Concerto in A Minor and the Piano Concerto in C Major by Rachmaninoff as Jenny had never heard them played before, and at the end of his performance the huge burst of applause from the audience was a tribute he well deserved.

"Wasn't he *marvellous*?" Her face glowing, Jenny turned eagerly to Raoul, still clapping her hands until they stung, almost shouting to make herself heard above the roaring wave of sound.

"He was." Raoul smiled at her and in her excitement and delight Jenny caught hold of his arm.

"*You* made it possible for me to hear him! I'll never forget that, ever!"

For a moment they stood there, very close together, and in that moment Jenny was vaguely aware that although she would have been thrilled by Max Weber's playing even if it had been David who had accompanied her, the mere fact of Raoul's presence enhanced her pleasure. When she was with him he lifted her to an intensity of feeling and living which she never experienced with anyone else.

The knowledge should have dismayed her, but it did not. Nor was the rest of the evening in any way an anti-climax. Raoul took her, for supper, to a little restaurant that was perched high in the hills. The dining room was crowded, but Jenny saw a note pass between Raoul and the head waiter and a few minutes later they were beckoned to the end of the room, where french windows led out on to a terrace. They stepped through these and found that a small lamp was casting a soft pool of light on to a table which, tucked away in a corner, was laid with fine silver and crystal and flowers.

"Are we going to have supper here? Oh, Raoul, look!" and Jenny ran across the terrace to lean over the stone balustrade. It seemed as though the whole of Nice lay at their feet, a sea of glimmering lights, and the sea itself was dark and mysterious, its edges laced with bobbing gold reflections.

Raoul was laughing, seemingly amused by her delight. "I thought you'd like it. What will you have to drink? Champagne, I think, is the only drink for a night like this, don't you?"

"I've never tasted it," Jenny said simply.

For a moment he looked startled and then he laughed again. "You know, tonight I keep forgetting what a puritanical upbringing you've had! You don't look a bit like a prim little English schoolteacher: Mrs. Grundy and Lord Baden-Powell would both, I'm sure, disown you! But me, I like the transformation!"

His blue eyes laughed at her across the table and Jenny crimsoned. She knew, however, when she caught sight of her reflection, that he was right. She didn't even recognise herself: it was just as though she glowed with an inner flame.

The champagne was marvellous and so was the food that was brought with it. Afterwards they went somewhere else to dance and then, insisting that she might as well be hung for a sheep as for a lamb, Raoul took her to the casino. He played and Jenny watched him, and then he persuaded her to play and she won and then won again.

"You can give the money to charity if your conscience troubles you tomorrow, *ma mie*!" Raoul said teasingly when at last the wonderful evening was over and at two o'clock in the morning they were speeding home. "But I think it would be more sensible to keep it and perhaps to buy yourself another dress as beautiful as that one." He touched the white cloud of the skirt as he spoke.

"Gabrielle helped me to choose it," Jenny told him.

"She has excellent taste. It is a pity that Dominique has not inherited more of it," Raoul said wryly.

Jenny shot him a startled glance. "But Dominique always looks beautiful!"

"I wasn't talking, in her case, about clothes." Raoul's brows drew together in a slight frown. "I assume you've met Count Alex?"

"I—yes, I have."

"Do you like him?"

Jenny hesitated, then answered him truthfully. "No. No, I don't. But that's really rather beside the point, isn't it, because it's not me he's in love with. Do—do you think Dominique is going to marry him?"

Raoul gave an exasperated little shrug. "I sincerely hope not! However, I know better than to stick my oar in! Dominique isn't the sort of girl to take kindly to any gratuitous advice, however well meant."

"I should have thought that you had a great deal of influence with her. She is certainly very fond of you," Jenny said quietly.

Raoul laughed. "Merely, I think, because I've never tried to interfere with anything she wanted to do! I've been content to leave the sermonising to Piers, who is certainly well equipped to do so!"

He spoke lightly, but Jenny detected a faint note of bitterness in his voice. How they disliked each other, those two—Piers and Raoul! Not wanting to answer, she turned her head and stared out of the window. The moon, a silver crescent in the indigo sky, was shining above the dark still sea, and there were myriads of stars.

"I never knew that stars could be so bright...." She spoke dreamily, grateful for the little breeze which was blowing in at the window and fanning her hot cheeks.

Raoul accepted her change of subject without comment. "The Côte d'Azur, then, has come up to your expectations?"

Jenny laughed, relieved that the awkward moment had passed. "I didn't know that I had any! The Mediterranean is as blue as I expected it to be, yes, and so is the sky, and the sun is as hot, but—" She hesitated.

"But?" he prompted.

"I can't help wishing that it didn't all seem so—well, so terribly artificial and—and commercialised. I don't suppose you'll agree with me, but—"

"On the contrary. That is exactly how I feel myself." Raoul, reaching in his pocket, produced a flat silver case and then, searching again, swore softly. "Damn ... I've forgotten my lighter. Will you look in the glove compartment, please, *chérie*, there may be a box of matches.... What was I saying? Ah yes, Nice has been ruined, but there are many other places in the south of France which remain comparatively unspoilt. Some day, Jenny, I would like to show you something of Provence ... the real Provence, stripped of the tinsel overlay. Sometimes fierce and mysterious, sometimes romantic, steeped in history but always telling a story of heat and sun." He paused, then added softly, "You and Provence have something important in common, *mignonne*. You are both so very beautiful...."

Jenny, groping in the glove compartment for the matches, heard a caressing note in his voice which made her heart thud madly against her ribs. Idiot! she adjured herself. Raoul probably said that kind of thing to every girl he took out for the evening. To him it would all be part of the exercise....

Even as the thought flashed through her mind her searching hand encountered, not the box of matches, but a small cylindrical object. She didn't need to see it to know what it was. A lipstick. The metal case was cold against her warm palm, but not so cold as the little shiver which chilled her heart. On her last but one visit to the Villa Buichi Céleste had mentioned, casually, that she had mislaid a favourite lipstick. No need to wonder what it was doing in Raoul's car . . . or why it had been necessary for her to make lightning repairs to her make-up! The picture was all too clear.

She dropped the lipstick as if it had been red-hot. It made a little clicking noise as it rolled back into the compartment. She said crisply, "I'm sorry, there don't seem to be any matches here."

"Never mind. Jenny—" He stopped, as if unsure what to say next, and then moved one hand off the wheel to drop it lightly over hers.

Her heart missing a beat, her throat constricting, Jenny snatched her hand away. The gesture of repudiation was so violent that almost immediately she was ashamed of herself, but Raoul, apparently, was more amused than anything else. He glanced at her with a sardonic, tilted eyebrow and said, lightly, "There was no need for such ferocity. I was only going to hold your hand. Would it have been so very terrible?"

She could not trust herself to speak and after a moment he laughed. "It seems as though the transformation I spoke of earlier has not been as thorough as I hoped! Or is it, perhaps, that my licentious behaviour is too much of a contrast with that of the estimable Dr. Chalmers?"

It was the first time since the night he had come home that he had spoken to her in that half-jeering way. She had the oddest feeling that he was angry with her and she wondered why. Then she remembered what Dominique had once said—"He will expect you to fall in love with him. . . ." She'd forgotten that recently, he so obviously hadn't expected anything of the sort, but perhaps tonight he'd imagined that moonlight and music and champagne and roses would predispose her to a light-hearted flirtation. She bit her lip. It didn't really matter if Raoul misconstrued the relationship between her and David. In fact, in a way she was glad. It would be so easy to give way to Raoul's overpowering physical attraction : to join all those other women who had found his good looks irresistible! And she wouldn't—oh, she wouldn't—ever give him that satisfaction!

It seemed as though the night—her lovely night!—was going to end in ruins, but again Raoul surprised her. His next remark was completely innocuous and for the rest of the way home it seemed to her that he was doing his utmost to dispel the slight awkwardness that had risen between them. Why, then, did her heart feel so leaden when, after thanking him and saying goodnight, she left him to put the car away and came up alone to her room? Why, when she was brushing her hair in front of her mirror, did she have to close her eyes because tears were pricking her lids? She was over-tired and over-excited, she told herself severely: she wasn't used to a night of such riotous pleasure! Yet, when she lay down to sleep, her last conscious thought was not of Max Weber's playing, nor of the champagne or the dancing or the casino, but of the chilling moment when, in the darkness of the car, she had held Céleste de Courville's expensive gilt-cased lipstick in the palm of her sun-browned hand.

Raoul had evidently meant what he said about introducing her to the real Provence, for in the days that followed it was thanks to him that she discovered that there was far more to the South of France than groves of lemon trees, a dancing sea, olives and scented pines under a gay blue sky. With Raoul driving, and usually either Dominique or Gabrielle as a fellow-passenger, she had her eyes opened to a whole world of mountains, gorges, canyons, and ancient hill-towns, all within a few miles of the sunshine and sophistication of the Riviera.

Roman cities, glowing under a luminous sky ... villages washed a warm pink or yellow, enclosed in olive groves and clinging to their hilltops like crowns . . . orchards and endless vineyards . . . dry, scrub-covered hills tufted with wind-bent trees ... Jenny saw them all with delighted eyes and began to understand the fascination that this rich, colourful land seemed to hold for Raoul, if not for his mother and sister.

"Me, I prefer civilisation!" Dominique said with a laugh and a shrug when at Aix-en-Provence Jenny, flushed and breathless, returned with Raoul from exploring the *Musée de Vieil Aix,* which housed a collection of Moustiers pottery, dolls, marionettes, ancient costumes, furnitures and pictures. "You English all seem to have this great thing about the past! Stephen, he is just as bad!"

"Not all the English are infected, though," Jenny said, laughing. She was thinking of David, with whom she had spent the previous day and who certainly showed no inclination to delve into history! David's idea of a relaxing day off was lots of swimming, plenty of sunbathing, a large meal and a visit to the cinema!

She suddenly found herself reflecting that it was a programme which might well appeal, under certain circumstances, to Dominique. Her handsome Count's ideas on entertainment appeared to be both sophisticated and glamorous, enough to turn the head of any girl, but Dominique was very much younger than he was and possessed, too, a *joie de vivre* which probably he had never known. Wasn't it possible that sometimes she longed for the chance to do something young and silly and gay with someone more of her own age? Someone who realised that happiness didn't always have to be bought with francs?

She sighed, and her brows contracted in a little frown. It was a pity that her stepsister cherished such an illogical grudge against David ... a pity, too, that he showed no signs of getting over his hopeless infatuation! Loving somebody when there was absolutely no chance of that person loving you back was such a sad and wasteful business. . . .

"Penny for your thoughts," Raoul said, and she looked up to find him watching her intently. In spite of herself she flushed. She had long ago given up trying to analyse the effect that Raoul had upon her or her feelings towards him. She only knew that she was very happy these days, even though beneath the happiness was buried something which she half-realised might one day very easily become active *un*happiness. One day, when Raoul's doctors decreed that he was fit to return to Colorado ... or when Céleste de Courville returned to Nice from Geneva. Whichever happened first.

She said lightly, "They aren't worth it, you'd only be wasting your money.—Where did you learn your idiomatic English, Raoul? Nobody would ever take you for a Frenchman!"

"I am quite aware, *chérie*, that you are trying to pay me a compliment, but I am not so sure that I do, in fact, feel complimented!" Raoul said, laughing.

Dominique looked up from repairing a broken finger nail. "We've always been bi-lingual. We had an English governess when we were small, and an English housekeeper for years and years before we had Berthe, and quite a lot of English friends."

"Not to mention an English stepfather!" Raoul said, grinning.

"It was one of the best things Maman ever did, marrying Stephen!" Dominique tossed back her dark hair, then added, with a laugh, "What is it they say? That the English make atrocious lovers but excellent husbands?"

"That seems to me to be an absurd generalisation!" Jenny said indignantly, and Raoul's eyes danced wickedly.

"Yes, indeed. Quite as absurd—and nearly as dangerous!—as believing that all respectable English girls are fat and ugly and very, very dull!" he said solemnly, and ducked as Jenny, searching for a suitable missile, flung an orange at him.

Dominique watched them with amusement, tinged a little with mystification. She couldn't understand the relationship between those two. Raoul treated Jenny exactly as if she were a real sister and not just a "step", she thought. It was odd, that: for up to now (Céleste or no Céleste) he had seemed unable to resist flirting with every passable girl he encountered. And Jenny was a lot, lot more than merely passable: she was quite lovely, especially now that she had grown so sun-tanned and her hair had gone so very fair! No wonder David Chalmers, seemingly impervious to the charms of his female patients, appeared to be so strongly attracted!

"But how you have changed since you first came here, Jenny!" she exclaimed, looking from one flushed laughing face to the other. "You did not find that kind of remark amusing, once! You were—oh, *très triste*!—when first we knew you, you hardly laughed at all! Now you laugh often and your eyes, they have a sparkle!

She was not the only one to notice the great change in Jenny. Stephen, too, noted it, and although he welcomed it he was also slightly uneasy. It wasn't the young Englishman, David Chalmers, who had brought the Sleeping Princess so suddenly to life. It was only since Raoul had come home that Jenny had learned to laugh freely and often, that light had begun to dance in her smoke-grey eyes and her face had lost its too-serious expression. Raoul's gaiety was, of course, infectious—it had always been so. But though at the moment there seemed to be nothing remotely lover-like about their relationship, was Jenny perhaps more strongly attracted to Raoul than at present she realised? It was this possibility which caused Stephen several pangs of very real anxiety: he had not realised, until now, how much his young daughter had come to mean to him. He was extremely fond of Raoul, too, but he had few illusions about him. He was a born philanderer. If Jenny fell in love with him and expected him to return that love she would be courting almost certain heartache. Raoul had never loved any woman, with the possible exception of Céleste de Courville.

He walked over to the window and knocked out his pipe. Raoul and Jenny were just coming up the steps, talking and laughing. The sun was making Jenny's hair gleam like burnished gold and she was wearing a short, sleeveless shift which revealed her faultless figure. Her arms and legs were bare and very brown. Remembering old lady Barrington, Stephen's lips twitched into a rueful smile. She would have had a fit if she had ever seen her cherished granddaughter looking so carefree and abandoned!

Now Jenny had one foot on the top step and her head was turned back towards Raoul, whose hand was on her arm, detaining her. Stephen could not see Raoul's face, but he could see Jenny's, and what he saw there made him turn abruptly away. The sooner Raoul removed himself from the Villa Buichi and returned to Colorado the better! Then he sighed, for he was a husband as well as a father, and although he felt that for Jenny's sake Raoul's disappearance from the scene would probably be a good thing, he knew that it would also mean renewed anxiety for Gabrielle. Raoul was the best-loved of her three children and she had never learned to accept with equanimity the risks which seemed, to him, the very breath of life.

CHAPTER EIGHT

ON Friday there was an unexpected letter for Jenny from old Mrs. Barrington's lawyer, who had been entrusted with the disposal of the contents of the house since it was a job which Jenny had not had the heart to tackle. He wrote explaining that a sheaf of documents and letters had been found crushed away at the back of an old chest-of-drawers and asked for permission to examine them in case the bundle contained anything of value. He had always been a family friend and his letter, after dealing with one or two other matters, ended with a suggestion that Jenny should eventually try to obtain a teaching post in Oxford.

"I have a widowed sister, several years younger than myself, who lives there and I know she would be delighted if you felt that you would like to make your home with her," he wrote. "Oxford is, of course, a delightful city, and my sister lives very quietly, has a charming house and garden and could, I think, make it possible for you to lead the kind of quiet and peaceful life you enjoyed with your grandmother. There is no need to come to a hasty decision, but I felt that during the next week or two you might like to consider a really concrete suggestion."

Jenny, who was sitting out on the patio—she had come to feel that she could never have too much sun—dropped the letter on to her lap and stared at the sky with unseeing eyes. Of course, Mr. Davidson meant to be kind and helpful. A few weeks ago she might even have jumped at his suggestion, but now.... The prospect of a quiet, peaceful life among Oxford's dreaming spires after the gaiety of these weeks on the Côte d'Azur seemed oddly unattractive, and the knowledge disturbed her profoundly. Had she become so inured to luxury, even after such a short time, that she now felt she could not do without it?

She bit her lip, forcing herself to face the truth. It wasn't the luxury of her new life she cared about. It was the feeling of being really and truly alive, for the first time in her twenty-two years of existence. Once she had been content to dwell within her ivory tower, but during the last few weeks she had watched its walls crumble and after the first shock of surprise she hadn't even minded!

And apart from everything else she most definitely did not want to go back to teaching. There *must* be an alternative! She sat looking down at her hands, gripped tightly together in her lap, while her mind struggled with the complexities of her situation.

"Why so glum? You haven't had bad news, I hope?" Dominique, wearing a completely backless white Tricel dress and a new and very vivid lipstick, flung herself on to a swing hammock and looked at her with questioning eyes.

"Oh no." Jenny forced a smile. "It's just that I've had a letter which has made me realise that I've simply got to make up my mind what I'm going to do. After this holiday, I mean."

Dominique plucked a flower and studied its petals carefully. "But I shouldn't have thought that there was any great difficulty about that. What about David?"

"What about him?"

"Well, it looks rather as though he might want to marry you one day." Dominique detached one of the crimson petals and it fell, a glowing blob of colour, on to the grey stone. "That would solve all your difficulties quite nicely, wouldn't it? If you want to marry him, that is."

"Well, I don't!" Jenny sat up straight and spoke

forcefully. Then, as Dominique laughed and raised her brows disbelievingly, "I just don't seem able to make you understand that there's nothing but friendship between David and me!"

"Just good friends!" Dominique gave a little crow of laughter. "That's just what Céleste says, about her and Raoul, and all the time she eyes him as hungrily as a dog eyes a bone!"

It was futile to protest any further about her feelings for David. Once Dominique got something into her head it appeared to be an *idée fixe*. Instead Jenny said shortly, "Well, what do you expect Céleste to do? Ignore Raoul completely?"

"No, but I *don't* expect her to write him long letters from Switzerland, when I bet Piers hasn't had as much as a single line!" Dominique retorted. "There was another letter from her this morning, I recognised her handwriting and the Swiss postmark! I don't know what was in it, of course, but I watched Raoul while he was reading it and he looked as black as thunder by the time he'd finished! I expect he's been hoping that she'll change her mind about marrying Piers, but she still can't bring herself to kiss his bank balance goodbye!"

Jenny was silent. It was absolutely nothing to her if Raoul and Céleste corresponded! Nevertheless, she felt as though a shadow had fallen on the golden day and she was glad when Dominique, who was never able to sit still for long, jumped to her feet and announced that she was driving in to Nice.

It was during lunch that Raoul, who seemed unusually silent and preoccupied, looked up and said, "I have to go to Avignon tomorrow, Maman. I shall probably be very late back, so don't start worrying about me and imagining all sorts of horrible disasters!" His smile was teasing but affectionate, for despite the grey hairs that she alleged that he had caused her he was very fond of his mother.

A faint line etched itself between Gabrielle's arched brows. "You're not planning to go alone, I hope?" Then, as he nodded, "But why not take the girls?" She looked hopefully at Jenny and Dominique as she spoke. Raoul was very much better: he had not had one of his severe headaches for days and he seemed confident that when he reported to the doctors at the end of the week they would pass him fit to return to Colorado. Nevertheless, she could not help thinking that at present it was inadvisable for him to drive such a long distance unaccompanied.

"Sorry." Dominique shook her head. "Alex has invited me to lunch aboard his yacht, to meet his mother and sister. I can't possibly get out of it."

"Then what about Jenny? I am sure she would enjoy the drive," Gabrielle persisted.

Was it her imagination, Jenny wondered, or did Raoul hesitate for the fraction of a second? She was almost sure that he did, but when he turned towards her there was genuine warmth in his voice and smile.

"Of course. I shall be delighted to have your company, if you have no other plans for tomorrow, Jenny?"

It was Jenny's turn to shake her head. She was not at all sure whether she wanted to spend a day alone with Raoul, but it was too difficult, on the spur of the moment, to think of an adequate excuse. In any case, she told herself, there was no need to worry. It was only on the night of the Weber concert that Raoul had given any sign of regarding her as a lovely and desirable woman rather than as a sister. And since then he had again reverted to his role as big brother, treating her as before with amused, laughing indulgence. She was relieved, of course, but at the same time, perversely, she was a little puzzled.

Raoul impressed upon her that he wanted to make an early start and so the next day Jenny was waiting by the car well before nine o'clock.

"I might have known that I could rely upon you to be punctual," Raoul said, laughing as he joined her. "If my baggage of a sister had been coming with us I should have resigned myself to the prospect of starting at least an hour later than I meant to! What time did you get up? The crack of dawn?"

Jenny laughed. "It doesn't take me long to get ready. I don't have Dominique's standards of extreme elegance to live up to!"

"No?" Raoul looked at her with an odd expression in his eyes. She was wearing a coffee-coloured shirt and a cream skirt and she had tied back her hair with a wide brown ribbon. The effect, although she did not realise it, was singularly fresh and charming. Raoul's glance ranged from her shining hair to her slim ankles, but all he said was, "You look very nice. Have you a hat? You may need one."

"Yes." Jenny pointed to the wide-brimmed straw hat which was lying on the back seat along with her camera and handbag, and then climbed into the car. For some reason she was feeling extraordinarily happy and light-hearted, but as they drove away she noticed, with a sudden pang of dismay, that Raoul's face was set in grimmer lines than usual. Had he not wanted her to accompany him to Avignon? Gabrielle had, after all, made it almost impossible for him to refuse! Unconsciously her brows puckered and she bit her lip.

"What's the matter? You look worried." Raoul spoke sharply—a little too sharply—and Jenny flushed.

"Nothing's the matter. Except—except that I was wondering whether you really wanted to be bothered with a passenger today. I should hate to feel that I was being a bit of a nuisance."

"Oh! Is that all?" For some inexplicable reason Raoul sounded distinctly relieved. "Don't be silly, *petite*. I'm glad you're with me: I should doubtless become very bored with my own company!" He paused, then added lightly, "Besides, I have a feeling that you and Diane will like each other."

"Diane?" Jenny stiffened in her seat.

"Diane Beauvais. She is the widow of Marcel Beauvais, who was my best friend and who was killed some months ago in South America." Raoul was looking straight ahead of him, his eyes narrowed against the sun. "It is because of Diane and her children that I am going to Avignon today. It is her elder son's birthday and I promised him faithfully that I wouldn't miss it."

Sheer, stunned surprise kept Jenny silent. After a few moments Raoul turned his head and smiled at her. "You needn't come with me to see them if you don't want to, you know. Perhaps you don't care for children very much?"

Jenny found her voice. "I'd love to see them. How—how old are they?"

"Pierre—who, incidentally, is my godchild—is eight today. Michel is six and Jacqueline is five."

Raoul's face was impassive, but Jenny felt that she knew what he was thinking. It was as though she had developed a sixth sense...a new sympathy for him. "Do they miss their father very much?"

"I'm afraid they do. They were a very close and devoted family. Diane is wonderful with them, though, of course. She loved Marcel so passionately that when he was killed it was just as though part of herself was wrenched away, but for the sake of the children she's made a marvellous recovery. I truly think she is one of the bravest women I've ever known." He paused, his eyes sombre. "Marcel was a fine person and his death was a tragedy. Nothing, for me, will ever be quite the same again."

Jenny said nothing, robbed of words by the sudden intensity of feeling in his deep voice. He had never ever revealed his inmost self like this before and the sudden response of her own feelings almost overwhelmed her. She felt choked, and for a long time they drove in silence.

When he next spoke, however, Raoul sounded his normal gay and cheerful self, and Jenny, quick to follow his lead, soon found herself laughing at his absurd jokes. This was the Raoul she knew best, though she would never forget that for one brief moment he had allowed her to glimpse a deeper side to his nature—a side she had never suspected.

They stopped for lunch at a little country inn right on the edge of a slow-moving river. A simple but superbly cooked meal was produced for them with the minimum of fuss and bother, and they ate it outside, on an attractive paved patio.

"All this and free entertainment thrown in, too!" Jenny said, laughing at the antics of a family of ducks. She put down her coffee cup with a sigh of satisfaction. "It doesn't seem possible that anyone should be able to produce such a marvellous meal at a moment's notice! I know what one would probably get under similar circumstances in England—a black look for having the temerity to feel hungry and perhaps a few soggy ham sandwiches and a packet of crisps!"

Raoul smiled. "In England you do not take food seriously. Here, we do."

"I'm rather glad, except that I shall probably end up by putting on so much weight that I won't be able to get into any of my clothes," Jenny said ruefully.

Raoul's glance flicked over her and something in his eyes ... an expression she had not seen for a long time ... made the colour rush into her cheeks and her pulses thudded. He reached towards her and, suddenly panic-stricken, she pushed her chair back. She saw his eyes narrow, but all he did was to drop his half-smoked cigarette in the ashtray on the table and say lightly, "Aphrodite with a bulge? I don't think it's very likely!" He glanced at his watch. "I think we'd better get going, don't you?"

He was annoyed, Jenny thought, and he had a right to be. What on earth had made her react so stupidly, as though she had expected him to lunge at her across the table? He *had* taken her off her guard once, of course, but that had been a very long time ago, at a moment when he had been temporarily shaken out of self-control by anger and other emotions. He wasn't at all likely to do it again!

He paid the bill and she followed him to the car in silence. There was, however, something she wanted to ask him and when after a few minutes he began humming softly to himself she plucked up the courage to do so.

"Do you think we'd have time to stop for a few minutes in Avignon, please, Raoul?" she said diffidently. "I'd rather like to buy Pierre a present, as it's his birthday. Perhaps—perhaps you'd help me to choose something he'd like?"

He shot her an amused look. "With pleasure. Not that my guesswork is likely to be any more inspired than yours! He's got my present already: a bicycle."

"He'll love that!"

"Yes. His father always promised that he should have one on his eighth birthday," Raoul said quietly.

So he had taken the trouble to remember that! Jenny turned her head and stared out of the window. The landscape seemed a patchwork quilt of dull golden crops, of emerald-green meadows, trellised vines and silver-grey olives. It was very lovely, a land of rich, smooth colour, and very peaceful.

"I've sometimes thought that I'd like to settle here." Raoul's voice broke into her thoughts. "Buy a vineyard, perhaps—if and when I have the money to do so."

Jenny looked at him uncertainly. "You're not serious?"

His lips twisted. "Any reason why I shouldn't be?"

"I—well—it just doesn't sound like you, that's all." Jenny floundered badly and Raoul laughed, though his laugh was tinged with something she could not quite analyse.

"You think it was merely an idle thought? Ah well, perhaps you are right. Doubtless you believe, *chérie*, that I shall never settle down? That all my life I shall be a rolling stone? A perpetual vagabond?"

"Well, you don't like ties of any kind, do you?" she countered.

"It depends very much upon the ties." His voice sounded lazily amused and Jenny decided to adopt the same flippant note.

"Well, when your mine in Colorado starts pouring out its gold you'll probably be a millionaire and then you'll be able to buy a dozen vineyards if you want to, won't you?"

"Correction number one, it isn't 'my' goldmine. Correction number two, I'll never be a millionaire. To start with, anything I get out of the mine will have to be split two ways, between Diane and myself. When Marcel was alive we shared everything, and as far as I'm concerned that still holds good. Correction number three, a mine never pours anything! You have to work damned hard to get it out!"

Raoul spoke with feeling and Jenny laughed. "Tell me about the mine! It sounds as though there ought to be an exciting story behind it."

"There's a story all right, but I don't know whether you'd call it exciting. An old tramp miner lost his way in the mountains and went to sleep in a sort of cavern. When he woke up he found that he'd been sitting with his back against a rounded mass of white quartz streaked with gold stains and specks. He knew at once what it was."

He paused. "Luckily for him he found the trail again, and three weeks later he was telling me his story. Nobody else believed him—he'd always been a bit of an eccentric—but I thought his claim was worth investigating. I helped him to find the exact location again—not too easy, though he'd had the sense to pile up a cairn to mark the spot—and then advised him to have an assay done. On the strength of that he decided to forge ahead and float a company. We're convinced it's a vein... what they call a bonanza... and we've expert opinion to back us up, but there *is* a slight risk that there's only a small pocket. What we are hoping to do is to hit the main vein. We've a competent geologist working for us, but he's made one or two mistakes and they've cost us time and money."

He glanced at her rapt, interested face and grinned. "Don't tell me that you, of all people, believe in fairy tales!" he said sardonically. "Tell me, just as a matter of interest—if you had any money would you find a goldmine in Colorado an attractive proposition or would you prefer to invest it in something safer?"

Jenny flushed, but she answered truthfully. "I haven't any money, so the question is purely hypothetical. But no, Raoul, I wouldn't put a penny into your mine. There's far too much risk attached!"

"Prudent little Jenny!" he mocked softly. "I don't believe you'd ever be prepared to take a risk, would you? Not in money nor in love!" His tone changed, became impersonal. "Not that I really blame you. It just happens to be lucky for the company and the people who *have* put their faith in us that there are men like Pierre Lamotte. God knows how he heard about the mine—I'd never even met the chap!—but he, at any rate, doesn't seem to mind taking a slight risk now and again!"

Jenny shot him a swift startled look. Surely Raoul knew of Pierre Lamotte's friendship with Céleste? Why, it was reasonable to suppose that it was Céleste who had told Pierre of Raoul's difficulty in raising a loan! She hesitated, on the point of mentioning how she had seen Céleste with Pierre Lamotte in the pavement café in Nice, but Raoul went on.

"Brother Piers, of course, thinks the whole thing is moonshine. That doesn't really surprise me, though I did hope that he'd allow me, under the circumstances, to sell my shares in the firm. If he had I wouldn't have needed such a big loan." He paused, then added wryly, "It was his refusal which led to the quarrel between us, the one you overheard."

So the quarrel hadn't been about Céleste, as she had supposed! Not stopping to analyse her relief, Jenny said indignantly, "But it wasn't fair of him to refuse, when he knew how badly you needed the money!"

"He didn't see it in quite that light, I'm afraid." Raoul's voice was grim.

"They are your shares. You ought to have been able to please yourself," Jenny protested.

Raoul grinned suddenly. "I don't ever seem to have much success in that direction!" he said cryptically, and then fell silent, leaving Jenny, completely bewildered, to adjust herself to some entirely new ideas.

When, finally, they arrived in Avignon Raoul said that they were early and that there was not only time to buy Pierre a birthday present but also time for Jenny to do a little exploring. Since she had fallen in love with the beautiful little walled town at first sight she was delighted, and spent a happy hour wandering round the ancient and mediaeval streets and gazing at the Palace of the Popes, with its massive golden walls and soaring buttresses, and the old bridge of the song, with its four remaining arches.

"You're a born tourist!" Raoul teased when they returned to the car. "How many photographs did you take? A dozen?"

Jenny laughed. "Not quite. The film ran out!" She carefully deposited her camera next to the large brown paper parcel that Raoul had been carrying for her.

It had been fun, choosing a present for Pierre. Finally, at Raoul's suggestion, she had chosen a model of a lunar rocket, an intricate affair which, he'd assured her, would delight the heart of any small boy. Jenny, with no experience at all of the eight-year-old male, only hoped he was right!

In actual fact she was feeling a little nervous about the welcome that might be in store for her, an uninvited guest, but she need not have worried. When they arrived at the Beauvais home, a large, shabby but comfortable-looking house set in a big garden, the three children were hanging over the gate and uttered shrieks of joy directly they caught sight of Raoul's big car nosing its way down the tree-lined street.

"Uncle Raoul! Uncle Raoul! Thank you for my bicycle!" A handsome, sturdy little boy with dark hair and eyes and very rosy cheeks tugged impatiently at the handle of the door.

"Uncle Raoul! We've got icecream and jelly for tea!" His younger brother spoke shrilly, while the youngest of the three, a small girl with dark ringlets and wearing a pink frock, danced up and down with excitement.

Although it was Pierre who managed to open the door of the car first it seemed to Jenny that all three children managed to surge in at once. For a few minutes there was turmoil, then Raoul, extricating himself with some difficulty from a welter of arms and legs, managed to introduce Jenny and the noise subsided as the children greeted her politely but cordially. At least, the two boys did. It seemed to Jenny that the small girl, Jacqueline, gave her a somewhat cautious, speculative look, but before she could attempt to establish friendly relations the children's mother had arrived on the scene, a small, shaggy-haired dog barking joyously at her heels.

Diane Beauvais was very slight and small, with softly curling brown hair and eyes which, seven months after her husband's death, were still dark and sad. The smile which greeted Raoul and Jenny, however, was warm and gay, and it was obvious that whatever her secret unhappiness she tried to present a brave front to the world.

"Raoul! How good it is to see you again! You are better, *mon cher*?" She looked up at him anxiously.

"Perfectly," Raoul assured her. Turning, he drew Jenny forward. "Diane, this is Jenny Barrington, my stepsister. She is staying in Nice for a few weeks. Jenny—Madame Beauvais, the mother of this noisy brood, although she looks so young that I don't suppose you'll be able to believe it!"

"Flatterer!" Diane said, smiling. "You have not lost your silver tongue, Raoul!" She turned to Jenny, holding out a thin hand. "How nice that Raoul has brought you! He is always monopolised so much by the children that I shall feel myself fortunate in having you to talk to!"

"I am glad to be here, Madame Beauvais," Jenny said shyly, and Diane laughed.

"Do call me Diane, won't you? And I shall call you Jenny. I cannot stand on ceremony with Raoul's sister!"

"Stepsister!" Pierre corrected her.

"A small difference, but a very important one," Raoul said. He spoke lightly, but for some reason Jenny crimsoned. Hastily, in order to divert attention from herself, she thrust the brown paper parcel into Pierre's arms and in the excitement of opening it and admiring the lunar rocket everything else was forgotten.

It was a delightful afternoon. Jenny, who had had very little to do with small children, was captivated by Pierre, Michel and Jacqueline, even though in point of fact at first they paid very little attention to her. It was Raoul they wanted: Raoul who had to mend a couple of broken toys, answer innumerable questions, inspect Michel's new pet rabbit, watch Pierre ride his new bicycle, take a thorn out of Michel's finger and tell Jacqueline a story. It was Raoul who had to settle a dispute between the two boys, Raoul who had to light the candles on the birthday cake and Raoul who had to comfort Jacqueline when she fell and hurt her knee.

Jenny, marvelling at his patience, good-humour and

gentleness, wondered why she had ever thought him arrogant and self-centred. Here he seemed a different person. But which was the real Raoul—this one or the gay philanderer?

She looked up to find Diane watching her shrewdly. "It surprises you, that Raoul should be at home among such domesticity?" she asked, smiling slightly.

"It does, a little," Jenny confessed.

"He has been kindness itself to me and to the children since my husband died." Diane spoke with grave deep feeling. "I cannot tell you how much, and in how many ways, he has helped us to build a new life without——without Marcel. I do not know what we should have done without him." She paused, then added with a lightness belied by her words, "He does not wear his heart on his sleeve, *mon cher* Raoul, but I can tell you this—it is made of gold!"

Jenny smiled politely, wondering how much Diane knew of Raoul's reputation. Yet, after all, what exactly did that amount to?

As if she guessed her thoughts Diane said quickly, "Not everyone would agree with me, of course. Raoul has a kind of reckless courage which takes delight sometimes in flying in the face of all safety, law and order and he has not always been—shall I say discreet? Perhaps, though, that is not altogether his fault, for he has had many temptations. Women, you know, have always found him attractive and have pursued him relentlessly since he was in his teens."

Her eyes rested thoughtfully on Jenny. There wasn't anything of the huntress about this English rose : with her quiet serenity she was a very different proposition from the usual run of Raoul's girl-friends. But stepsister or not, she was very charming and pretty.

She drew a deep breath. "What he needs, of course, is a wife. When he has someone of his own to love and to cherish Raoul will leave his swashbuckling ways and his philandering behind him, you may be very sure of that," she said firmly, and her meaning was so plain that Jenny felt her cheeks grow warm.

Luckily at that moment they were interrupted. Raoul was helping Pierre to launch his lunar rocket and

Jacqueline, momentarily bored with technicalities that were beyond her, decided that it was time she paid some attention to Jenny.

"Would you like to see my dolls, *mademoiselle*?"

"I'd love to," Jenny said warmly, and Jacqueline, holding out her hand, led her to a small, sunny bedroom where a long row of dolls sat propped up against the wall.

"Babette — Cleone — Vivienne — Priscille — Lucie — Françoise — Lisette." Jacqueline recited their names at express speed. "Look! This one is my favourite," and she picked up Lucie, a rosy-cheeked brunette wearing a blue velvet coat trimmed with fur. "Uncle Raoul gave her to me and she has real hair that can be washed and she says *'Maman'*!"

"She's beautiful. This one is nice, too," and Jenny picked up a golden-haired beauty with long curls and eyelashes who had not as yet been formally introduced.

"Oh, that's Céleste. I called her after a great friend of Uncle Raoul's because I thought she looked so much like her. I often do that kind of thing, you know," Jacqueline said carelessly.

Jenny's lips felt stiff. "You mean—Mademoiselle Céleste de Courville?"

"Yes, that's right. She used to come to Avignon with Uncle Raoul and we met her once, at the Pont du Gard. They were sightseeing," Jacqueline said. She sighed. "Me, I thought they were going to be married and then I would have been a bridesmaid, but Maman said no, she had decided to marry someone else." She slid off the bed. "I don't really mind. I shall probably marry Uncle Raoul myself, now. Come and see my kitten! It's so sweet!"

So Raoul had been in the habit of bringing Céleste to Avignon! They'd probably lunched together at the same little inn by the river... laughed at the same ducks! The magic that had laid its spell on her, Jenny, this afternoon, would have worked for them too... only more so, because they had been lovers!

At the thought Jenny was shaken by such a storm of jealousy that she was appalled. Desperately she tried to forget everything except Jacqueline and her fluffy grey kitten, but the joy had gone out of the afternoon. In fact, she began to feel oddly depressed and she was more than a little relieved when, amidst wails and lamentations, Raoul announced regretfully that it was time that he and Jenny started for home.

"Please do come again," Diane said to Jenny as they were leaving, and much to Jenny's surprise the children echoed their mother's words. She had not realised that during the afternoon she had been inspected, weighed up and not found wanting!

Jacqueline, especially, seemed sorry to see her go. "I'll call my next doll after you, if it's a nice one!" were the child's parting words, and Raoul laughed as he let in the clutch.

"What does she mean?" His voice was lazy, amused. "It sounds a bit like celebrity treatment!"

He was back in character. Sudden tears stung Jenny's eyelids. To her horror she found herself saying, in a voice which sounded hard and brittle even to her own ears, "She has a habit of calling her dolls after people she knows. One is called Céleste, after your brother's fiancée. Only, of course, she wasn't Piers' fiancée at the time!"

Her heart gave a painful twist as she saw his eyes flicker and darken at the mention of Céleste's name. He said nothing, but she was conscious of his withdrawal from her and felt oddly cold and forlorn. Sitting beside him as they drove through the bat-haunted twilight she knew that he wished that it was Céleste who was his companion, and the knowledge hurt her so much that she could no longer ignore the truth she had fought against for so long. Despite her certainty that such a thing could never happen to her, sensible, well-balanced Jenny Barrington, she had fallen head over heels in love with Raoul de Vaisseau.

Before she had come to Nice the prospect of falling in love had always seemed extremely remote to Jenny. Immured in her ivory tower, she had felt safe and secure: invulnerable, the mistress of her emotions. Other people's gyrations when they became interested in a member of the opposite sex never failed to astonish her: in fact, she was slightly contemptuous. Some day, she'd vaguely supposed, she might meet someone suitable, someone whose tastes and background were similar to her own, and then it was just possible that she might fall in love quietly and decorously, marry and live happily ever after. She had not reckoned on loving someone like Raoul, someone gay and brilliant and unpredictable, nor had she reckoned on this sudden mad fire in her bones.

But what could be kindled could also be stamped out, and Jenny, after her initial dismay, was determined to do it. She didn't want to love Raoul—oh, she didn't! Gambler, adventurer, vagabond—what did she, Jenny Barrington, have in common with a man like that? Even if by some miracle he did love her, he'd make an impossible husband. With Raoul there'd be no home, no stability, no settled future and probably no money. No, whispered a small treacherous voice within her heart, but there'd be gaiety and laughter and loving and living. . . .

For just one moment she yielded to temptation and gave herself up to the kind of daydream that she knew was mere foolishness, and then her native common sense reasserted itself. Raoul was not for her. Her lips twisted a little in self-derision. Once, Raoul had been sufficiently attracted by her to want to flirt with her, despite the rebuffs she had given him. Now he seemed to regard her merely as a member of the family: another little sister to amuse or entertain him when no other diversions were available. While Céleste was away. . . .

Remembering the way Raoul's mood had changed at the mention of Piers' fiancée, Jenny felt bleak. Well, he would not have to wait long now before he saw her again and found out whether she really intended to become Piers' wife. She was planning, apparently, to return to Nice next week: just in time, Gabrielle said without any noticeable enthusiasm, for a party she had planned to celebrate hers and Stephen's wedding anniversary.

David had been invited to this party. He had, at first, intended to refuse but Jenny persuaded him to change his mind. At the moment she badly wanted the reassurance of his friendship. She had to be so much on her guard with everyone else, lest by look or word she betray her love for Raoul, whereas even if David did guess her secret it did not particularly matter. They were both in the same boat, both longing for the unattainable.

Although David did not ask questions, Jenny knew that he realised that she was not happy. He seemed to have jumped to the conclusion that she was lonely and worried about her future, and out of sheer kindheartedness he did his best to spend as much of his free time with her as he possibly could.

Returning from one afternoon expedition with David, she met Raoul coming down the terrace steps, and his brows lifted enquiringly when he saw a handkerchief tied around her upper arm.

"What on earth have you been doing to yourself?" His glance flicked to the departing car. "Or has your boy-friend been practising his first-aid?"

Jenny laughed. "I wanted some flowers, but they were high up and I slipped and fell on a rock when I was trying to reach them." She touched the makeshift bandage. "It's only a slight scratch, but David insisted on tying it up."

Raoul frowned. "*You* were trying to reach the flowers? But why didn't Chalmers get them for you?"

"I thought I could manage." Not for worlds would she have told Raoul that David had stated quite bluntly that the flowers were out of reach and that it wasn't worth risking life or limb to clamber after them. And that his first remark, after he'd satisfied himself that she was not badly hurt, had been "I told you so!"

Raoul, however, said with uncanny perspicacity, "I suppose if they were high up Chalmers thought the climb was too risky? He was quite right, of course. The only thing that puzzles me is why you obviously didn't agree with him?"

Jenny flushed. She didn't know the answer to that herself. She only knew that for some reason she had found herself excessively irritated by David's caution and that for once in her life she'd thrown common

140

sense to the winds. The flowers had symbolised something : she didn't quite know what. She looked down at them, already wilting in her hands. At least she'd got them, even if she *had* come to grief in the process!

Raoul watched her for a moment. "Cautious type, your David. I rather thought that that was probably what attracted you to him in the first place," he said softly.

The cool irony of his tone stung. "I don't see anything wrong with being cautious! It—it's stupid to do things out of sheer bravado, as—as some people do!"

Raoul grinned. "Meaning me?"

Jenny thought of all the stories she had heard about Raoul's recklessness and said crossly, "Yes, if you like."

He bowed ironically. "I accept your criticism. All the same, *chérie*, Dr. Chalmers might do well to remember that even if it pays to look before you leap, fortune is said to favour the bold—and faint heart never yet won fair lady!"

Before she could answer he had deftly plucked one of the flowers from her hands, stuck it in his buttonhole and continued his way down the steps, humming softly under his breath.

In the house Jenny found Gabrielle writing out party invitations. She looked up with a smile as her stepdaughter entered, and shook her head when Jenny apologised for interrupting her.

"I need a rest. So many invitations to write—so many preparations to be made! I ask myself, is it worth it?"

Jenny knew her too well to be deceived. "You're enjoying every moment!" she said, laughing, and Gabrielle's eyes glimmered.

"Well, perhaps I am. For both Stephen and myself this year's anniversary celebrations will be especially important," she said, pushing a pile of envelopes away from her and flexing her cramped fingers. "This year, for the first time, we shall have our entire family around us. You, and Piers and Céleste, and even Raoul."

"But I thought—isn't he anxious to return to Colorado immediately he's had his final check-up?" Jenny's surprise showed in her face.

"Yes, but if he stays for the party it will only mean a few days' delay, and as he knows how much it will mean to me to have him here he has decided to postpone his departure," Gabrielle explained.

Jenny turned quickly aside. Was Raoul staying for Gabrielle's sake—or for his own? How much had his decision to postpone his return to Colorado been influenced by the fact that the guests at the anniversary party would include—Céleste?

She wondered, painfully, what he would do if Céleste, when she returned from Geneva, refused to change her mind about marrying Piers. Perhaps he would leave home for good...perhaps under the circumstances he would feel that that was the only course open to him. But if, on the other hand, Céleste decided to marry for love instead of money, what then? Apart from her own feelings it was a situation Jenny did not like to contemplate, for it was obvious that the repercussions would split the family from top to bottom.

The following evening Jenny had been invited by Sally to an informal party to celebrate her engagement to Louis, and David had arranged to call for her. She did not really feel in the mood for festivities and while she was dressing she reflected, wryly, how much more care she would have lavished on her appearance if it had been for Raoul she was getting ready, and not David.

She stared at herself in her bedroom mirror. She supposed, detachedly, that she did look quite nice. The blue dress she was wearing—a present from Gabrielle and Stephen which she had felt unable to refuse—suited her admirably, though she could not help feeling that the neckline was rather too low. Her lips curved into a rueful smile. Since she had come to Nice many of her prejudices had disappeared, but the habits and attitudes of twenty-two years were hard to shed all at once. There were many things which Gabrielle and Dominique accepted as a matter of course but to which she found it extremely difficult to accustom herself. This plunging neckline, for instance....

She searched in a small box which stood on her dressing table and drew out a dainty blue necklace which had once belonged to her mother. She had not worn it much lately because the clasp was faulty, but it was the only necklace which would go with this dress. She fastened it around her neck, picked up her evening bag and made her way downstairs. David was calling for her at eight . . . she had only five minutes to wait.

Raoul was in *le petit salon* . . . alone. When Jenny saw him she would have retreated hurriedly, but he saw her and sprang to his feet. For a moment he stood looking at her, then he said lightly, "I hope your David knows how to pay pretty compliments, but in case he doesn't . . . you look ravishing, *chérie*!"

"Thank you." She knew she sounded stiff, but she couldn't help it. And she could not resist adding, tartly, "I wish you wouldn't keep on calling him 'my' David. He's not!"

"No?" He looked at her intently, an odd little smile in his eyes. "I find it hard to believe that he would not like to be. I have no faith in platonic friendships, especially when the man—even though he is a cautious Englishman!—is young and personable and the girl is as pretty and charming as you, *petite*!"

That's the way he would talk to Dominique, Jenny thought. Half-serious, half-teasing. She said childishly, "Well, I don't want to discuss it!" and turned to leave the room.

The next moment she felt Raoul's hand on her arm. He said quickly, "One moment . . . your necklace is undone."

She stood still obediently, but as his warm strong fingers touched her bare neck she shivered. As she did so she heard him suck in his breath and his fingers closed over her shoulders and gripped. It seemed to her, for one startled moment, that there was anger in the grip, but when he released her and turned her to face him he was smiling. She knew why almost immediately: Stephen was standing in the doorway watching them.

CHAPTER NINE

"YOU look charming, my dear. That dress is a very pretty shade of blue." Stephen's eyes were on his daughter's flushed, all-too-revealing face: they narrowed a little, but he lost nothing of his usual urbanity.

For just a moment Raoul hesitated and then with a somewhat brusque "Excuse me" he brushed past Jenny and left the room. Jenny's gaze followed his tall, lithe figure. Her heart was still pounding against her ribs. What would have happened if her father had not come in just then? Raoul had been on the brink of some furious outburst, she was almost sure of that. But why? What on earth had she done to make him angry?

Her father's voice cut across her thoughts. "We shall all miss Raoul very much when he returns to Colorado."

"Yes." Raoul was the very last person she wanted to discuss, especially with someone as shrewd as Stephen, and she glanced at her watch. David, for once, was late.

Stephen pulled pipe and pouch from the pocket of his tweed jacket and began to pack the pipe reflectively. He was not sure what to say. The policy he had always followed with his three stepchildren was one of total non-interference and he was certain that it was the right one. But wasn't a different policy called for in Jenny's case? The incredibly sheltered, almost cloistered, life she had led with her grandmother had made her extraordinarily vulnerable: he could not stand by and risk her getting hurt.

He cleared his throat. "Will you forgive me, my dear, if I suggest that perhaps you'll miss him more than anyone else will? Oh, don't worry!"—as Jenny, her eyes wide with alarm, swung round to face him—"it isn't at all obvious. You've put up a pretty good smoke screen. It's just that—well, I've been watching you quite closely and I couldn't help realising which way the wind was blowing. It's natural, of course:

Raoul is a very attractive young man. You're by no means the first—" He stopped abruptly. He had been about to say "You're by no means the first to discover that", which, although true, was hardly likely to console her. He realised from the expression on her face that she knew quite well what he had been about to say and cursed himself for a blundering fool.

She said, in a small, stifled voice, "You must think I'm very stupid. I—it's not as though he's given me any encouragement. It's not his fault, Stephen."

"Nor yours. These things happen. And I don't think you're in the least stupid, my dear." Stephen spoke gently, but though he smiled the smile did not reach his eyes. "For you to fall in love with Raoul was perhaps inevitable." He paused, then added, still gently, "What is also inevitable is that it can never come to anything. You do know that, don't you?"

"Oh yes," Jenny said, "I know that."

Stephen sighed. "That's something, at any rate. I was half afraid that you might be building castles in the air." He got his pipe going and blew a cloud of smoke into the air before forcing himself to go on. "Raoul has never been attracted to your type—the quiet, gentle, domesticated type. But even if he *had* managed to fall in love with you, Jenny, it would be no good. He would never be able to make you happy, simply because his way of life is not yours and your outlooks are poles apart. When you marry you'll want a home and children, a husband in a settled job and a peaceful, orderly life. Raoul will always crave gaiety and change and excitement. One of you would have to change—and resent, always, the fact that the change had been forced upon you."

His voice was tinged with bitterness. He had loved Jenny's mother until the shackles that had bound him to his dull nine-to-five job, the utter monotony of suburbia, had become a daily burden almost too heavy to bear.

Jenny was silent, but in her silence Stephen read acquiescence. After a moment he said with forced cheerfulness, "Your young man is there: I heard his voice. You and he make an excellent combination, Jenny,

I've always thought so. Shake the stardust out of your eyes, my darling, and try to forget Raoul as quickly as you can. Believe me, it's the best thing you can do."

It was, Jenny thought desolately, sensible advice, but in the days that followed she realised how hopeless it was to try to act on it. Raoul was now so much a part of her life that she could never forget him. Even when he returned, as he quite soon must, to Colorado he would leave so many memories behind him.

Bitter-sweet memories... some gay, some gentle. Raoul rubbing her hair dry after she'd lost her bathing cap in the sea, then twining brightly-coloured flowers in the still-damp tresses and threatening to beat the life out of her if she ever let a hairdresser touch it... Raoul driving her home along the Grande Corniche one moonlit night and stopping en route to tell her the names of the stars that clustered the blue-black sky ... Raoul singing her an old French lullaby that he had learned as a little boy, his voice so tender that instinctively she'd wondered if he was thinking of the child he might one day have... Raoul, discovering that she was afraid of thunder, making her stand with him at an open window and watch the storm rolling among the hills. (Incredibly she'd enjoyed the experience: in Raoul's company fear could not make a third.)

Yet, given time, even the most precious memories faded, she told herself desperately. And perhaps even time wasn't all that important... perhaps, as Grandmother would undoubtedly have said, it was all a matter of willpower and common sense. Jenny sighed at the thought. Love had rushed into her life like a wind-blown flame and was to end in nothing, and she could almost hear old Mrs. Barrington saying, "I told you so! That's what comes of tangling with foreigners!"

Dominique was another one who seemed to dread Raoul's departure, even though she saw little enough of him. Lately more and more of her time was being spent with Alex and her family, realising with dismay that his intentions were serious, began to suspect that an engagement might be imminent. Because of his play-boy reputation Alex was not the sort of man that, ideally, Gabrielle and Stephen would have chosen for their son-in-law, but they had to admit that from a worldly point of view Dominique would be making an excellent match. Apart from his title he also had wealth and possessions : what he lacked, Jenny thought, were the qualities ... the dynamic charm and vitality ... which made Raoul and Dominique so much alike.

Dominique herself seemed undecided about her feelings towards Alex. Jenny suspected that she was flattered by his attentions and a little dazzled by his assets, but that she was not really in love with him. Even so she seemed to be willing to turn a blind eye to his faults ... faults which were distressingly obvious to everyone else ! He was rather like a spoilt child in some ways, except that no child had quite such a streak of arrogance in his nature, nor such an overweening assurance of his own worth !

He certainly spared no expense in his courtship of Dominique.

"Heavens, more flowers !" Dominique, sitting in the garden with Jenny, raised her brows and laughed as yet another box of delicate, fragrant blooms was delivered to the Villa and she found the Count's card inside. "Maman says she simply doesn't know what to *do* with them all ! Raoul wants to open a florist's shop : says with people like Alex about it ought to be even more rewarding than a goldmine in Colorado !"

She paused, then added inconsequentially, "I do wish he liked Alex more. He doesn't, you know; I can tell. He likes your David, though."

Jenny's head jerked up. David and Raoul had met on several occasions, but there had been very little conversation between them. "How do you know?"

"He told me so. He also said that he thought you would probably make each other very happy." She shot Jenny a quick glance, as if to see how that remark had been taken, then added, "I think he was quite relieved. He is very fond of you, you know, Jenny. He says you have the most valuable quality a woman can possess—tranquillity. We are such an excitable family, and he finds you restful."

Jenny's cheeks were burning. She said, managing

to laugh, "I expect that 'restful' is just a euphemism for 'dull'."

Dominique considered. "No, I do not think so. You have been very good for Raoul since his illness, Maman says. If Céleste had been here—and thank goodness she wasn't!—there would have been no quiet moments listening to Chopin. She would have expected him to do far too much."

"Well, I'm certainly glad to have been useful in my own small way," Jenny said; and was unable to keep her voice from being tinged with bitterness.

She saw Dominique looking at her in astonishment and jumped to her feet. "I must go and get ready: I'm going swimming with David and Sally. What are you doing today, Dominique? I suppose you're seeing Alex?"

"I'm not, as a matter of fact. He's been away this week, looking after some business interests in Paris. He's got shares in a bank and some industrial concerns, I believe." Dominique yawned and stretched her slim brown arms above her head. "I'm at a loose end and I can't say I like it much."

Jenny hesitated. Then she said, "Why not come with us? I'm sure Sally and David would be awfully pleased." They wouldn't, she thought wryly, but just at the moment she couldn't help feeling sorry for her stepsister. She looked and sounded so oddly forlorn.

"Nice of you, but don't you and David prefer to be alone? Why does Sally insist on tagging along? Hasn't she got a boy-friend of her own?"

"Yes, she's engaged to a very nice young architect. I've met him. And there's no question of her playing gooseberry! She'd be the first one to realise it if there was any danger of that, but there isn't!" Jenny said sharply.

Dominique laughed but did not argue the point. "All right! I'll come with you. I suppose it will be better than being left entirely to my own devices."

She might have accepted the invitation more graciously, Jenny thought, half-amused, half-annoyed. Obviously she didn't expect to enjoy herself very much! For one uneasy moment she wondered whether Dominique would contrive to spoil the day for her and David and Sally, then she shrugged her misgivings aside. It was too late to have second thoughts now.

Certainly dismay registered on Sally's face when she realised that the swimming party was to include Dominique, although her greeting was cordial. Jenny, watching David anxiously, saw him go a little pale under his tan, but he, too, was equal to the occasion.

"Nice to see you, Dominique," he said, as casually as though there had never been any friction between them. Perhaps, Jenny thought, his love was wearing out ... as hers for Raoul would, one day, impossible though now it seemed.

It was Dominique who seemed oddly ill at ease. She was looking enchanting, wearing a white sun-suit patterned with scarlet poppies, and with her dark hair swept up into a topknot, but she wasn't talkative.

Sally, an enthusiastic but unspectacular swimmer, was the first one in the water. Jenny followed, leaving David and Dominique together on the beach. What passed between them she did not know, but certainly when she and Sally emerged from the sea Dominique was noticeably brighter and for the rest of the day she seemed her usual vivacious self.

It was a pleasant day. Jenny soon realised with relief that all her earlier misgivings had been without foundation. They picnicked on the beach and spent most of the afternoon lazing on the hot sand, then they drove over to St. Raphael for dinner and returned to David's flat for coffee. Surprisingly, Dominique insisted on making it—"as the only Frenchwoman here I think it's my privilege!" she said, laughing.

"Right-o! I'll show you where everything is," David said cheerfully, and they disappeared into the tiny kitchen which was always kept in apple-pie order.

Sally looked at Jenny, her brows raised. "Heavens! She *has* changed! I'd hardly recognise her as the same girl! Is that your influence, Jenny?"

Jenny shook her head. "You saw the worst side of her before."

The sound of laughter came from the kitchen. "Well, she certainly seems to be hitting it off better with

David. She hardly spoke a civil word to him when she was his patient." It was obvious that Dominique's difficult behaviour at that time still rankled a little with Sally, since she had borne the brunt of it.

It was a line of discussion which Jenny felt was unsafe to follow. She said briefly, "She doesn't take kindly to authority, but then quite a lot of people don't—What a lovely brooch, Sally! Is it a present from Louis?"

As she had hoped, Sally's face lit up at the mention of her fiancé, and until David and Dominique came back into the sitting-room, carrying coffee and sandwiches, they discussed wedding plans. Sally was to be married in the small country church where she had also been baptised and confirmed, and she was already busy preparing her trousseau.

"Of course it will be quite a simple wedding: nothing like the terrific splash there'll be when your stepbrother marries Céleste de Courville, for instance!" she said, laughing. "When is it to be, Jenny? Haven't they fixed the date yet?"

Jenny shook her head. "Not yet." What would Sally say, she wondered, if she told her that there was a possibility that the marriage between Piers Vaisseau and Céleste de Courville might not take place after all? That instead of Piers it might be his younger brother, Raoul, who led beautiful, golden Céleste to the altar?

On the way home Dominique was again very quiet and Jenny glanced at her once or twice, a little puzzled. She had been gay enough all evening and so, thank goodness, had David. A Frenchman under such circumstances, she thought wryly, might have been so emotionally disturbed that he could not behave naturally, but not David. Perhaps he had more than his fair share of British phlegm!

After a time she asked tentatively, "Are you tired, Dominique?"

"Oh—just a little," her stepsister admitted. She hesitated and then added, as though with an effort, "But it has been an agreeable day. Your David is very much nicer when he is off duty than when he is prowling around that horrible nursing home ordering his patients to behave themselves!"

"You and Raoul both have a habit of getting your personal pronouns wrong!" Jenny spoke tartly, and then, as Dominique did not answer, she added, "At any rate I'm glad you've enjoyed yourself. I was afraid that perhaps you'd find the programme a little flat, after the kind of entertainment you're used to!"

Dominique gave an odd little laugh. "I didn't miss the caviare and champagne treatment, if that's what you mean. One can have a surfeit of that kind of thing, you know."

"If you marry Alex they'll be part of your daily diet," Jenny retorted.

"*If.* I don't know whether I want to or not."

"Surely if you're in any doubt—" Jenny began, and Dominique laughed again. "But I'm not—not really. I'm not likely to be given another chance of acquiring such an eligible husband! Don't you know that I'm the envy of half the women on the Côte d'Azur?"

"You're as bad as Céleste!" Jenny protested, and Dominique shrugged.

"*Peut-être.* Except that you have forgotten that we do not know what Céleste has decided, alone among the Swiss mountains! She may have decided not to marry Piers after all. That is certainly what *mon cher* Raoul is hoping—have you not noticed how restless and how much on edge he has been these last few days?"

Jenny had noticed. She had tried to put it down to a natural preoccupation with his plans for his return to Colorado, but Dominique's suggestion—that he was waiting on tenterhooks for Céleste's final decision—seemed far more feasible.

Jenny was in the music room the following evening when Raoul came and joined her for the first time in many days. He stood by her side in silence, listening to the Beethoven sonata she was playing, then when she had finished he caught hold of her wrist. His fingers felt firm and very cool.

"Will you come with me to the opera tomorrow evening, Jenny? They're doing 'La Bohème', one of your favourites, I believe." He paused, then added casually,

"Just you and I ... nobody else in this unenlightened family cares for opera, I fear. Even Maman went to sleep when I once rashly invited her to accompany me to 'Madam Butterfly'!"

Jenny caught her breath. One last evening alone with Raoul! An evening to remember ... something to take out and recall when she was back in England and Raoul was many thousands of miles away!

She said breathlessly, "Thank you. I'd like that very much."

"Good." There was a smile in his eyes. "Can you be ready by seven? I've a business appointment in the late afternoon, but I'll be back by then." He paused, then added lightly, "Wear the white dress I like so much, won't you? It makes you look like the fairy on top of the Christmas tree!"

Jenny remembered his words when she was getting ready the following evening and laughed softly to herself, as she studied her reflection in the full-length looking glass. The dress *was* beautiful ... she was glad now that she had bought it, although at the time she had felt guilty about her extravagance. There was a glow in her cheeks which matched the glow in her heart, because with only three more nights at home Raoul had wanted to spend one alone with her. Tomorrow, of course, was Gabrielle's and Stephen's party and the house would be crowded with guests, but tonight Raoul was hers and she wouldn't have to share him with anyone else. Tonight she wouldn't even let the shadow of Céleste intrude on her happiness! She'd be here in person tomorrow, of course, but tomorrow was another day ... in fact, tomorrow might not even come!

She laughed again, amazed at herself for producing such an un-Barrington-like piece of philosophy and ran lightly down the stairs. She had hoped that Raoul would be waiting for her in the hall and that he would look up to see her descending the wide staircase in a drift of white but she was disappointed. Only Gabrielle was there.

"*Ma fille*, Raoul has not yet returned." Gabrielle's eyes were anxious. "I cannot understand it! He must have been detained, but there has been no message—nothing!"

Jenny laughed. In the crystal world that contained her, and Raoul, and 'La Bohème' there was no space for inquietude.

"It's only five to seven. He'll be here," she said confidently, and sat down to wait.

It was at ten minutes past seven that she felt the first stirrings of anxiety. Her misgivings increased as the hands of the clock swept remorselessly on ... quarter-past seven ... half-past seven ... quarter to eight ... and by eight o'clock the crystal world had completely evaporated, leaving her cold with apprehension and doubt. There *couldn't* have been another accident! There couldn't have been! He must have been delayed somewhere, unable to reach a telephone. She had only to wait a little longer and the phone would ring, or else he would be here, explaining, apologising, rushing her out of the house so that after all they wouldn't miss more of 'La Bohème' than the first act....

She was so sure of this that when at last she heard a quick firm tread in the hall and the door of *le petit salon* opened she sprang to her feet with a little cry of relief. It was not, however, Raoul who stood framed in the doorway, but David.

He must have seen her incredulous disappointment written plainly on her face, for he came quickly to her side.

"Sorry if I startled you, Jenny. I know you're going out—your stepmother has just told me—but I was passing and I thought I'd return your cardigan. You left it in the car the other day and I was afraid you might be needing it."

Jenny swallowed. "I—that's nice of you, David. Thank you very much." Mechanically she took the pale b᷉ ᷉cardigan that he held out to her.

"You look beautiful." David's eyes were admiring as he took in every detail of her appearance. "You're off to the opera, aren't you? Not my cup of tea, but there's no doubt that you'll enjoy it!" He glanced at his watch, his face suddenly registering surprise. "You're going to be a bit late, though, aren't you?"

"Raoul is taking me, but he's not home yet." Jenny's voice was taut as she felt the necessity to confide in someone. "I—I can't help feeling worried. I feel sure he would have got in touch if he knew that he was going to be unavoidably delayed!"

"Raoul?" David stared, and his voice was suddenly sharp. "But, my dear girl, I've just seen him! He was strolling down the Promenade des Angelais as large as life, with a beautiful blonde beside him—" He stopped short as he noticed her stricken expression. Then, as comprehension dawned, "Oh, lord!" he said ruefully. "Trust me to put my great foot in it!"

So Raoul was still philandering! So much, Jenny thought bleakly, for her foolish dreams. Who was the beautiful blonde who had caught his eye this time? She felt tears of anger, shame and disappointment prick her eyelids and she turned quickly away so that David should not see her shed them. Too late. The next thing she knew his arms were round her, holding her tenderly, comfortingly.

"Oh, Jenny! Jenny darling, I had no idea...we *are* a silly pair, aren't we?"

"At last we both know the score." Jenny looked up into his face and tried to smile through her tears.

The sight moved David profoundly. He swore softly under his breath and bending his head, brushed her quivering lips with his own. It was a kiss and yet it was not a kiss, and Jenny knew perfectly well what he wanted to convey.

Then, as she searched for words to alleviate the situation, a movement in the doorway caught her eye and she turned her head. As she did so every vestige of colour receded from her face and she tore herself from David's arms with a little gasp.

"Oh, please don't mind me." Smoothly, his face so mask-like that for the first time Jenny noticed a resemblance to his brother Piers, Raoul strolled forward.

"I came to apologise to you, Jenny, and to explain why I am so late, but I see that even if explanations and apologies are still called for there is no reason why they should not wait." He gave a sarcastic little smile. "You've obviously managed to fill the time you've been waiting for me remarkably well, and though I'm sorry you've missed the opera I can at least console myself with the thought that there have been—compensations!"

If his face was expressionless his voice was not. It was raw with anger, betraying the fact that he was having trouble hanging on to his temper. He walked out before either Jenny or David could answer, leaving them both staring blankly after his retreating figure. For a moment Jenny felt stunned, then a flood of furious colour flooded into her pale cheeks. What right had *he* to mind because he had found her in David's arms? How *dared* he look at her like that . . . speak to her like that . . . as if *she* was somehow in the wrong! What had he done with the blonde, she thought bitterly—somehow shaken her off when (belatedly) he'd realised the time?

"I say, I think I'd better be going." David looked and sounded acutely uncomfortable and Jenny did not attempt to detain him. Seething with anger and resentment, the only thing she wanted to do at this particular moment was to seek out Raoul and tell him, before her temper cooled, exactly what she thought of him and his behaviour! This was one time when he wasn't going to get away with his outrageous conduct!

He was not in the study or the Blue Salon. Jenny, determined systematically to search every inch of house and garden until eventually she found him, was just approaching the music room when she suddenly stood stockstill, a startled expression on her face. Someone was playing the piano . . . and yet no one in the Villa Buichi ever touched the instrument with the exception of herself! Could it possibly be . . . Raoul?

She flung open the door of the music room and marched in, indignant words already on her lips. Then she stood still with a shock of incredulous surprise and dismay. Céleste de Courville, slim and graceful and wearing a dress that was the colour of spring leaves, was seated at the piano, playing the Beethoven sonata that Jenny had played to Raoul the previous night.

CHAPTER TEN

CÉLÈSTE looked up with a cool, brilliant smile and Jenny thought, inconsequentially, "Why, her eyes are green...witch eyes...funny how I've never really noticed them before!"

"Hello, Jenny." Céleste went on playing the sonata, very correctly and with a great deal of showy technique but without the slightest trace of feeling. Jenny was irresistibly reminded of a musical box.

Aloud, she said feebly, "Oh, hello! You're back!" and was immediately annoyed with herself for producing such an inane remark. Surely, even if she *had* been taken by surprise she could have achieved something better than that!

Céleste laughed, and her laugh was like the chime of faraway bells. "As you say, I'm back." She took her slender, red-tipped fingers off the keyboard and flexed them. "I saw the piano open and I suddenly had an urge to play it. I used to be rather good once, though of course I don't get much chance to practise these days." She rose and replaced the sonata on top of the pile of music that Jenny had been playing earlier. "I suppose all this is yours? I must say I had a little difficulty in finding a piece to suit my taste, it's all rather romantic, nostalgic stuff, isn't it? I prefer something with a little more verve myself, though of course if one is trying to set a scene..." She laughed again, and swept one hand across the keyboard in a rippling movement.

Jenny stiffened. "Set a scene? What do you mean?"

"Oh, come, Jenny, don't try to be naive! Raoul has told me all about your musical evenings! Actually he seems to think you play quite well." Céleste's voice was indulgent, amused. "He's very fond of music, of course. We often used to go to concerts together—in the old days." She played just two notes, a fifth in a low register, over and over. "I suppose if I married Piers concert-going would be something else I'd have to forgo. He can't tell one note from another!"

Instinctively Jenny glanced at Céleste's left hand. The huge emerald ring still blazed upon her finger.

"If?" she echoed.

"Well, there isn't actually any 'if' about it. Not any more. I've decided that I simply can't give Raoul up after all." Céleste spoke calmly. "I suppose you know what happened—that I threw him over for Piers because I couldn't bear the thought of being poor? He met me at the airport tonight and I told him that at long last I had discovered that I'd made an awful mistake and that it's quite right what they say, love *does* matter more than money." There was a soft luminous look in her green eyes and then her mouth curved ruefully. "The only thing is, I'm such a frightful coward that I haven't dared to tell Piers yet. He doesn't even know I'm home: he thought I was coming tomorrow, only I had the chance of an earlier flight and I was so longing to put poor Raoul out of his misery that I jumped at it."

"I—see." Jenny's voice sounded, even to herself, to be coming from a long, long way away.

"I hope you do, because of course a lot of people are going to think I've behaved frightfully badly. There's bound to be an absolutely ghastly row, I'm afraid. For that reason we—Raoul and I—aren't telling anyone until after the party: we don't want to spoil things for poor Gabrielle. In fact, we may even wait until after Raoul has gone back to Colorado, to avoid any unpleasantness, so you will keep our secret, won't you, Jenny darling?"

Jenny thought that if Céleste didn't stop playing that low fifth she would scream. She said huskily, "I'm amazed that you've made me your confidante!"

"Oh, the English never sneak! Everyone knows that!" Céleste's voice was honey-sweet. "Besides—" she stopped.

"Go on. Besides?"

Céleste seemed to hesitate. "W-e-e-ll, I rather think Raoul wanted you to know the truth. He's feeling just the teeniest bit guilty about you, you know. You've got quite a thing about him, haven't you? At least, that's what he seems to think, and heaven knows he's had enough experience of lovelorn maidens to be able to tell!"

The colour burned into Jenny's cheeks. For a moment she stared at Céleste, speechless, then, afraid that if she stayed any longer her precarious self-control would snap, she whirled round and fled, pursued by the sound of a triumphant chord. When, breathless and more hurt than she had ever been in her life before, she reached the sanctuary of her own bedroom she flung herself on to her bed and buried her face in the soft, sweet-scented pillow.

Raoul had guessed her secret! He'd probably realised that she was falling in love with him long before she'd realised it herself. That must be why he had treated her in such a brotherly fashion, because he hadn't wanted to be embarrassed by a love he couldn't return! It had always been Céleste with him ... always. No wonder tonight he had forgotten about the opera! Once he'd known that she was coming home a day early ... that she wanted him to meet her ... everything else would have been driven clean out of his head!

Sick with humiliation and misery, she tore off her lovely white dress. Forgotten now was Raoul's inexplicable anger when he had walked into *le petit salon* and found her in David's arms, and even if she had remembered she would have put it down to hurt vanity. Probably, she thought wretchedly, everyone ... the whole family ... guessed that she was in love with Raoul ... were amused or sympathetic. "Poor little Jenny ... and she thinking herself so sensible, too!" She could almost hear them saying it, and her fingernails drove into her palms. Oh, it *was* funny, really, no doubt about that! No wonder Céleste had laughed ... no wonder her low, husky voice had held that hateful, underlying note of amusement!

She looked at her dress, now lying in a crumpled, forlorn little heap on the floor, and a lump came into her throat. "It makes you look like the fairy on top of the Christmas tree...." Some fairy! she thought bitterly. Fairies could wave a magic wand and make all troubles disappear. *They* did not fall in love with unsuitable people and then cry because they got their fingers burned!

Mechanically, because tidiness was a thing she had grown up with, she picked up the dress and put it on a hanger. The way she felt now, she never wanted to wear it again. Quick, hot tears stung her lids as she remembered the way her heart had sung every hour of the day, just thinking of tonight, and the care she had taken over her appearance. She had wanted so little ... just one evening to remember for the rest of her life ... and even that had been denied her!

She kicked off her shoes and slipped her feet into the soft mules that had been a gift from Gabrielle. She couldn't go downstairs again tonight ... she simply couldn't! She'd plead a headache ... anything. She couldn't face Raoul, not after what Céleste had said. Tomorrow, though, please God, perhaps she would be able to salvage her pride ... stick her chin in the air and pretend she didn't care! She didn't know how well she could act, but if she could possibly help it neither Raoul nor Céleste should have the satisfaction of knowing how cruelly they had hurt her, or what leaden misery lay like a dull weight inside her!

But there was, after all, no need for an elaborate pretence. Raoul was not at breakfast and she discovered that he had left the villa shortly before eight o'clock, leaving a message for Gabrielle that he would be away for most of the day. Greatly relieved, Jenny spent most of the morning in her bedroom carefully composing a letter to Mr. Davidson, the family lawyer who had written suggesting that she make her home in Oxford with his widowed sister.

Although at first the prospect had not appealed in the least, after all that had happened she was now beginning to think it was quite a good idea. Stephen and Gabrielle would probably be hurt and disappointed, but it couldn't be helped. She didn't want to stay here and become involved in the family crisis which was bound to be precipitated once Raoul and Céleste made their plans known. Living quietly, peacefully ... wasn't that better than being torn in twain by conflicting emotions? Wasn't it better to eschew love completely since when it came it seemed to bring pain, not ecstasy, in its wake? Perhaps, if she really tried, she might one day efface the memory of the last few weeks, recapture the serenity that had been hers before Raoul had disrupted it. Perhaps, in time, she might even manage to forget him altogether.

Consequently, she wrote in her letter that she was very grateful for Mr. Davidson's suggestion and that she would very much like, on her return to England, to call upon his sister.

"I am not expecting to stay in France much longer—possibly only another week or so," she wrote, and then stopped, staring down at the page with eyes that were blurred with sudden tears. It was going to be so hard, saying goodbye to Gabrielle and Stephen, who had been so good to her and whom she had learned to love ... Dominique ... David, who had been such a kind and dependable friend ... France itself, which had been revealed even to her prejudiced eyes as a beautiful and gracious country. And as for saying goodbye to Raoul. ...

She drew a deep breath, firmly pushed her painful thoughts away, and finished the letter before her resolution could falter. She sealed the envelope, addressed and stamped it, and put it on her bedside table. Tomorrow she would post it, and then she would tell Stephen and Gabrielle that she wanted to make immediate plans to return to England.

Like Raoul and Céleste, she certainly did not intend to do anything which might mar Stephen's and Gabrielle's anniversary celebrations. Gabrielle loved parties and this one was to be extra-special, marking as it did nine years of a perfect marriage. The Villa Buichi seemed literally to hum with activity and pleased expectation, and when she had written her letter even Jenny, despite her heavy heart, forced herself for Gabrielle's sake to take an interest in what was going on.

Neither Raoul nor Céleste made an appearance, but an unexpected caller during the afternoon was David, who was enjoying a long spell off duty.

"I'm just on my way to get a haircut," he said with

a grin, running his fingers through his thick, unruly hair. "Can't disgrace you by turning up tonight looking like a hairy monster. Oh, and I thought you might like these to wear on your dress. They're rather pretty," and a little sheepishly he handed Jenny a cluster of tiny, star-shaped flowers which, for all their seeming simplicity, she realised had probably cost him a small fortune.

"Oh, David!" As always Jenny was touched by his kindness and she sniffed the flowers rapturously. "They're simply lovely!"

David shifted his weight from one leg to the other as he prepared to make the real reason for his visit known. "Everything all right?" He asked the question awkwardly and in evident embarrassment.

"Oh yes," Jenny said drearily. "Everything's fine. Truly, David. There's no need to worry about me."

He stuck his hands into his pockets and there was a deep crease between his brows. "Well, I do worry about you, Jenny. More than ever now, since I gather that we're more or less in the same boat." He cleared his throat. "I suppose I'm a bit dense, but I never thought —that is, de Vaisseau just didn't seem your type, somehow."

Jenny smiled mirthlessly. "I think you mean that I'm not his. But it's all right, David. As I told you last night, I do know the score." She forced herself to laugh. "I guess it must be something to do with the climate. When I'm back in England I shall wonder how on earth I ever came to be so silly!"

"You're going back? When?" David asked the question sharply.

"Oh, pretty soon," and Jenny told him about the letter she had written to John Davidson. "I shall like Oxford—I'm told it is a beautiful city," she said lightly.

"It doesn't sound a particularly lively future!" David was still frowning. Suddenly he swung round and looked into her eyes searchingly. "Do you really want to return to teaching, Jenny?"

Jenny couldn't hold his gaze. Her eyelids flickered and she tried to turn away.

161

"Obviously you don't." There was an odd note in David's voice. He hesitated, then went on, "If I offer you an alternative will you promise to think it over carefully before you say no?"

"An alternative?" Jenny looked at him blankly.

"You could marry me." David's voice was steady, almost impersonal. "I can't have Dominique, and you can't have Raoul de Vaisseau, but what we could have is—each other. We're good friends, Jenny, and I honestly believe that despite the—unusual—circumstances we could make a good marriage. Temperamentally we're much alike, our tastes and backgrounds are very similar. Don't *you* think that we could make a go of it, if we really tried? That one day we might even come to care for each other very deeply?"

It was the kind of proposal, Jenny thought, that would have found favour with her grandmother. Cool, calm and rational. David had evidently thought the matter over very carefully, and she answered him with the same coolness, the same care.

"David, you've paid me a tremendous compliment. I—I do like you, more than anyone else I've ever met and I expect you're right, we could make a go of it if we tried. But—"

David laughed. "I was waiting for that one little word! Jenny, all I ask is that you think about it. I'm not going to try to bludgeon you into anything. I just want you to know that you don't *have* to return to teaching, that you don't *have* to live a cloistered, sterile life just because you were unlucky enough to fall in love with the wrong bloke!" He paused. "As far as I'm concerned, I want to put an end to dreaming. I'm not going to spend the rest of my life sighing for the might-have-been." For the first time his voice became slightly bitter. "I'm told that Dominique and her Count are likely to be announcing their engagement soon, and de Vaisseau is returning to Colorado within the next day or two, isn't he? It seems an appropriate time for us to bury the past and to think about the future. *Our* future, if you want it that way."

But did she? Long after David had gone Jenny sat still and silent, thinking troubled thoughts, until a shadow fell over her shoulder. Startled, for in her pre-occupation she had not heard the sound of footsteps, she looked up swiftly.

Raoul.

He wasn't smiling, and again she was struck by his resemblance to his elder brother. It was only their expressions which made them look so different, usually: when Raoul looked stern, as he did now, one could see how much alike they really were.

He did not waste time on preambles. "I want to talk to you, Jenny—about last night. As I said then, I owe you both an explanation and an apology."

Jenny's throat felt oddly constricted, but she answered him steadily, ignoring the wild thumping of her heart.

"I don't think anything of the sort is at all necessary, Raoul. Can't we just forget the whole thing? After all" —she managed quite a convincing laugh—"it wasn't the end of the world. It isn't as though I'd never seen 'La Bohème' before, or that I never will again!"

An odd expression crossed his face. He said slowly, "That's all my non-appearance meant to you, then— the forgoing of an evening's entertainment?"

"Well, of course." Jenny, looking him straight in the eye, felt as though she was daring him to think anything else. He might believe that she had fallen in love with him, but he didn't actually *know*, therefore she was spared the final humiliation.

For a moment he said nothing and then he smiled, and at the smile Jenny took instant fright. It held tenderness as well as amusement, and she was not proof against Raoul the gentle, only against Raoul the gay and mercurial. She had not meant to mention David, but now she added, "Anyway, the evening was not entirely wasted. As you yourself pointed out at the time, there were certain compensations!"

He gave a twisted little smile. "I assume you mean your 'good friend', David."

The cool irony of his tone stung. She said sharply, "That's something of a misnomer, actually, since he's just asked me to marry him!" She saw the startled expression in his dark blue eyes and felt a surge of satisfaction.

163

It was short-lived, however. After a moment Raoul said coolly, "And are you?"

He *would* have to ask that! Jenny stuck her hands into the pockets of her skirt, gave him a brilliant smile and said, "I'm going to think it over."

Raoul laughed, and suddenly his face was once more full of mockery. "You make it sound just like a business transaction! What is there to think over, *ma chère?* Either you love him or you don't—and frankly, I'm inclined to think you don't, despite that charming little scene I witnessed last night!"

The colour surged into Jenny's cheeks. "You know nothing at all about it!" She was going to add, "And, anyway, what's it got to do with you? You've got your own love affair to sort out and I wouldn't mind betting that that will take a lot longer than mine!" but she didn't, because just at that moment Dominique joined them. She had been to the hairdresser and wanted Raoul's opinion of her new hairstyle, which, although too elaborate for Jenny's taste, certainly looked very glamorous.

There was no further opportunity for a private conversation with Raoul. It wasn't till afterwards that Jenny realised that the "explanation and apology" he had mentioned were still owing to her, though of course it did not matter. She knew already what he had been going to tell her.

By evening the Villa Buichi was *en fête,* brilliant with lights and fragrant with the scent of massed, exotic blooms. In her room Jenny dressed slowly, strangely reluctant to go downstairs and mingle with the guests who had already begun to arrive. Piers, much to Gabrielle's relief, had driven up not half an hour ago, looking tired and harassed and carrying an impressive looking briefcase (he had, he explained, driven straight from an important meeting), but at least he had come. Jenny could not help wondering what Céleste's attitude would be towards him, or how she would manage to stall for extra time. Obviously, since she did not wish for an immediate revelation of her change of heart, she would have to do a certain amount of pretending. Jenny felt a stab of compassion for Piers, who, whatever his faults, did not deserve to be deceived and lied to. He would not readily forgive either Raoul or Céleste when he learned the real truth: the animosity between himself and his brother was bound to be increased and it would be Gabrielle who suffered the most.

The strains of music reminded her that it was time she joined the party. She was too pale, she thought, looking into the mirror. She ought to have asked Dominique if she could borrow some rouge. She was wearing not the white dress Raoul liked—at the moment she could not even bear to look at it—but the blue one Gabrielle and Stephen had given her. And instead of wearing her hair loose, as Raoul liked to see it, she piled it on the top of her head. It made her look older ... more sophisticated, and she wished she'd done it before.

She gathered up her skirts and went reluctantly towards the door. From downstairs came the sound of voices and laughter. She must have taken longer to dress than she'd thought, it sounded as though the party was already well under way.

The main *salon* had been cleared completely for dancing. Jenny, finding a more or less secluded corner, stood and watched for a few moments, her eyes searching, in spite of herself, for a glimpse of Raoul's tall, debonair figure. She couldn't see him, but there was Piers, and Céleste, looking as cool and beautiful as a waterlily, was in his arms. Dominique, wearing a coral dress which enhanced her vivid colouring, was dancing with Alex, and she saw Gabrielle, looking wonderful in a gown the colour of rich burgundy, exchanging a few words with Stephen. Handsome and immaculate in evening dress, he looked years younger than his actual age, and Jenny felt a sudden surge of pride and affection. Despite her bruised heart she was glad that she had come to France. She would never have learned to love her father if she had not.

"Jenny! I've been looking for you everywhere!" said a voice from behind her, and she turned to see David smiling down at her.

"Oh, David, I'm sorry ... have you been here long? I think I must have taken too long over dressing,"

Jenny said, and shook her mind free of the tantalising question re Raoul's whereabouts.

"Well, if you have I'd certainly say that the result justifies the hold-up," David said lightly. "You're the belle of the ball."

"Then you can't have seen Dominique yet!" Jenny retorted.

The smile vanished from David's eyes. "Oh, but I have." He hesitated, then added with would-be casualness, "I may even ask her to dance with me later on, though I don't suppose she will."

"I don't see why not. I rather got the impression that you'd both buried the hatchet," Jenny said, matching his tone.

"Well, she did have the decency to apologise for the letter she wrote to me after I'd dragged her out of the swimming pool. Said she'd been feeling sore about making a fool of herself or she wouldn't have done it. That did sort of disarm me, I must admit," David said drily. "All the same, what is it they say?—something about one swallow not making a summer? Perhaps it's not terribly applicable in this case, but you'll probably gather what I'm trying to say." His grin was so cheerful that she was almost—but not quite—deceived. "Anyway, as I told you this afternoon I'm not worrying about Dominique any more. May I have the pleasure of this dance, Miss Barrington?"

Although not a particularly good dancer, David had a relaxed, uncomplicated style which was easy to follow. Jenny danced with him twice, and was then claimed by a tall, dark-haired young man whom she vaguely recognised as one of Dominique's friends. It was impossible to do what she wanted to do... keep an eye on the door, though since she knew that at any moment Raoul might make an appearance she could feel her heart beating fast and jerkily under the strain of waiting.

It was in a state of high-strung tension that she sank into a chair at the end of the dance while her partner departed in search of cool drinks. She just had time to exchange a smile with the pretty, brown-haired girl sitting next to her when the sound of a deep familiar voice made her heart skip a beat.

"May I have the next dance, Jenny?" Raoul's tall figure loomed up in front of her and she caught her breath convulsively. Raoul at last . . . Raoul looking more handsome than ever, his smile a little crooked and a glint in his eyes which somehow rang alarm bells in her mind.

Fiercely determined not to betray herself, and knowing that propinquity was the worst hazard she could face, Jenny said (and was surprised how calm, even indifferent, she sounded!), "Thank you, Raoul, but I don't want to dance again just yet. I simply must get my breath back."

He held out his hand. "Then come with me into the garden." His voice and eyes held a caress, but they were compelling—so compelling that she almost obeyed.

Then pride came to her rescue. Out of the corner of her eye she saw her last partner approaching and said quickly, "I'm sorry, I can't. I'm thirsty and Henri has been kind enough to bring me a drink."

For a moment their eyes met and Jenny saw the expression in his change. Something twisted inside her and then Raoul said coolly, "I see. Perhaps later— when you have quenched your thirst?" He bowed, turned on his heel and walked away. Two minutes later Jenny saw him dancing, his partner a slender brunette with slanting eyes and a beautiful provocative mouth. She was dancing very close to him, smiling up into his face, and Jenny, watching, felt her little show of independence turn to dust and ashes in her mouth.

She looked round for David, and saw him dancing with Dominique. She was laughing at something he'd said, her eyes as bright as the sparkling crystals at her ears, the skirt of her filmy dress floating out behind her. Nothing wrong there. . . .

"You would like to dance again, yes?" Henri asked, and automatically Jenny assented. Leaving her lemonade practically untasted, she again took the floor, though this time she followed her partner's steps mechanically and without enjoyment. Céleste drifted past in the arms of a tall, bearded man . . . had she seen Raoul yet? (Oh, Raoul, Raoul . . .) David was still dancing with Dominique . . . where, then, was Alex? Oh, yes, there he was, dancing with quite a pretty girl in turquoise blue, but she couldn't be enjoying herself much because he was paying her only the most cursory attention. He kept looking over his shoulder at David and Dominique, his expression lowering. What was Dominique doing ... trying to make him jealous?

"Mademoiselle Jenny, you do not pay attention!" Henri murmured reproachfully as she trod on his toes for the second time. "Your thoughts, they are miles away!"

"Oh dear, I'm sorry!" Conscience-stricken, Jenny tried to concentrate on her partner, but before she had time to make amends Henri received a light tap on his shoulder.

"This is my dance, I believe, *mon ami*," Raoul said with cool effrontery, and before Henri could utter a word of protest he had drawn Jenny into his arms and they were circling the floor.

"Since you will not dance with me of your own free will, it seems I must act the pirate!" Raoul said suavely.

It was impossible to resist without making a scene. Jenny, her cheeks burning, unable to trust herself to speak, tried to hold herself rigidly, as far away from him as possible. She was not successful. Raoul, his mouth a hard, straight line, merely drew her closer, so close that his tanned cheek brushed her temple as they swung into a turn and she thought, panic-stricken, that he must surely hear the pounding of her heart above the nostalgic waltz that the orchestra was playing. She was almost frighteningly aware of the physical contact with his lean, hard body and was only thankful that he did not seem to expect her to talk.

On a swirl of music the dancers near them swung and parted and Jenny saw Céleste. Their eyes met, and Jenny saw the elder girl's eyebrows lift and an expression of mocking amusement cross her beautiful face. Then she laughed and said something to her partner and he, too, looked in Jenny's and Raoul's direction before some other couples came between them and cut them off from view.

It was then that the music stopped. Realising that

they were at the edge of the room, near the french windows which stood open, Jenny tried to pull away, but Raoul gripped her hands tightly.

"Oh no, you don't!" His voice was pleasant and his lips smiled, but there was a glitter in his blue eyes which belied both. "I told you this afternoon I wanted to talk to you—remember? You can spare me a few minutes, I'm sure."

His grip was inexorable. Without waiting for her answer he led her out into the garden and the music, which had started again, followed them out through the long windows. It was not until they were some little distance from the house and screened from view by bushes that he stopped and turned to face her. Several times before she had suspected that he was angry with her, but this time she realised, with almost a shock of fear, that he was simply furious. His eyes were as cold as a winter sky and when he spoke his voice almost crackled.

"What have I ever done to make you so afraid of me? Why do you shrink from me every time I come near you? Do you think I enjoy the feeling that either you find me physically repulsive or else I scare you out of your wits?" A muscle was twitching in his lean brown cheek and he almost hurled the words at her.

"I've done every damned thing I could think of to try to win your confidence ... to eradicate the memory of that one time when I admit that I behaved like a brute and a boor! Instead of making love to you, which God knows I've wanted to do, I've treated you almost like a sister ... and as a reward for my pains you've made it painfully obvious, tonight, that you don't even trust me to behave decently on a dance floor!"

He paused for breath. Horrified, incredulous, Jenny stared at him. "Raoul, I didn't ... I haven't ... you don't understand!"

He gave a short savage laugh. "On the contrary, I understand only too well! And since you obviously fear my unbridled lusts, and I equally obviously have nothing to lose, I may as well prove your point!"

With a swift, almost violent movement he swept her

into his arms and bent his face to hers. The next instant he crushed her lips with his own, holding her with steel-hard arms so that no resistance was possible.

"Monsieur Raoul!" An urgent, apologetic voice spoke from somewhere behind them ... Berthe's voice. *"Mille pardons, monsieur ... excusez-moi ...* but I have been searching for you everywhere. It is the telephone, a call from Colorado. You are wanted urgently, *monsieur."*

At the sound of Berthe's voice Raoul had let Jenny go so abruptly that she had almost fallen. For a moment he stood staring at her with a look on his face which she had never seen before, then, without a word, he turned and followed the housekeeper back towards the house. Jenny, left standing in the garden, did not move. She might have been a statue made of stone.

CHAPTER ELEVEN

JENNY was never able to recall, afterwards, anything that happened between the moment that Raoul left her in the garden and the moment when, as the house gradually emptied itself of its tired but happy guests, she at last found herself alone in her ivory bedroom. She supposed that she had danced, laughed, made conversation, even drunk champagne, but she could not consciously remember having done any of those things.

When they weren't chasing each other around and around in her mind her thoughts were all snarled up like a tangle of barbed wire, and her head was one vast ache. Over and over again, as she lay with her face pressed into her pillow, she re-lived those few dramatic moments in the garden ... heard again Raoul's bitter, accusing voice and felt the aching pressure of his lips upon hers. She did not even begin to understand his attitude or the reason for his anger, and the more she tried to think herself into his personality the more bewildered she became.

Perhaps she would have lain awake all night wrestling

with her troubled thoughts had the door of her bedroom not suddenly burst open. A moment later Dominique had flung herself on Jenny's bed and burst into a fit of violent weeping.

"Dominique!" Startled into sitting bolt upright, Jenny stared in consternation at her stepsister's heaving shoulders. "Whatever is the matter? What has happened?"

For answer Dominique only sobbed louder than ever. That she was crying as much from rage as from anything else was painfully apparent, for her clenched fists were pounding the silken counterpane and the only words that Jenny, now thoroughly alarmed, could distinguish were "I hate him! Oh, I hate him!"

"Hate whom? Dominique, who are you talking about? Tell me what has happened!" Jenny spoke with all the authority she could muster, and it seemed to have some effect, for after a few moments some of the tension went out of Dominique's slim body and the storm of angry sobs began to abate.

Jenny went to fetch her a glass of water from the bathroom, and when she returned she found her scrubbing furiously at her eyes. Even tears could not mar Dominique's loveliness: she managed to look entrancing even though mascara had streaked her cheeks and her breath was still coming in shuddering gasps.

"Here, drink this." In her anxiety on Dominique's behalf Jenny had almost forgotten her own problems. "Can't you tell me what's wrong? Who—or what—has upset you so badly?"

"Alex, of course!" Dominique crumpled her damp handkerchief into a little ball and threw it savagely across the room. "I hate him! I hate him, do you hear? And I never want to see or speak to him again!"

"But I thought—Dominique, what *has* happened?" Jenny spoke sharply, the memory of the Count's sullen resentful expression as he had watched Dominique dancing with David returning forcibly to her mind.

"He didn't want me to dance with anyone but him!" Dominique's eyes still glittered with anger. "He—he *forbade* me to, Jenny! And—and when I said phooey, I'd dance with whoever I liked, he s-said beastly things about David and that he wasn't going to allow an English nobody to paw the future Countess Venescu!"

She flung back her lovely head. "And that just made me see *red*, Jenny, because I hadn't even said that I *would* marry him! And when I pointed that out he got terribly excited and went on and on about the great honour he was paying me and how he would expect me to behave when I bore his illustrious name, and—and I was so furious that I said nothing would ever induce me to marry him! He didn't believe me at first and then—and then he saw I was serious, and Jenny, he was simply *seething*! The things he said!" In spite of herself she shivered at the memory. "Luckily it wasn't all one-sided! I had quite a bit to say myself!"

Jenny's face was grave. "Dominique, was that wise? I've got an idea that Alex isn't the best person to cross. You've hurt his pride, and he isn't likely to forgive you for it."

"I don't care!" A wild cat would have looked gentle in comparison with Dominique's expression. "I *won't* be treated as though I'm one of his chattels, and I won't have him saying things about my friends! I meant it when I said I hoped I'd never see him again!"

Jenny looked at her. "But it isn't so long ago that you were seriously thinking of becoming the Countess Venescu," she pointed out quietly.

For a moment Dominique was silent, then she gave an odd little laugh. "I know. I really meant to marry him, whatever. Then I—well, then I suddenly realised last night that I couldn't possibly go through with it." She jumped to her feet. "And don't lecture me, Jenny, or ask me any more questions because I want to forget all about it!"

"But, Dominique—"

"But nothing!" Dominique retorted, and Jenny realised that she had undergone one of her lightning changes of mood. "There are plenty of other fish in the sea, thank goodness! I won't necessarily end up on the shelf just because I'm not now going to marry Count Alex Venescu!"

With an angry, defiant little laugh she swept out of the room, leaving Jenny with something else to occupy her mind. She seized upon it thankfully and worn out with thinking and worrying, eventually she dozed, finding when she next awoke that the morning light was streaming into her room.

A glance at her bedside clock told her that it was nearly half-past nine. Gabrielle and Dominique would be having breakfast in bed around about now. That was their usual habit after a late night, though Jenny had laughingly rejected Gabrielle's suggestion that she should enjoy the same privilege. She had been brought up with the belief that the only time one breakfasted in bed was when one was too ill to get out of it!

It was unlikely, she thought as she showered and dressed, that after the revelries of a few hours ago anyone else would be up, but when a few moments later she passed Raoul's room she saw that the door was wide open. Impossible not to notice that the room was empty, the curtains drawn and the bedclothes flung back.

Momentarily she hesitated. If Raoul was having breakfast downstairs, alone, then the last thing she wanted was to join him. She would infinitely prefer to return to her room and forgo breakfast altogether, even though she was dying for a cup of coffee.

She was still undecided when she caught sight of Berthe, who was carrying a silver breakfast tray garnished with a single red rose to Gabrielle's room.

"*Bonjour, mademoiselle!* You are not tired after last night?" The housekeeper's smile was beaming, for her devotion to all the members of the de Vaisseau family had long ago been extended to include Jenny.

"Not at all." Jenny managed to smile back, hoping that her shadowed eyes would not betray the fib. "I was just going downstairs. That coffee smells delicious, Berthe! Is—is anyone else in the breakfast room at the moment?"

"*Mais oui, mademoiselle.* Monsieur Challoner, he has been up a very long time. It was he who picked this red rose for Madame's tray. He is having breakfast now, with Monsieur Piers."

"And—and Monsieur Raoul?"

"Gone, *mademoiselle*—to Paris, I believe."

It was the last answer Jenny had expected. For a moment she was sure that her astonishment must show in her face, though luckily Berthe did not seem to notice. At least, she thought ruefully as she descended the stairs, she could drink her coffee in peace! But what on earth had made Raoul rush off so early? And why, come to that, had he gone at all? He had promised Gabrielle that he would spend this, his last day, with her!

Her brow was still creased into a puzzled frown when she walked into the breakfast room. Her father and Piers were both seated at the table, but though they sprang to their feet immediately they saw her she knew at once that she had interrupted something. Her father was looking anxious, and Piers' face was set in the grim lines that she had come to know quite well.

"My dear Jenny! We didn't expect you so early! Come and sit down next to me." Stephen pulled a chair out for her as he spoke, but his smile was a trifle forced.

Uneasiness suddenly engulfing her, Jenny stayed where she was, still grasping the door handle. "Is—is anything wrong? Sure I'm not interrupting anything?" she asked hesitantly.

"Not at all." It was Piers who answered since Stephen seemed to be taking an unconscionable time to do so. His voice was clipped and hard. "We were merely discussing the bad news that my brother Raoul has received this morning."

Jenny went white. "Bad news?"

Stephen, an annoyed expression crossing his handsome features, interposed swiftly. "It's all right, Jenny. I'm afraid that the bad news is that now, at what is quite literally the eleventh hour, Pierre Lamotte, who promised Raoul the loan he needs to finance his mining venture, has gone back on his word. He says that after all he thinks the venture is too risky and that he cannot afford the gamble."

"Oh no!" Jenny scarcely breathed the words. She felt as though she had been jerked into complete wakefulness with horrible suddenness. Raoul had been depending so utterly on that loan! What on earth would he do without it?

Piers banged his coffee cup down with such force that the saucer rattled. "All I can say is that Raoul has only himself to blame! Why on earth didn't he get an agreement in writing, a contract signed? The damned young fool has absolutely no head for business, I've always said so and I'll say it again!"

"Lamotte pooh-poohed the idea of a formal agreement, assured Raoul that the money would be available the day he left France. Raoul had no reason whatsoever to doubt his good faith," Stephen said sharply. "He was far too trusting, I admit, but he happens to believe —wrongly in this case, of course—that a man's word is his bond!"

Piers gave something that was a cross between a snort and a groan. "Rubbish! You can't do business like that! Heaven only knows I don't blame Lamotte for getting cold feet—it amazes me that he was ever attracted to the idea in the first place!—but I do blame Raoul for not getting the whole thing put on a proper legal basis! It was madness to rely on a verbal agreement!"

"What will happen now?" Jenny spoke through lips that felt strangely stiff.

Stephen ran his fingers through his greying hair. "Raoul has gone tearing off to Paris to try to see Lamotte and find out what has caused his sudden change of heart. If he doesn't succeed—"He gave a hopeless little shrug and left the sentence unfinished. "I suppose he'll try to obtain the loan from elsewhere but he didn't have much luck in that direction before and time is now so short. It's that, I'm afraid, that will defeat him."

Jenny's eyes were wide and dark in her pale face. She turned swiftly to Piers. "Why can't *you* help him?" she asked indignantly.

She did not see Piers' eyes narrow, nor would she have cared if she had. He said shortly, "I cannot. And, frankly, even if I could I wouldn't. Like Pierre Lamotte, I've no wish to throw good money after bad!"

"You don't believe the mine is any good?"

Piers looked and sounded exasperated. "My dear Jenny, I'm not a complete greenhorn! Of course it's no good! Oh, it's true they've struck a small pocket of gold, but it won't amount to anything. I'm sure of that!"

There was irritation in his voice but—yes, something else, too. Why, Piers *minded*, Jenny thought blankly. He did not believe that Raoul was right, that the mine was a worthwhile proposition, but at the same time he was sorry for his brother's predicament. It was such a revelation that she stared at him almost disbelievingly.

"There's nothing any of us can do, unfortunately—except to hope that Raoul can either persuade Lamotte to reverse his decision or find another backer within the next twenty-four hours." Stephen spoke quietly. "He'll do his best, you may be sure of that."

Jenny suddenly stiffened. "But perhaps there *is* someone who could help him! *Céleste*!" The words were out before she realised that, under all the circumstances, they were scarcely tactful.

"Céleste?" Piers stared at her, his rather thin mouth tightening. "What do you mean? How could she possibly help?"

Jenny flushed scarlet under his piercing gaze. "I—I only meant, I know she's friendly with Monsieur Lamotte—"

She was not allowed to finish the sentence. "I was not aware of that fact. How is it that you have knowledge which I have not?" Piers' voice sounded like the crack of a whip and she saw his jaw set.

Wishing desperately that she had held her tongue but feeling that she had already said too much to be able to retract, Jenny forced herself to meet his gaze.

"I—well, I saw them having coffee together, in Nice. I didn't know who it was, but the friend who was with me said it was Pierre Lamotte, the financier. She was quite sure." She swallowed. "It—it was just after that that Raoul said he'd got the loan he wanted. He—he said he didn't know how Monsieur Lamotte had come to hear about the mine, but I've always assumed that it was Céleste who told him."

In the little silence that followed the petals fell suddenly from a rose in the silver bowl on the table. Piers' hands clenched at his sides and he said slowly, in a voice that Jenny hardly recognised, "Céleste ... I wonder!"

She looked at him, wide-eyed, and then abruptly, without another word, he turned on his heel and walked out of the room. Jenny watched him go, feeling suddenly cold. Why had he looked like that, as if he had suddenly made a very unpleasant discovery? What had she said, to have had such a drastic effect?

She turned imploringly to her father. He was frowning heavily, but he did not meet her gaze, nor, whatever he thought about her disclosure, did he seem inclined to discuss the matter with her. Instead, he rose to his feet with a quick, abrupt movement and said rather shortly, "I must go and tell Gabrielle what has happened. I am afraid she will be very upset—Dominique, too."

Dominique! With a shock of dismay Jenny realised that she had forgotten all about her stepsister. Was she awake and if so, how was she feeling? Would she regret, in the cold light of day, what had happened last night?

If she did she certainly gave no sign of it when, an hour or so later, she came downstairs. She had, in fact, no thought for anyone but Raoul, for she had heard from her mother and stepfather about the blow that had fallen on her beloved brother and her indignation knew no bounds.

Jenny, listening to her furious denunciation of Pierre Lamotte, felt her thoughts going round and round like a prayer wheel. Oh, if only she could help Raoul! But of course, there was nothing she or anyone else could do without money. Wrong. Céleste might be able to help, if she really did have any influence at all with Pierre Lamotte. It was certainly in her own interests to try, since whatever affected Raoul affected her also. Jenny bit her lip at the thought. Where *was* Céleste now? Not at her parents' villa, apparently: Piers had been there and found it shuttered and bolted. Perhaps Raoul had taken her to Paris with him this morning.

Jenny felt suddenly acutely sorry not only for Raoul

but also for Piers, who had left the villa at midday. Almost certainly, now, he would have to learn the truth about his fiancée's clandestine relationship with his younger brother. It wouldn't be possible for them to keep it a secret much longer.

There was no communication of any kind from Raoul either that day or the next morning. Jenny, who had not slept a wink all night, looked at Dominique's heavy eyes and realised that the same was probably true of her also.

"It is tonight that Raoul is due to fly back to Colorado," she said tragically at breakfast. "I cannot believe that he will go without saying goodbye to us! It would be too cruel!"

"There won't be much point in his going, if he hasn't got the loan," Stephen said rather grimly.

Dominique put her hand to her head. "I cannot bear to think of it! My poor Raoul!"

Jenny could not trust herself to speak. Instead she picked up the mail that she had found lying by her plate. One letter was from Susan Round, a teacher she had been quite friendly with at the High School. (Aeons ago ... !) She would know that black italic handwriting anywhere, Susan had been so fond of pinning notices up all over the place. The other letter was from Mr. Davidson, the family lawyer. That thin, rather spidery handwriting—his letters to her were never dictated to his secretary—was also unmistakable.

Jenny slipped both letters into her pocket. She'd read them both later on. With a little shock of surprise she remembered that she had not yet posted the letter she had written the day before yesterday. Well, it could wait now until she discovered what else John Davidson had to say!

"I think I'll go into Nice this morning. You will come with me, Jenny?" Dominique looked at her enquiringly.

Jenny assented readily. Anything was better than sitting here, waiting and wondering.

Before they left there was a telephone call for Dominique from Alex. She refused to speak to him and asked

Berthe, who had brought the message, to tell him that she was unavailable. Jenny felt uneasily that this was not perhaps the wisest way in which to treat someone like Count Alex Venescu, but knew from bitter experience that Dominique would not readily listen to advice.

Dominique's complete *volte-face* had, in fact, puzzled her, though she could not help but feel relieved that the break had been made. Whatever his wordly goods, Alex was not the type to make a good husband, and especially not for someone like Dominique. She needed a man with a certain amount of stability to counteract her own mercurial temperament. Someone like David. . . .

Jenny sighed at the thought. Despite David's proposal, she knew quite well that he loved Dominique as much as ever. Absurd to suppose that what he had suggested would ever work. He had not got Dominique out of his system and she would never get Raoul out of hers. It was just one of those things.

Dominique certainly did not seem to have any regrets regarding her former suitor. In Nice she bought a hat and a very pretty flame-coloured dress, and then insisted that she would treat Jenny to lunch. They were standing at the kerb, waiting for a break in the traffic so that they could cross the road, when a voice said "Hello, there" and turning, they found David beside them.

"Why . . . hello." Jenny smiled and then glanced quickly at Dominique. She was smiling, too.

David's glance swept over them, taking in their cool, crisp suits, wide-brimmed hats and elegant gloves. (It had been Dominique's idea that they should "dress up". "It's good for one's morale," she said firmly.)

"You are both looking very elegant! I suppose you wouldn't like to make me the most envied man in Nice and come and have lunch with me, would you?" he asked laughing. "I'm not on duty until four, so there's plenty of time."

They both hesitated, whereupon David said, "I warn you that I'm not going to take no for an answer! What about La Mediterranée? They do an excellent meal, I'm told."

"It's frightfully expensive," Dominique said quickly, and David laughed.

"Not to worry! I'm in funds at the moment," and he hailed a passing cab.

Jenny darted a swift glance at her stepsister. David couldn't possibly know, of course, but La Mediterranée had been a favourite meeting place for Dominique and Alex. Still, if she didn't mind. . . .

La Mediterranée was justly famous for its *cuisine*, but Jenny found that she had very little appetite for her lunch. Not only could she not remove Raoul from her thoughts, but she felt that she was acting as a sort of buffer between David and Dominique. They both seemed very shy and constrained with each other, and that was odd, considering the way they had seemed to enjoy dancing together at Gabrielle's party! She felt just a little annoyed with them both, for the tension certainly made her own position rather uncomfortable.

She was just wishing that they had, after all, refused David's invitation when she suddenly saw Dominique stiffen. Following the direction of her gaze, Jenny saw that Count Alex Venescu, accompanied by several friends, had arrived at a neighbouring table, where they sat down and noisily ordered some drinks. It seemed to Jenny that Alex had probably been drinking already, for his black eyes were brilliant and there was a flush on his tawny cheekbones.

After that first glance Dominique had turned her head away, but Alex, his hard eyes raking the room, had already noticed her. The flush on his cheekbones became deeper, and he spoke in a low voice to the waiter who was hovering over their table. A few moments later the man brought a note over to Dominique.

She read it, flushed, then grew very pale. Screwing up the paper and tossing it into the ashtray she said, forcing a smile, "Alex seems to think, mistakenly, that I should enjoy his company more than yours, David." She turned to the waiter. "Please convey my regrets to the Count, but it is impossible for me to join him at his table. I am lunching with friends."

The waiter delivered her message and the Count's

handsome face darkened. Then, before anyone realised what he meant to do, he got up and swaggered over to their table.

Ignoring both David and Jenny, he spoke to Dominique. "Stop sulking, little one! I wish to talk to you!"

"I'm afraid you can't, not at this moment." Dominique spoke calmly, but Jenny, beside him, felt David tense.

"No?" Alex laughed derisively and picked up Dominique's glass, drank out of it. "How do you propose to stop me?"

"Put that glass down and go back to your friends." David leant across the table, his voice ominously quiet. "You heard what the lady said. She can't talk to you now."

"Ah, Dr. Chalmers!" For the first time Alex deigned to notice David and his lip curled unpleasantly. "I must say I'm surprised to see *you* here. I wouldn't have thought that you could afford La Mediterranée prices—unless, of course, you mean to leave it to Mademoiselle de Vaisseau to pay the bill?"

"Alex!" Dominique was white with rage, but the Count merely laughed and catching hold of her wrist, jerked her to her feet.

"You belong at *my* table, *chérie*! Come!"

David was ice-pale but perfectly controlled. He got up. "You will kindly release Mademoiselle de Vaisseau at once and return to your own table, or I shall be forced to summon the manager," he said steadily.

Black eyes stared into blue, and it was the black eyes which fell first. Jenny thought that David had won, but what Alex did next was completely unexpected. Dominique had kindled a blazing passion in him and this, coupled with his hurt vanity and the alcohol he had consumed, made him lose his head entirely. He let go of Dominique's wrist, but in one swift movement picked up the wine bottle and swung it at David's head.

Luckily it did not break, but David, momentarily stunned, went down like a ninepin. The next moment there was pandemonium. The Count's friends, horrified by what he had done, rushed over to the table and escorted him, protesting and struggling, back to his own table. The manager, pale with alarm, ordered them to leave and then rushed to David's side, but Dominique had forestalled him.

"David! Oh, David darling, has he hurt you?" Careless of her expensive suit, she knelt on the floor beside him, her lips quivering and her eyes swimming with tears. She looked wildly up at Jenny. "Oh, Jenny, he's all right, isn't he? I can't bear it if he isn't. I—I love him, Jenny!"

David opened his eyes. "*What* did you say?" he asked faintly, and the next instant struggled to a sitting position. "What did you say?" he repeated.

"David! I thought you were unconscious!" A vivid blush suffused Dominique's pale cheeks, but when David, his eyes bluely triumphant, looking like a man who had seen the gates of heaven open, grabbed hold of her hand she made not the slightest attempt to pull away. For all the attention they paid to anyone else they might have been on a desert island instead of being the focus of attention in an extremely crowded restaurant!

"She says she's been in love with him ever since she first met him, only she couldn't bring herself to admit it!"

Jenny, arriving home in Dominique's car to break the news to Gabrielle and Stephen while Dominique accompanied David to the nursing home—he needed a couple of stitches in an ugly gash in his head—could not help laughing at her stepmother's stupefied expression.

"You're glad, aren't you?" she asked. "I know David hasn't got an awful lot of money, but he's very clever and I'm sure he'll reach the top of his profession one day. He's just the right person for Dominique and they really are quite crazy about each other, just wait until you see them! It's quite impossible, at the moment, to drag a sensible word out of either of them!"

Gabrielle put her hand to her head. "Indeed I am glad! I have always liked Dr. Chalmers immensely.

But Jenny, my dear, we all thought that you and he—" she stopped helplessly.

"We were never anything but very good friends," Jenny assured her, smiling. "I've known almost from the first about David's feelings for Dominique but, like him, I thought it was hopeless! I'd no idea that in her case hate was very akin to love!"

"So it would seem! Well, it is good to know that one of my children, at least, is happy." There was a note of sadness in Gabrielle's voice and Jenny looked at her quickly.

"What do you mean?"

"I mean," said Gabrielle, "that Piers telephoned me a short while ago to tell me that his engagement to Céleste is broken. The marriage will not now take place."

Jenny's throat felt dry. "Then—Céleste has told him that she is going to marry Raoul?"

There was a moment's silence. Then Gabrielle, her brows drawing into a puzzled little frown, said, "Marry Raoul? I do not understand you, Jenny. Most assuredly she is not going to marry Raoul! The reason that Piers has broken their engagement is that he has discovered her treachery with regard to poor Raoul and he has been sickened by her behaviour!" She paused. "There has been much friction between those two, Piers and Raoul, in the past, but they are nevertheless loyal to each other in their own way. It is because of that loyalty that Piers cannot forgive Céleste for the way in which she has deliberately tried to ruin Raoul's hopes!"

Jenny felt as though her head was spinning. What *was* Gabrielle talking about?

"It was you, of course, who gave Piers the clue to what Céleste had done," Gabrielle went on. "Had you not spoken of her friendship with Pierre Lamotte he would never have suspected that it was Céleste who persuaded him first to grant Raoul the loan and then, when it was too late for him to make other arrangements, to withhold it. Piers frightened her a little, and she has admitted it all."

"But why? Why should she do such a terrible thing?" Jenny's voice was little more than a shaken whisper.

Gabrielle sighed. "I can only think that it was her method of revenging herself on Raoul because he did not love her. She wanted, you see, to marry him, and she was very angry when he made it clear that he was not interested. It was then, I suppose, that she conceived the idea of becoming engaged to Piers, who had always been very attracted to her. She knew, of course, that such an engagement would afford her the opportunity to go on seeing Raoul and I can only think that she hoped, eventually, to persuade him to change his mind."

"But—but everyone believed that it was Céleste who had thrown Raoul over! He *let* people believe that!"

"That was for Piers' sake," Gabrielle said quietly. "Only I knew the truth, from Raoul's own lips, and I promised him I would never divulge it, not even to Stephen. Raoul knew, you see, what a terrible blow it would be to Piers' pride if he discovered that Céleste was merely making use of him, that she had no real love for him at all." She sighed. "We both hoped, Raoul and I, that either Céleste would undergo a change of heart or else that Piers would realise for himself what a mistake he was making. As, indeed, he now has, though I think his disillusionment began a long time ago."

Jenny felt dazed. Céleste had lied! All that she had told her the other night, in the music room, was a complete fabrication! But why? Why had she lied?

Gabrielle was still speaking. "Unfortunately, of course, knowing about Céleste's duplicity does not really help matters, at least from Raoul's point of view. He still has not got the money he needs and has no hope now, I fear of obtaining it in time to save the mine."

"You've heard from him?" Jenny's voice was sharp.

Gabrielle shook her head. "No. But his plane leaves tonight and I hope he will telephone me before then. We have no idea where he is staying, so we cannot get in touch with him as we should like to do."

Stephen came into the room at this point and while Gabrielle was telling him about Dominique's engagement Jenny went upstairs to her room to change. She felt as though she was in the grip of some kind of nightmare. Regret and rebellion and bitterness were surging over her and it was with the slow, jerky movements of an automaton that she removed her elegant suit and put on the cooler, more comfortable cotton dress that she had been wearing earlier in the day. As she did so she heard the crackle of paper and realised that the two letters she had received that morning were still in the pocket, unread.

Sitting down on the edge of her bed, she tossed Susan's aside—it was bound to be full of school gossip and she couldn't be bothered with that kind of stuff at the moment—and opened the lawyer's. It was short, but she read it with widening eyes, and when she had finished it she gave an incredulous gasp and read it all over again.

When, finally, she put the letter down the words were still dancing in front of her dazed and bewildered eyes. Far from her grandmother dying practically penniless, as everyone had believed, she had actually been a rich woman. The papers which the lawyer had discovered stuffed away at the back of an old chest-of-drawers had proved, on inspection, to include a large number of share certificates which had been of little value when purchased but which were now worth a very great deal.

"Since you are your grandmother's sole heir I am delighted to be able to inform you that you will now enjoy a measure of financial independence. Safely invested, the proceeds from the sale of the shares will bring you in a considerable annual income," Mr. Davidson wrote, and went on to name a sum which to Jenny seemed astronomical.

Safely invested.... Suddenly she gave a gasp. Raoul! She could help Raoul! She looked at her watch and sprang to her feet. Oh, if only she knew where he was ... could get in touch with him by phone! She had to tell him, at once, that there was no need for him to return to Colorado to admit defeat, that although Pierre Lamotte had not kept his word she, Jenny, could lend him the money he wanted!

The airport. She would have to reach the airport before his flight left. That meant either taking

Dominique's car or else hiring a taxi. The taxi would probably be quicker, since the driver would doubtless know the way and she did not.

Pausing only to snatch up her handbag, Jenny flew downstairs to the telephone. Luckily there was no one about. Neither Stephen nor Gabrielle must know where she was going or why, because if they knew they would probably try to stop her. Not that they, or anyone else, would succeed. Mr. Davidson was hardly likely to call it a "safe" investment—in fact, he'd doubtless be horrified—but she had the power, now, to save Raoul's mine and she meant to use it! If only she could get to the airport in time. . . .

The taxi arrived at the huge Paris airport with twenty minutes to spare. On the way the driver, a wizened little man with an ugly, cheerful face, had broken just about every traffic regulation that existed, and Jenny, respectable, law-abiding Jenny Barrington, had egged him on. Now, as she flung herself out of the cab and raced across to the terminal buildings, the taxi driver settled himself in his seat, folded his arms across his chest and waited philosophically for her to remember that she had not paid her fare. She was, of course, in love, and when one was in love, he thought sentimentally, one did strange things. Funny, she didn't look the type to go overboard over a man, yet one never could tell!

Jenny found Raoul standing with a number of other passengers. Oblivious of dishevelled hair, creased dress and missing belt—she had forgotten to put it on—she stood still, suddenly shaking, as she caught sight of him, and tried to draw several deep breaths. Her heart was hammering against her ribs and now that it came to the point she was suddenly too shy to approach him.

Raoul looked up and saw her and she saw the incredulous amazement in his eyes. Then he dropped the paper he was reading and reached her side in two strides. She moved towards him and melted into his arms as he seized her.

Raoul held her in a crushing embrace, fiercely kissing her, and Jenny, her blood pounding, responded.

Whatever qualms or doubts had assailed her vanished into limbo: she did not even care that this was a very public place and a very public embrace!

It was Raoul who seemed to recollect himself first. Slackening his hold, he said in a voice which shook a little, "Jenny! What on earth are you doing here?"

It was very difficult, Jenny decided, to think at all clearly when one had just been very thoroughly kissed! She said breathlessly, "Raoul, I know all about your loan falling through! There's so little time to explain, but—"

He cut her short. "On the contrary, there's all the time in the world!" His brilliant, lapis lazuli eyes laughed down into hers. "My sweet Jenny, I have never believed until now that dreams really do come true! If you seriously imagine that I am going to board a plane to Colorado under circumstances such as these then you're very, very much mistaken! Colorado can wait!"

"But, Raoul—"

"No buts!" he said firmly. He put his arm round her shoulders, then looked round impatiently. "There's nowhere here where we can talk! We'll have to hire a cab if we want to be alone!"

"Heaven!" Jenny's hand flew to her mouth. "My cab! I haven't paid him! And he's brought me all the way from—Nice!"

Raoul's brows shot up. His voice was solemn, but there was laughter dancing in his eyes as he said, "My dear Miss Barrington! *What* extravagance! You must have wanted to see me very badly!"

Jenny was scarlet. "It was either a taxi or Dominique's car. I nearly borrowed that, then I decided I wouldn't be able to go fast enough on roads that I didn't know," she explained. A horrid thought occurred to her. "Raoul, will the taxi cost very much? I—I don't think I've enough money on me to pay for it!"

"Darling, how I love the Jenny who is extravagant, improvident and quite absurdly irresponsible!" Raoul said solemnly. "Is that your cab? The driver seems to know you!"

He strode forward and exchanged a few rapid words with the driver, whose grin was splitting his face from ear to ear. Then, "Get in the back, *chérie*!" he said gently, and immediately she had obeyed his command climbed in beside her and took possession of her hands.

"Now tell me what all this is about!" he said firmly. "And be quick about it, *mignonne*, because there is something that I want to tell you—something that cannot wait!"

"I—it's about the loan you want, Raoul." Shyly and a little incoherently Jenny told him about the letter she had just received from John Davidson. "So, you see, I've got money to invest and—and I'd like to put it into your mine, if—if you'll let me, please, Raoul," she finished breathlessly.

There was a short silence. Then Raoul said, in a peculiar voice, "You really mean that, Jenny? You'd willingly invest your money in a mine you don't even believe in? You'd run the risk of losing it all?" Then, very softly, "Why, *ma mie*?"

"Because—" Jenny could not go on and with a little exclamation Raoul caught her in his arms and strained her to him so fiercely that she could scarcely breathe.

"You *do* love me!" There was wonderment and quick, incredulous joy in his voice. "Oh, Jenny, I can't believe it! I thought I'd spoiled everything!" He drew a deep breath, then put his face down and kissed her, kissed her hard.

When, finally, he raised his head he said huskily, "I fell in love with you weeks ago, do you know that, *mignonne*? Even though you thought the worst of me and treated me with the freezing contempt that I fear I thoroughly deserved!" He gave a soft, rueful laugh. "It was because of you that I discharged myself from that damned hospital and because of you that I was quite content that my convalescence should take so long! I did not want to return to Colorado and leave you behind!" His fingers touched her hair. "They say a leopard cannot change his spots, but oh, Jenny, you'll never know how hard I tried to change mine! Whenever I was with you I wanted so desperately to make love to you, and instead I had to treat you almost like a sister so that you would stop feeling afraid of me and give me your confidence. It hurt so much, your fear of me, Jenny."

"I wasn't really afraid of you." Jenny, feeling as though she was in a wonderful dream, spoke quickly. "It was Céleste. I—I thought, you see, until Gabrielle told me the truth today, that you were in love with her. She told me, the night we were supposed to be going to the opera, that you and she were going to be married."

Raoul listened with a darkening face to her account of her meeting with Céleste in the music room. When she had finished he said grimly, "I was never in love with Céleste, nor did I give her any reason to think that I was. When she became engaged to Piers I let people assume, for his sake, that she'd thrown me over, but it was a bad mistake. And another bad mistake was letting her know that I was attracted to you. It was the first time I asked you to go to the opera with me—remember? She rang up to ask me to go to a party with her and I had to tell her that I had other plans. Her reaction should have warned me."

He paused. "The day she came home from Geneva I met her quite by chance, when I was rushing home to you. I daren't leave her, she was emotional ... almost hysterical, kept saying that she should never have become engaged to Piers and that I'd only to say the word and she'd fling his ring in his face. Finally, in sheer desperation, I told her that she was wasting her time ... that it was you I loved and that if I could I meant to make you my wife." He paused. "Her last words were that I'd be sorry. I took it as an idle threat, but I know now what she meant."

Jenny looked at him. "You know about Pierre Lamotte?"

"I telephoned Maman—I suppose it must have been just after you'd started out, at any rate she hadn't missed you—and she told me the whole story." He paused again.

"She also told me about Dominique's engagement. I am very glad. Chalmers will make her an excellent husband though he wouldn't have done for you, *mignonne*, at all!"

Jenny laughed and Raoul laughed too, and kissed her.

"I was sure, you know, that you were not in love with Chalmers, and yet the night I came home to find you in his arms I was nearly crazy with jealousy! And Stephen didn't help. He let me know, in the nicest possible way, that he would very much prefer to see his only daughter married to a nice steady young doctor than a penniless adventurer, and I have to admit that I saw his point!" He looked into her eyes. "You're not afraid, *chérie*, to marry someone who has always been considered the black sheep of the family?"

Jenny snuggled into his arms. "You're a reformed character, but in any case I much prefer black sheep to white ones! Besides, Stephen doesn't know you half as well as I do! One day I think you'll want to stop adventuring and settle down to vineyards, but until you do I'll be quite content to have adventures, too!"

"Stephen doesn't know *you* very well, either," Raoul told her, amusement in his voice. "You're very much more his daughter than any one of us thought!"

Jenny suddenly decided that it was time to become strictly practical. "When do you want the money, Raoul? As soon as I can get it?"

She became aware that he was smiling. "I don't need it, *ma mie*. You see, you were not the only one to receive good news this morning. I put a call through to Colorado this morning, to prepare them for the worst, and the information I received was that we've hit the main vein, weeks sooner than expected." He gave a triumphant and satisfied laugh as she gasped aloud.

"That vineyard will be a reality before we are very much older, that I promise you, *ma belle*. I wish to be a vagabond no longer. I shall become a staid and respectable farmer, and everyone will look up to me as a pillar of the community and say what a pity it is that I have such a giddy and harum-scarum wife!"

Jenny caught her breath. "Raoul, you're sure that's what you want? Stephen said—he said that you'd always crave gaiety and change and excitement, that you'd always want adventures!"

Raoul's eyes were very tender. "With you, my darling, every day will seem like the start of a new adventure," he said huskily, and kissed her hard on the mouth.

Over his shoulder, through the taxi window, Jenny saw the first evening star. She thought of an old nursery rhyme she had learnt as a little girl and gave voice to it when she was allowed to.

> "Star light, star bright,
> First star I've seen tonight,
> Wish I may, wish I might
> Have this wish I wish tonight."

The smile in Raoul's eyes deepened. "And what is it that you wish, *ma chérie*?"

Jenny shook her head. "Nothing. I haven't got a single thing left to wish for," she said simply, and only she and the Recording Angel knew that what she said was the exact truth.

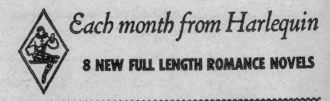

Each month from Harlequin

8 NEW FULL LENGTH ROMANCE NOVELS

Listed below are the latest three months' releases:

ALL BOOKS 60c

These titles are available at your local bookseller, or through the Harlequin Reader Service, M.P.O. Box 707, Niagara Falls, N.Y. 14302; Canadian address 649 Ontario St., Stratford, Ont.

A